THE DACHSHU ... DES

Book 4

A
DACHSHUND'S
TRIBUTE

Mavis Duke Hinton

A Dachshund's Tribute
THE DACHSHUND ESCAPADES, Book 4

A Dachshund's Tribute is a work of fiction. References to real people, events, establishments, organizations, or locales are intended only to provide a sense of authenticity and are used fictitiously. All other characters, incidents, and dialogue are drawn from the author's imagination.

ISBN-13: 978-1505440126

ISBN-10: 1505440122

Printed in the U.S.A.

❧ DEDICATION ☙

For the grandchildren:

THE DACHSHUND ESCAPADES
were written for you as a record
of our family's fond memories of your
remarkable great grandparents,
Robert "Papa" Duke
and
Ramelle "Nana" Duke!

THE DACHSHUND ESCAPADES

I AM SARGE
BOOK 1

I AM DACHSHUND
BOOK 2

DACHSHUNDS FOREVER
BOOK 3

A DACHSHUND'S TRIBUTE
BOOK 4

A DACHSHUND'S MERRY-GO-ROUND LIFE
BOOK 5
2015

∂ Preface ∞

WHY I WRITE FROM THE DACHSHUND'S VIEWPOINT

It is a running joke in our family that we know, without a doubt, what a dachshund is thinking by its facial expression and body language. My late father used to tell us what our dachshunds were thinking, and I believe I have inherited that "gene" for doing so. These interpretations are tongue in cheek, of course—and make for many a laugh around our house.

For example, I watch my dachshund Duke closely if I think he's up to something. If he's looking at Clark imploringly, I "interpret" his wishes for my husband: "I wish you'd put down that newspaper and throw my ball for me. Mama has been at the computer all day, ignoring me. I need to have some fun around here, you know!" Voilà— Duke's thoughts. It's not necessarily a talent (maybe even a bit silly to those who are not dog lovers), but we all get a good chuckle out of my interpretations.

In addition, Duke, like most dogs, exhibits traits quite similar to humans. Here are some actual examples of his "people-like" traits, so you just might find situations in my books that sound familiar:

He often **annoys** Shadow, our doxie granddawg, by taking a squeak toy and running with it, growling: *C'mon, boy! See if you can take this away from me!* Duke even flaunts the toy in Shadow's face, daring him to take it. (Note: Shadow thinks all toys are his).

He **argues** by barking at me when I tell him he can't do something (like get on my lap when I'm drinking hot coffee). He also knows when we are making fun of him, and he doesn't like that, either!

He is **loving** by giving doggie kisses and wanting to be close.

Another particularly appealing trait is **playfulness**; Duke is downright comical! He seems to get pleasure from including his human companions whenever possible. One night, seven of us: Holly, Philip, Clark, and I, along with the three grandchildren, were flying paper airplanes around the living room. Duke joined right in, jumping up and trying to snatch one out of the air. He finally succeeded, then ran off with it, much to the delight of the grandchildren. He likes to snatch balloons when we are batting them around in the air, too, but doesn't care too much for the noise they make when his sharp teeth cause them to pop.

But perhaps one of the most endearing traits I've found is his **concern** for someone who is sick or upset. After my two surgeries in the hospital this year, Duke stayed right by my side while I recuperated at home. I appreciated how well he took care of me! I know he would have made me a cup of hot chocolate if he could have done so, too. I have incorporated that caring attitude into my books, as Sarge often relates his feelings about family members or some happening in particular.

My other reasons (besides the "gene" thing) for writing from the dog's viewpoint are:

1) I enjoy imagining how day-to-day happenings must appear to the family dog;

2) I can shift reality to share with readers what dogs think about life situations;

3) I have a zany sense of humor (my family can attest to that), and can use such humor when incorporating it into the dog's viewpoint;

4) I love and appreciate dogs as man's best friend. They show us unconditional love, like God has for us. In THE DACHSHUND ESCAPADES series, Papa Duke so aptly states my feelings about dogs:

"A dawg loves you no matter what. You can be ugly, old, even dumb--but a dawg don't care. All he wants is your love and some food now and then. I think dawgs represent the unconditional love God has for us--maybe that's why He created them, to show that to us."

Papa Duke, as readers know, was my late father. He loved dogs tremendously, and they returned the favor. So in my books, he lives on, just like he does in our hearts.

For those of us who love our dogs, my doggie stories give us a glimpse into our dogs' views on life. Oh, they're not Shakespeare, but they read just fine for us dog lovers.

Or so I'm told.

M.D.H.

"For by grace are you saved through faith, and that not of yourselves: it is the gift of God, not of works, lest any man should boast." Ephesians 2:8-9

1
Grab Your Plate: Annika Is Eight!

"Mama, I want to have a different kind of party for my birthday," Annika told Mama one day last spring. Apparently, it was only a few weeks until her eighth birthday, and she wanted Mama to come up with something as special as Alexa and Asher's birthdays had been last year: Alexa's was a princess-themed party, and Asher's was a cow-themed party.

"Honey, do you have any idea what kind of party you'd like to have?" asked Mama, who was folding laundry. It was after school, almost time for Mama to start dinner, and my nose was looking forward to smelling those delicious aromas. Alexa and Asher were in the playroom, whereas Annika, Mama, and I were in the living room.

"I don't want a baby party," Annika replied. "I mean, I'm gonna be eight, so I'm getting big. I want to invite a bunch of my friends from church and from school, so I want girls *and* boys to enjoy it. Girls I know wouldn't like cars or superheroes, and boys I know wouldn't like princess stuff, dolls, or other frilly stuff."

"Tell you what," said Mama. "I'll think about it for a day or two, and I just know we can come up with something that both girls and boys will like. They all like to eat, right? So right there we have common ground for all your friends to enjoy."

"Food is always fun and everybody likes it," replied Annika, nodding. *You got that right, Sister. Every dawg I know likes it, too. In fact, I don't know anybody—be they human or animal—who does not like food!* "Why can't I have a food party??"

"Hey, that gives me an great idea for the party," exclaimed Mama. "I remember one of my friends who lives in another state had such a party for her daughter several

1

years ago. It was called a chef party, and the kids loved it—I know I did—well, at least the ideas, because we couldn't attend since it was too far away."

"What do you do at a chef party?" asked Annika. "I don't think my friends want to cook. Oh, we like to eat, but we want to do some fun things."

"Hmmm. Here's an idea: have chef hats and aprons for each boy and girl. We could let them decorate their own aprons with sequins, fuzzy balls, jewels, and so on—I have plenty of things with my scrapbooking materials." Mama thought for a moment. "I've got another idea: we could do a little cooking with the kids. We could provide the individual crusts, and then they could each make a personal pizza! I could put bowls of different toppings on the counter, and they could decide what to put on their pizzas!"

"But what kind of pizza crusts, Mama?" Annika asked.

Mama snapped her fingers. "My mom did this for one of Aunt Bethany's birthdays when we were growing up. Those refrigerator biscuits that come in tubes! You know—I have to stick a fork in the side of the tube to open it? Well, I could show them how to flatten their biscuit for a crust, and there you go—they could put toppings on it, and I could put it in the oven!"

"That would be fun! I like that, Mama—and those biscuits taste good. What kind of toppings could we have?"

Mama thought a moment. "The usual pepperoni, of course. Shredded mozzarella, too—and I could chop up some ham, green pepper, and mushrooms." Annika opened her mouth to say something, but Mama stopped her. "Oh, I know everyone doesn't like some of those toppings, but some will. We need to have a variety."

"We need to think of something else to do, too, because making pizzas wouldn't take very long. I'd have a really short birthday party!" Annika exclaimed.

"I can order chef hats and aprons on the internet. It

will take a little time for you and your friends to decorate your aprons. I'll get stick-on letters so you can put your names on them, and the other materials I mentioned for decorating them. I might even want to do one for myself!" Mama added. "Oh, and I'll ask Miss Janet from church to help me—together we'll come up with other things to do at your chef party. I can even design invitations on the computer. You'll see. Now that I've finished folding the clothes, you children can put them away. Asher and Alexa! Come help Annika put away the clothes."

And Mama started dinner.

The next few days were very busy with school and church activities. She even called Miss Janet, asking her to help, and invited her to come over one afternoon to work on ideas for the chef party together. I did see Mama sitting with her laptop computer a few times, and she worked on something one day for about an hour. Since I was the only one home at the time (Asher was napping, so he didn't count), Mama looked at me and said: "Oh, Sargie! These birthday invitations are so cute. I made a border of all kinds of food: hamburgers and hot dogs, fruit and veggies, even ice cream cones. Here's what the invitations say:

<u>*Grab Your Plate: Annika is Eight!*</u>

You are invited to a Chef Birthday Party
On Saturday, May 10, 11:30 – 1:30
At the Blinsons' home - right across from the church.
With chef hats and aprons (which you will decorate),
You'll make your own pizza,
Enjoy a Food Hunt,
And win prizes, too!

RSVP 555-1947
By Thursday, May 8

"What do you think, Sargie? Isn't that cute?" *Of course it is, Mama! You know I like anything to do with human food—and with all those kids here, someone is certain to drop something my way. Oh, yes. It is perfect,* I barked to her.

"All right, then. It sounds like you approve, so I'll go ahead and make up some copies so Annika can hand them out to her classmates at school, and on Sunday, she can hand them out to her friends there, too. We'll have a houseful, but thankfully, this house and kitchen are large enough for so many chefs," laughed Mama. "They say 'too many cooks spoil the broth,' but since we're making pizzas, that should be fine." *Oh, I don't mind at all myself. The more, the merrier, especially when FOOD is involved.*

Mama always gets into planning parties and children's activities at church, so she and her friend Janet, who often work together on children's activities, planned to make this party a real success. One afternoon, Janet came over so they could plan and discuss. Now I really like "Miss" Janet. She's married, but that's what the children call her. She laughs and smiles a lot, and I've heard Mama say that Miss Janet loves animals so much that she has twelve (yes, twelve) dogs! And even a dawg can tell when a human is creative, just like Mama is. They come up with some very interesting ideas when they plan something together.

"Miss Janet!" shouted Asher. "You coming to see Asher? See my toys?" And he brought her one of his figurines. She looked it over while rubbing my back as I lay on the couch. *Ah, that's very nice. A little to the left. Yes.*

"Asher, this is a very nice toy, and Miss Janet is so glad to see you," she replied, hugging him. "But I am going to help your mama plan Annika's birthday party. You'll get to come, too, so we want to do things that will be fun. What do you think of that?"

"Good," he answered. "I want LOTS of fun at sissie's

party!" Then he went back over to his toys. *What a good boy he is. No argument, no tantrum. Just a good kid.*

Mama had asked me to keep an eye on Asher in the living room, but my boy had gone back to playing with his little figurines, making up a story with them. All I had to do was lie on the couch, something I was really good at. I could also hear everything Mama and Miss Janet were discussing at the dining table from my comfy position.

The chef hats and aprons that Mama had ordered had already arrived, so Mama and Janet were looking through Mama's scrapbooking supplies to decide which items would be best for decorating those aprons. "Look, Janet," said Mama. "I bought these stick-on letters yesterday so the children can put their names on their aprons. After they do that, then they can decorate them like they want. Which of these small decorations do you think they would enjoy putting on their aprons?"

Miss Janet must have been looking at the items, because I could hear the plastic containers being moved on the table. In a moment she replied: "Holly, you have some stick-on veggies here! Those would be perfect—and what about these small pompoms in different colors? Oh, look—you have fake jewels, like rubies, emeralds, amethysts, to attach to the aprons. Every kid—either boy or girl—likes a little bling, you know."

"I like all those, too, Janet," I heard Mama say. "But we need at least one more thing to put on those aprons." I heard Mama moving plastic containers around. "Here you go," announced Mama. "I had forgotten that I had these. What do you think?"

"Yes, I like the small stickers of kitchen utensils," agreed Miss Janet. "Those will be just the right size, and they are also peel-and-stick pieces like the others. Oh, those aprons will be so much fun. I hope you have a few extra, because I might want to decorate one myself!"

"Of course I do, because I plan on decorating one,"

laughed Mama. *You two are just girls on the inside, aren't you? I like to see grownups having fun.* "I'm having the small pizzas—I'll show them how to flatten the refrigerator biscuits. They can lay the 'crusts' on the baking sheets I'll have ready, and I'll also have bowls of toppings on the counter over there so they can choose their own toppings. With something to drink, the pizza, and cake and ice cream, that will be enough for them to eat, don't you think?"

"Of course. I know that some of those little boys can probably eat several—and I know Annika can," laughed Miss Janet. "I will be here to help you with the kids so one boy doesn't put all the toppings on his first pizza!" she chuckled. "I know how kids are." *Oh, so do I. They might be sloppy and drop pepperoni or cheese. I'll be there to 'help clean up,' so to speak.* "What are you gonna do with these plastic foods in this bag, Holly?"

"I racked my brain to come up with some kind of game that fits in with the chef theme. Then it hit me: what about a food hunt—you know, like an Easter Egg hunt? We'll hide the plastic foods in the yard before the children arrive on Saturday, and after the pizzas, we'll give them each a plastic bowl so they can go outside and 'hunt' the food. The one with the most pieces will win a prize. I think we should also have a second and a third prize, too. How 'bout that?" Mama sounded pleased with her idea.

"What a fun idea," replied Miss Janet. "I see that you have apples, oranges, bananas, pineapples, and tomatoes, potatoes, corn, onions, and even some broccoli!" I heard some movement on the table, probably from Miss Janet looking over the plastic food. "Oh, and here are some slices of cake, pie, and ice cream cones. Well, the kids will certainly have a ball hunting for these." *Too bad they're fake, though. I could have my own party with them if they were real.*

"I'm getting Annika's cake from the bakery this time," added Mama. "We've been so busy lately, I just didn't have the time to make it myself, but Annika won't mind at all. I did request that they put candy fruit and veggies on it, so it would be in keeping with our chef theme. I'll get Philip to pick it up Friday afternoon."

"It appears that you've gotten everything organized," said Miss Janet. "We haven't really discussed decorations yet, though. How are you going to decorate for the party?"

"I have this cute tablecloth I got the other day." *I hear plastic being moved again.* "And these plastic plates and napkins also have fruits and veggies on them. All I'm planning to do is just have a centerpiece on this table, since I'll have to use the counter for placing the pizza toppings. The children will be moving around a bit here in the kitchen and dining room, so too many decorations will just get in the way. Any ideas for a table centerpiece, Janet?"

It was quiet for a moment or two, then Janet exclaimed, "I've got it! Just put kitchen utensils in mason jars—like serving spoons, spatulas, a wire whisk, maybe even a potato masher, a rolling pin, a pizza slicer—whatever you have on hand—then tie bright bows around the jars! How does that sound for a chef party centerpiece? And, we could tie a few balloons up high here and there, just to make it festive and party-like."

"Love it. We can even use the utensils if need be, too. The balloons are a good idea, and not much trouble if we attach them above the windows and door frames, out of the way. I think we are finished, don't you? Annika will be overjoyed. I'm excited about the party, too." *I bet Mama must be smiling right now.*

Miss Janet then announced, "I'll come early on Saturday to help you get everything ready. Do you suppose Philip can keep the children busy so they won't be underfoot while we get the kitchen and dining room in order for the party?" *Underfoot? You mean you would actually step on the sisters and Asher? Oh, wait. This is probably just another 'figure of speech' like Mavis is so fond of using all the time.*

"Knowing him," replied Mama, "he'll take them out to breakfast. I think it is his favorite meal, and he dearly loves his Southern breakfasts—eggs, sausage or bacon, grits or hash browns, biscuits—and even pancakes! We won't have to worry about anyone being in the way here!" *Gee, thanks, Mama. The cats will probably stay hidden, but I won't be in the way, you know. However, I am very interested in seeing what y'all do since it's a FOOD party. I wouldn't dream of getting 'underfoot' as you call it— dawgs don't like to get stepped on,* I barked to remind them that this *chopped liver* had ears. And so did Asher. He overheard Mama's remark about breakfast and went into the dining room. I trotted after him.

"Daddy taking Asher out to breakfast?" asked my boy. "Asher likes pancakes."

Mama and Miss Janet laughed. "Not yet, Asher. It's only Tuesday, and Annika's birthday party is Saturday. Daddy will take you and the girls out to breakfast on Saturday."

And I like eggs, bacon, grits, hash browns, biscuits, pancakes—oh yeah. I won't get to go. That's the story of my life, it seems. But I will be prepared to catch any food that drops at that party—there's no doubt about that.

The rest of the week flew by, as it usually does when Mama is in her "party preparation" mode. She checked with the bakery to make sure the cake would be like she wanted, she and Miss Janet talked on the phone several times, and parents called, replying to the RVSP on the party invitations. I heard Mama tell Daddy that about twenty children would be coming. *Wow. That's a lot of kids—the better for me when they drop food!*

The Sunday right after the party would be Mother's

Day, too. I didn't know that bit of information, but Daddy said he was preparing a special sermon for mothers at church that morning. He also said he didn't want Mama to have to cook on Mother's Day, so they could go out. Mama protested, replying that all the restaurants for miles around would be jammed, because *everybody* goes out to eat on Mother's Day! Daddy was in a fix—he didn't have time to cook, Mama shouldn't cook on her day, so what to do? *I can't cook, either, Daddy, or I would do it for Mama.*

Actually, it was Asher who came up with a brilliant idea for Mother's Day. I've always thought my boy was smart, and this idea of his proved it. He told Daddy just to buy some food and bring it home! So, on Saturday, when Daddy took the children out to breakfast, he would stop by the deli at the grocery store and get some prepared foods for Mother's Day lunch: sliced ham, potato salad, macaroni salad, rolls, and whatever else he thought would be good. That way, when they got home from church (and it would probably be a little later than usual), he and the children could easily get lunch ready for Mama: the sisters could set the table, and Asher could help Daddy bring the foods to the table from the fridge. He told the sisters that the children could help him pick out presents for Mama, too— BUT they were not to say anything to her. He even trusted Asher with that secret, and to my amazement, all three kiddos kept the secret. *I think it's because they love Mama so much and didn't want to spoil the surprise for her.*

The day of the party arrived. Miss Janet came over, Daddy and the children left, and the two ladies got busy. As they were talking, Mama mentioned that Clark and Mavis couldn't come to the party this year. They were in New York City all week with their senior class for the senior trip, and wouldn't arrive home until late Saturday night. The great grandparents wouldn't be coming to Annika's party this year, either, because it was getting harder for them to travel as often. They did send Annika's presents, which were hidden in Mama's closet. Miss Janet asked if Annika was upset about that, but Mama said she thought Annika understood, especially since Papa had been in the hospital last year. *I understand, too, but I will miss Papa and Nana so much. We haven't seen them much since Christmas, so I hope we can soon—and maybe have a cookout with lots of yummy FOOD??*

The table looked really nice: the "food" tablecloth, plates, and napkins; the mason jars with kitchen utensils were adorned with large red bows, and at each place were a chef hat and apron. Mama had stacked the plates on the counter, since the children were going to decorate their aprons before making pizza. She had the apron supplies in plastic bowls on the tables; Mama, Daddy, and Miss Janet would help the children find their letters to spell their names, and then help them choose decorations. *Hey, maybe I want an apron, too, but I can't reach any of the letters and decorations myself.*

Next, she and Miss Janet went outside to hide the plastic foods all over the yard. It didn't take them long, because they were back inside in no time. Mama commented that it had been easy with all the trees in the yard as well as several bushes.

Mama then set the cake on the counter, and it was colorful with little candy foods all around the sheet cake. Miss Janet read the inscription aloud: "Grab Your Plate. Annika is Eight! HAPPY BIRTHDAY, Chef Annika." I thought that was appropriate, since the party invitations also had the same thing on them. Mama looked at her watch. "Janet, kids should be arriving before long. Hey—I hear a car." She looked out the window. "Ah. Philip and the kids are back—just in time, I might add." The door opened, and the children burst in.

"Is it the party now?" asked Asher excitedly. "Make pizza and eat cake! Yay!"

"Mama, PLEASE help me change," wailed Annika.

"I spilled syrup on my shirt, and my hair is a mess. I wanna look nice for my party." *She might be growing up, but in some ways she still seems like a little girl to me. I feel kinda sad that she's already eight years old.*

"Of course, sweetie," soothed Mama. Taking a quick look at Asher and Alexa, Mama seemed satisfied with the way they looked, but she did ask Daddy to wipe off their faces and hands. He agreed as Mama and Annika disappeared into her room. They were back in a flash, with Annika sporting a new shirt and freshly styled hair in a ponytail and red bow. She was smiling. *'All's well that ends well.' I heard Mavis say that once; she also said that somebody named Shakey-spear wrote a play called that a long time ago. With a name like his, who would even remember what he said??*

"You look very nice, dear," commented Miss Janet, giving Annika a hug. The doorbell rang, which was my cue to bark madly. *Oh, goody! Somebody is coming to see me! Who is it? Where are they?*

"Hush, Sargie," chided Mama. "It's probably the first children for the birthday party! Annika, you answer the door—after all, it's your party."

So it began. Children, some tall and some short, arrived and kept arriving. Girls squealed, boys acted shy, but most of them gave me a hug, which I really enjoyed. I did my best to give doggie kisses to each and every child who arrived. *It's like I'm on the welcoming committee. And that makes me important.*

Miss Janet directed them to put their presents for Annika on the small table at the back of the dining room. Mama had them all wash their hands at the sink since they were going to be making food soon. *I don't get that. I eat several times a day, and I NEVER wash my paws first. Humans!* The children were seated at the dining table and the other hastily set-up tables around the dining room to accommodate all of them. Mama had even put a small table for four just beside the hallway outside the dining area. She showed them their hats and aprons, and began helping them to find the letters to spell their names. Miss Janet soon joined in, and of course Alexa and Asher were enjoying the party, too. Daddy helped Asher get the letters to spell his name, and Asher was so happy and laughing. I must admit, he did look cute wearing his chef hat.

As the children arrived, the dining room and kitchen were beehives of activity. A couple of chef hats were left over, so one boy named J.T. stuck a hat on my head. All the children laughed, and Daddy snapped my picture. *Oh my goodness. It isn't my party, Daddy. Somebody get this contraption off my head! Wait—I must be getting old: I really don't mind, and in fact, I kinda like wearing it and getting attention.* Daddy walked around, snapping several other pictures of the children decorating their aprons.

It took a while for the aprons to be properly decorated, and there weren't too many decorations on the floor. I didn't bother them, because after all, they weren't *food.* The cats didn't show themselves, but that's not unusual for them. They don't seem to like a lot of noise and confusion, so they stay hidden. *That's fine with me, anyway. Who needs cats?*

Mama clapped her hands and shouted, "Are all the aprons decorated?" Heads nodded around the room, and children laughed, smiling. "All right, then, it's time for you young 'chefs' to prepare your very own pizzas! Before we do, however, Annika's daddy, Pastor Philip, is going to say grace. Let's all bow our heads and close our eyes." Daddy said a nice prayer, I thought, as much as a dawg can understand such things. When he finished, the children clapped and responded with "Yay!" "I love pizza!" "How many do I get to eat?" *(I think that last comment came from a boy).*

Daddy, Miss Janet, and Mama helped the young "chefs" flatten and carefully stretch out their biscuits and put them on a baking sheets near the stove, then choose their toppings. Daddy snapped more pictures. The grownups made sure they didn't choose too many, probably because the pizzas were not very big. The grownups put the pizza sauce on the flattened biscuits first. Then, they guided the young hands to place their toppings carefully. Mama popped the pizzas into the oven. While they were waiting for the pizzas to cook, she explained about the "food hunt" they would do after eating pizzas. She showed them the prizes, too. First place (the child with the most pieces of plastic food) was a $5.00 gift certificate to the local hamburger restaurant; second place was an assortment of hair bows if a girl won, or miniature cars if a boy; and third place was a joke book.

The activities were so noisy and fast paced that I'm not quite certain I recall everything exactly, but I do know they enjoyed their pizzas—some requested seconds and even thirds—and I did manage to scrounge up a few bites of pepperoni and cheese. Children are, after all, a bit sloppy. *Thank goodness.*

The food hunt was a big hit, too. When they finished eating, Mama directed them outside and laid down a few rules before they started the hunt: no stealing food items from others; no pushing, shoving, or rude behavior; stop immediately when she blew the whistle.

"All right, then," shouted Mama. "On your mark, get set . . . GO!" You would have thought this was a horse race, for goodness sake! Kids started galloping all over the yard, with first one and then another shouting, "I found a banana!" or "I got some celery!" Then another shouted, "Look! I found a tomato AND an onion behind this tree!" They gleefully covered our yard like a fleet of detectives looking for clues. Mama, Daddy, and Miss Janet laughed so much as they watched the children seeking out their food treasures. Even Asher held his own, although he was several years younger than any other children. *I'm proud of you, my boy. You think you are as big as the rest of them—and in a way, you are.*

After a number of minutes, Mama shouted, "Three more minutes! Hurry, children!" They moved with a frenzy after Mama said that. Daddy looked at his watch again. In no time, he signaled to Mama that time was up, so she blew the whistle. The children stopped and ran over to where Mama and Miss Janet were standing. "We grownups will count the pieces of food you have to see who has the most, the second most, and the third most. Then we'll give out the prizes. So, just wait your turn. Annika's daddy will keep a record, and Miss Janet and I will count."

So that is what they did. When all the children's foods had been counted, Mama, Miss Janet, and Daddy conferred, and Mama then announced the winners: "First place with the most food goes to . . ." Mama waited, building up the excitement: "J.T.!" The boy shyly came up and Miss Janet pinned his first prize blue ribbon on his shirt, and Daddy gave him his prize of the gift certificate. The children jumped up and down again, clapping and yelling. He showed the certificate to some of the boys. One boy pretended to steal it from J.T., but didn't manage to do so.

"Second prize goes to . . . Jean Raquel! Come on up and receive your prize!" Jean Raquel skipped up to Mama, Miss Janet pinned the red second prize ribbon on her, and Daddy gave her the hair bows. She shyly thanked Mama, then ran back to the other girls, who all wanted to see the hair bows, too.

And last, Mama announced, "And, third prize goes to . . . Claire!" The smiling girl with curly blond hair ran up to Mama. Miss Janet pinned the white third place ribbon on her, and Daddy gave her the joke book.

Claire exclaimed, "Oh, thank you, Miss Holly! I love to tell jokes, and now I'll have some new ones!" She ran back to her friends who all wanted to see her prize, too.

It was now time for Annika to open her gifts. So everyone trooped back into the house, with Mama directing them to sit on the carpet in the living room. Daddy and Miss Janet showed them where to sit, and several of the children helped Asher and Alexa bring the presents into the living room. Annika was to sit in the "seat of honor," or the recliner, to open her presents. The children were all talking in excited voices, and I overheard several calling to Annika to open theirs first. Miss Janet solved that dilemma: she stood by the gifts and handed them one at a time to Annika. *Well done, Miss Janet. Well done.*

All this excitement had worn me out, so I didn't follow every detail of the gift opening. Annika squealed with glee a few times, I heard her say "thank you" a number of times, and there was lots of wrapping paper on the floor, which the grownups picked up quickly. When it was time for cake and ice cream, I got up really fast, because there was a stampede into the kitchen. Kinda reminded me of a herd of cattle in the Old West! Of course, I've never seen one in person, but I do watch TV on occasion.

I knew I wouldn't get any cake and ice cream, so I stayed put in the corner of the living room. In fact, I actually fell asleep and missed the singing, Annika blowing out her candles, and all the cake and ice cream being consumed. I even missed it when the children went home, only waking up as the last child, J.T., went out the door with his grandma, Miss Marlene.

That's just plain terrible. But a dawg does need his rest, 'cause I'm not as young as I used to be.

2

Happy Mother's Day, Mama

The next morning was a beautiful sunny day as my family left for church. Mama was wearing a new dress and a rose corsage that Daddy had gotten for her. She looked very pretty in that yellow dress, I thought. *Of course, Mama always looks pretty to me.*

When they got home, I heard Mama tell Daddy that she really enjoyed his sermon about mothers in the Bible. And she liked it that he recognized all the mothers and grandmothers who were at church. Annika said a young man and woman were there she had never seen before, and they had the tiniest new baby who was so cute. Daddy told the children that they lived in Thomasville and were visiting the young lady's parents, Mr. John and Miss Lizzie. Alexa added that the baby must have been a girl since it had on a pink dress and pink frilly cap. Asher also added that Mama was the prettiest mama of all, though. Mama hugged him and thanked him for being so sweet.

Daddy then told Mama to just sit down on the couch while he and the children prepared lunch. She said she could get used to that, as she sank down onto the couch with a smile. I jumped up beside her. *I'm sorry I don't have a present for you, Mama,* as I licked her hand. *I just never got to the store this week.*

"Oh, Sargie, I do believe you're telling me 'Happy Mother's Day.' Thank you, buddy. It is a happy day for me." *I'm so glad, Mama. You deserve it.*

"C'mon, Mama!" shouted Annika from the dining room a few minutes later. "Lunch is ready!" Asher and Alexa came into the living room to escort Mama to the table. I followed, because I wanted to see what they had done for Mama, too.

In the dining room, Mama gasped. There was her

white linen tablecloth, and Daddy had lighted several candles and placed them in the center of the table, making a soft glow in the room. The dining room lights were turned down, so it seemed like we were in a restaurant. Beside Mama's plate was a vase with beautiful red roses. Soft music played in the background.

The children were excited. "Do you like it, Mama?" asked Alexa. "Happy Mother's Day! Love you so much!" She hugged and kissed Mama, and so did Annika and Asher.

Daddy came over and did the same. "Holly, we hope you enjoy your Mother's Day lunch. Today, we are serving sliced ham, potato salad, macaroni salad, rolls, and a strawberry and gelatin salad. Help yourself! You get to serve yourself first." Mama looked so surprised, but she was smiling all the while.

"Oh, this is so sweet, Philip and children. Thank you so much!" Mama proceeded to fill her plate while the children sat and waited patiently. *Now this is a day for the record book. Nobody complaining, whining, or saying anything about how hungry they are. Wow.*

After Mama finished filling her plate, Daddy looked at Asher, who proceeded to say grace: "Everybody bow your heads," said my boy. They did. He continued: "Dear God, thank you for my mama. We love her a whole lot. Make it be a good Mother's Day 'cause Mama loves You. Ummm . . . Amen—wait! Thank You for our food. Amen." The sisters clapped, and Mama got up and gave him a kiss. *That was a good job, Asher. I am proud of you, too.*

Daddy got Asher's food, then the sisters got theirs. They had a delicious meal (I even got a few bites of ham from Asher), and afterwards, the sisters cleaned off the table. Daddy left for a moment and came back with a couple of wrapped gifts. He cleared his throat: "Holly, we have some presents for you now. You are so special to all of us, we love you so much, and we thank the Lord for giving me such a wonderful wife, and the children such a loving and caring mother. Now, please open our gifts."

Mama thanked him and picked up the first package, which was small and white, with a silver bow on top. She opened it and gasped. "Oh Philip! You shouldn't have! These earrings are beautiful! Honestly, I hope they're not diamonds—those are too costly. But they are gorgeous. Thank you."

"No, I can assure you they aren't diamonds, but Austrian crystals. I thought you'd like them." Mama nodded, and couldn't seem to take her eyes away from the earrings.

"Open ours now, Mama," inserted Annika. As if coming back from a place far away, Mama proceeded to pick up the other package. "This present is from me, Alexa, and Asher."

The package was in a gift bag that had "Happy Mother's Day" printed on the outside. Mama lifted out a pretty blue summer blouse. She was smiling. "Blue looks pretty on you, Mama," said Alexa. "I helped pick it out."

"So did I," added Annika. "Asher did, too—and we didn't even argue about it!"

Mama laughed and held it up to herself. "This is beautiful, children. I can't wait to wear it to church next Sunday with my blue butterfly scarf and my black skirt! My new earrings will make it all a beautiful outfit! Thank you all so much." And Mama got up and hugged every one of them—even me.

She then got her cell phone and called Mavis to wish her a happy Mother's Day. Mama hoped that Mavis would enjoy the gift certificate to her favorite bookstore. After that, Daddy called his mom Sheila to wish her a happy Mother's Day, too. *I know Mama and Daddy wish they could have seen their mothers today. I'm glad I could see my mama today, and I think she realizes how much I love her, too. I am her oldest child, after all.*

3
A Phone Call from Papa!

Sometimes I wish all of our family lived nearby. I mean, we live in northern Georgia, while Kurt, Bethany, and their two cats, Tate and Joey (whom I call the Fuzz Brothers) live in Arizona. The rest of my family live in North Carolina: Uncle Steve and Aunt Dorothy and their menagerie (Zoe and Charlie their dogs, and Gizmo, their gabby bird) live in Cary; Clark, Mavis, and my doxie buddy Duke live in Garner; and Papa and Nana Duke live in Sanford. Sellars and Renata live in southern Georgia outside of Thomasville near the Florida state line, so it's like they are as far away as North Carolina.

I don't know how some families all manage to live next door to each other or on the same street—or at least in the same town! I just don't get to see everybody as much as I would like to, and I miss them so much. That is why I was thrilled several months after Mother's Day when Papa Duke called Mama. Notice I said *Papa called Mama.* He very seldom calls us, but that's because Mama calls them regularly to say hi and lets the children and me talk to him and Nana. I bark to them, but Papa is one of few humans who can pretty much understand what I am saying. When his call came that evening after we had finished eating dinner, we were all very happy. Mama answered the phone in her usual way, with "Blinson residence."

"Hey there, sweet girl!" said Papa in that booming voice of his. It was easy to hear him since I was standing beside Mama at the dining room table. She immediately put him on speaker. "Ray-melle and me was just talkin' about how much we miss y'all. We wanna ask y'all somethin'."

"Papa, we miss you and Nana, too," Mama replied. "It's a nice surprise to hear from you, too!" she happily told

19

Papa. "Is everything okay there in Sanford?"

"Why, hit shore is," laughed Papa. "I'm beginnin' to feel like my old self—at least as good as I'm ever gonna feel. Ray-melle and me was talkin' about comin' to see y'all if that's okay. We ain't never been to see y'all since you moved to Georgia, an' we wanted to come while we can still git around—we ain't gittin' no younger, you know," he laughed.

"Oh, Papa, when are you coming to see us??" asked Annika, with a lilt to her voice. "You mean you are coming to OUR HOUSE and staying WITH US??"

"Yep, if yore mom and dad can fit us in somewhere. We ain't got a motor home like Sellars and Renata, but if you got a corner we can sleep in, we'd love to come see y'all in two weeks, if that is okay."

Nana chimed in: "Holly, it just seems so long since we've been anywhere, and since we're both feeling pretty good—for old people, ha ha—we want to come see y'all, take in how it looks around there in Georgia, and go to church with you on Sunday so we can hear Philip preach. Seems like ages since we got to hear him. We wouldn't mind too much if you'd sing us a solo that Sunday, too. Seems like you oughta be able to do that for your grandpa and grandma, right?"

"Uh, well, I'll see what I can do, Grandma. I'm not scheduled to sing that Sunday, but I'll check our music schedule, since it's your special request."

"Papa come see Asher?" asked the little boy. "Nana come see Asher, too?" He began smiling and clapping.

"Yep, Asher, we's comin' to see all of y'all 'cause we miss you SO much," answered Papa.

"Oh, Papa, we miss you, too," added Alexa. "I want to sit on your lap and listen to you tell us some funny stories! And Nana, will you sit beside me when we eat?"

Nana answered first: "Of course I'll sit beside you— I'll just take turns sitting beside each one of you while we're there. How does that sound?"

Annika answered, "That's a good idea, Nana. I don't want Alexa to hog you or Papa while you're here!"

"An' I'll see if I can come up with any new stories I ain't tole y'all," added Papa. "Ray-melle, mebbe you kin hep me remember some I ain't never tole 'em, okay?"

"I'll try, Robert," she answered. "But we'd better nail down the details for coming, right Holly?" *Hmmmm. How do you use a hammer and nails with words, Nana?* Mama replied that it would be a good idea. "How 'bout if we leave here on that Thursday after lunch and get there to eat dinner with y'all? We'll stay until Monday, and head on back here to Sanford about midafternoon. How does that sound?"

"That sounds great," commented Daddy, who had as yet added nothing to the conversation. In fact, I hadn't either—and nobody seemed to even remember that I was part of the family, so I barked to remind them: *I wish y'all could just move here to be near me, Papa. A dawg needs his Papa more than I get to see you.*

"I do believe I hear my favorite dash-hound tryin' to tell me somethin,'" laughed Papa. "Yep, we cain't wait to see you, too, Sarge! We'll have us a good ol' time while we're there, that's for sure. I might even break down and cook some while we're there. How would you like that?" *Oh, Papa, I would love to have some of your cooking! Mama's a good cook, but there's nobody who can cook better than you and Nana!* I barked to him. *Oh, I am so happy that you are coming to see ME.*

"Then that's settled, Sarge," boomed Papa. "I know what you said, even if nobody else kin figger it out. You want me to cook you up somethin' good, don't ya?" he laughed. *Oh Papa. You are my favorite human for many reasons, and understanding what I say is one of them.*

"What would y'all like to do while you're here?" asked Mama. "Our community is very small, but we live near some larger towns, Taccoa Falls, Helen, a little touristy town with quaint shops, Commerce with all the outlet stores, the mountains are not too far, either, so if you want to visit any of those places—and maybe eat out a couple of times—that would be fun. And the girls' school is just a few minutes away. If you get here early enough on that Thursday, maybe you could go with me to pick them up from school." She looked at the girls who nodded *yes* enthusiastically.

"If you aren't too tired when you get here," added Annika, "would you come in and see my classroom and my teacher?"

"Me, too!" yelled Alexa. "My classroom is not far from hers. Oh, please say you will! I've been telling my teacher about my nana and papa, and now they'll get to meet you!"

"Holly, anything you want to do is fine with us," replied Nana. "In fact, Robert and I would just love to come see the girls' school and meet their teachers, wouldn't we, Robert?"

"Why, we shore would," he answered. "It's been many a year since I set foot inside a school, an' with all the new stuff they got now, like computers, dvd's, an' movin' sidewalks, y'all will probly have to explain everthang to yore ol' papa."

The sisters laughed. "Papa, we don't have moving sidewalks at school," Annika replied.

"Oh, I know it. I was just bein' a little silly," laughed Papa.

"Ahem." Daddy cleared his throat. "You know, Ramelle, if y'all wanted to bring us some of your delicious baked goods, we'd be happy to show our appreciation by eating them," he said, smiling. *Why Daddy, you are a 'closet' chow hound just like I figured out a while back, aren't you? You really like to eat as much as Annika, Papa, and I do—but you're just quieter about it than we are!*

""Philip, you must have ESP," Nana replied, "because just today I baked one of those delicious crunch cakes and put it in the freezer—with you in mind. I figured if it worked out for y'all to have us, then I'd bring that, along with some frozen strawberry topping to go with it." *What is ESP? Extra Special Philip??*

"Nana," asked Annika, "What does ESP mean? *Bless you, child.*

"Oh, it means 'extra sensory perception'—er, in other words, being able to figure something out without anyone telling you." *Oh—kinda like Mama does when I think something and she usually mentions what I was thinking about. Crazy.*

"That sounds wonderful," smiled Daddy, rubbing his tummy. "I'll really appreciate that."

Asher piped up, "Asher like cake, Nana. It for Asher to eat—nobody else!" But he was smiling.

"Sweet boy," replied Nana with a smile in her voice, "if Mama says it's okay, you can have all of that cake you want." Asher clapped, and Mama raised her eyebrows, but smiled. *And I'll be glad to help him, Nana. It's just a thought, 'cause I know that dawgs aren't supposed to have sweets. They must be delicious, though—that's one of the things humans talk about a lot, and commercials on TV do, too.*

"And I plan on brangin' a blackberry cobbler," said Papa. "We had plenty of blackberries in the freezer that we put up last summer, so I'll throw one together and brang that. Y'all know that a blackberry cobbler has always been my favorite. How's that?"

"Oh, I would love that, with a scoop of vanilla ice cream on top," declared Mama. "Of course, we'll have the ice cream here—don't try to bring that, too! And you know we do have a guest room here with a king-sized bed, so I think you'll find it to your liking. We've got it decorated with UNC Tarheel memorabilia—hope y'all don't mind that!"

"No, not at all," stated Nana. "Since Steve graduated from there years ago, we've been UNC fans for years—but maybe not to the degree that y'all are."

"As long as y'all can put up with our UNC décor in the guest room, that's fine," said Mama. "So glad you're coming—that's only two weeks away, and we can't wait to see you! Call us when you leave so we'll know when to expect you. I'll have you a good supper when you get here that Thursday, too," said Mama happily. *I know she misses her grandparents as much as I miss them.*

"It'll take us about five hours, Holly, 'cause we ain't as quick as you youngins are," said Papa. "And with Raymelle, we'll probly need to stop at every rest stop between Sanford an' yore house, you know!" he laughed.

"Well," retorted Nana, "I sure hope you stop more than you used to—Mavis always said that unless YOU needed to stop, nobody else got to, either!" I heard them laughing.

"We'll be jumping up and down to see you," Mama said. *And I thought only the sisters did that, Mama.* "And I can't wait to introduce you to our church on Sunday, either. Everyone has heard so much about y'all that they feel that they know you, anyway."

"Love you, Papa and Nana," said Asher shyly. "Want you to see Asher's room, too."

"Why, we shore will, won't we, Raymelle?" laughed Papa. "I bet yore room is the best one in the whole house!" That made Asher smile a big smile. *He is getting big enough to join in with the rest of us, isn't he?*

They said their good-byes, and the call ended. I was thrilled, because Papa and Nana had never been to our house here in Georgia. I remember when I got to visit Sellars and Renata with them in southern Georgia, but they've never been here to this house. I will have him mostly to myself, too, since Duke won't be here. *Now that's a pleasant thought. Oh, Duke is my buddy, but he's so energetic that he makes me tired competing for Papa's lap!*

The rest of the evening involved homework for the sisters, baths for all three children, family devotions, and their usual bedtime rituals: family prayer, hugs, more hugs, a glass of water for Annika, the covers rearranged for Alexa, and his door open just the right amount for Asher. *Good grief—why don't they just go to bed, for heaven's sake??* Once the children were finally in bed and Mama had finished making school lunches for the sisters, she and Daddy sat on the couch and discussed the upcoming visit. I plopped down on the couch beside Mama so I could hear what they said—since nobody tells me anything! *I have to sneak around, put my ear to closed doors, eavesdrop on phone conversations, sidle up to my humans, and the like. I want to stay informed since I am part of this family, too.*

Mama commented, "You know, Philip, I am so glad Papa and Nana are coming. I was dreading the time when they could no longer travel anywhere much. Too bad Sellars and Renata can't see them, since they live in southern Georgia. Wouldn't that be something if they could come and be with us all, too?" *Oh yes. I like that idea, Mama,* I boofed, wagging my tail.

"Look, Philip! I think Sarge likes the idea of having Sellars and Renata around, too!"

Daddy thought a moment, then said, "So, Holly, why don't you just call up Renata tomorrow and see if they can come? Since they have their motor home, we wouldn't have to come up with a place where they'd sleep. And we could keep it a secret in order to surprise your papa and grandma. What do you think?"

"Philip, that is an absolutely brilliant idea! Hmmm. Seems like I looked up how far it is to where they live—I believe it's over 300 miles and takes at least five hours' driving to get here from there. That should be manageable for them if they can get away. I'll be sure to call her in the

25

morning after the girls leave for school and I get Asher down for his nap. Maybe we'll keep this a secret from the children so they don't 'spill the beans' in case we talk to Papa again before they come." *Spill the beans? Sounds messy—oh yeah—I remember now that it means giving away a secret. I'm wiser now than I used to be.*

Mama and Daddy talked a while longer, discussing things they could do during the visit, Mama reminding herself to check the music schedule about singing that Sunday at church, what she could fix for dinner that night when they arrived—my head was spinning with all the details.

I'm glad I'm just a dawg and don't have to keep up with all those details OR accomplish any of them. I'm just happy to look forward to having some company who will FEED me, SPOIL me, and PAY ATTENTION to me.

4
Have Motor Home, Will Travel

The next morning, which of course was a school day, Mama stayed busy getting the sisters ready for school—preparing their breakfast, helping them get dressed and fixing their hair, and all of them joyfully discussing Nana and Papa's impending visit. Even Asher, who normally isn't a "morning person," was in an extremely good mood, squealing with delight every time anyone mentioned that Nana and Papa were coming.

"Yay! Nana coming! Papa coming! Papa play ball with Asher! Nana give Asher cookies! Yay!" And he just smiled all through breakfast. The sisters were excited, too, laughing each time Asher squealed. It made for a very jolly breakfast, a bit different than the usual half-asleep, non-talkative children I normally encountered at the breakfast table. The sisters didn't seem to dawdle as much as they usually did; I suppose the excitement of having their great grandparents coming for a visit just added buoyancy to their already-high spirits.

Daddy took the sisters to school, and Mama busied herself around the house while Asher and I played in the playroom. I was to watch over him while she finished up the kitchen and straightened up the dining room and living room, too. Oh, Mama was never far away, keeping an eye on us all the while. I didn't resent it at all, because I knew that was as much for my safety as it was for Asher's. He was lining up those beloved figurines of his again, and to my mind, I could not find what the attraction was. They were just made of plastic or vinyl, and I was forbidden to touch them. I must admit that I have been known to chew up some toys around here when I was younger, but not lately. I think I have gotten over that phase of my life, since I haven't seen anything around here I'm the least bit

27

interested in chewing on except human food, but I seldom get any of that.

Before long, Mama whisked Asher away for his morning nap, which meant I could now go and relax, too—*I might even take a little nap myself,* I thought. I trotted into the living room, jumped up onto the couch, and burrowed up under my blanket. *Now this is the life.*

Mama returned from Asher's room and said to me, "Sargie, I know you're under your blanket, but I'm gonna call Renata to see if she and Sellars can come when Papa and Nana are here. You keep quiet, and even if a loud truck goes by on the highway out there, DO NOT BARK." *Geez, Mama. I'm not stupid. And I'm not deaf, either.*

From underneath my blanket, I heard Mama pick up her cell phone and presumably dial Sellars and Renata's number, since her phone keypad didn't make any noise when she dialed. In a little while, she said, "Hi, Renata! This is Holly." Apparently, Renata asked if everyone was well, since Mama answered, "Oh, everything is just fine. In fact, I'm calling to ask if you and Sellars would like to come for a short visit to our house—Nana and Papa are coming weekend after next, and I thought it would be fun to invite you to come, too—and surprise them. Wouldn't that be fun?"

I could faintly hear Renata exclaiming how much they'd like to do that. "They're coming Thursday afternoon of next week—let's see—today's Tuesday, so it's about a week and a half. I hope that's enough notice for you. I checked with our GPS, and you're about five hours from us. Yes, see what Sellars says." Mama waited a short while. "Really? Oh, that would be fantastic! We live right on Georgia Highway 320, so since you already have our address, you shouldn't have much trouble finding us. And our church is right across the street, too. Nana and Papa are coming Thursday and will stay until Monday afternoon. You can come and leave like you want, but we'll be so glad to have you! We have a guest room for them, but if you could drive your motor home up here, we have a big yard where you could park it. Sure—they want to see our little town and 'all the nearby attractions,' so we'll just all go along. Thank you, and we can't wait to see you, either.

"What? Oh, that's what Nana said—she wants to hear Philip preach, too. And yes, at her request, I'm gonna sing Sunday morning, too. All right—that sounds like a great plan! Tell Sellars to bring his fishing rod, 'cause a church member has a pond with fish where he and Papa might actually catch some fish this time!" Mama laughed. "Yes, we'll have a camera ready to record the moment—and should I call the local TV station so they can run that on the evening news? It would be a newsworthy event, that's for sure!" I could hear Renata laughing in the background.

"Now don't forget: we want to surprise Nana and Papa when they get here, okay? Oh, that will be so fun! We love you guys, too. See you soon!" She ended the call.

"Can you believe that, Sargie? Nana, Papa, Sellars, and Renata are coming to see us in just a few days! And we'll all go over to Mr. Cecil's farm and take Papa and Sellars fishing. The children would enjoy that again, too. Remember we went fishing over there a few months ago? Alexa caught two fish, so I know Papa and Sellars oughta catch at least one each." *Oh, I don't know. To hear Nana and Renata tell it, I don't know if they've EVER caught any fish since Alaska. And we'll never hear the end of it if they do catch something. One good thing, though—I don't have to go out on that pond in a boat with them like I did when I was a young dawg. Nosiree—I didn't like that at all. Who knows? Sellars or Papa might hook one of my ears this time and throw me out into that pond. OUCH.*

Mama was making another phone call, probably to Daddy, who was across the street in his office at the church. "Philip—guess what! Sellars and Renata are gonna come while Nana and Papa are here! And we thought of something they can do: go fishing at Mr. Cecil's farm—remember how much fun the children had when we went that time?" Daddy apparently thought that was a good idea. "Okay—love you, too."

"Goodness, Sargie, things are really coming together, and I can hardly wait for their visit! Now, I'd better get cracking to think up what I'm going to cook for dinner when they all arrive. Oh, I'm so excited, and I know our church family will love them all as much as we do." *I agree, Mama. Papa and Sellars really know how to feed a poor, starving dawg. And they also know how to pay attention to him, too.*

Oh, I love being the center of attention—but I seldom get to do that around here these days, since Asher usually steals the show. But I honestly don't mind, since Asher is such a sweet boy.

5
They're Coming!

During the next week and a half, we were all excited and thrilled at the prospect of having company—but not just any company—it was family, and two of my favorite humans in the whole world: Papa and Sellars. Oh, I love Nana and Renata, too, but Papa and Sellars just seem to understand this dawg (and dawgs in general) better than anybody else.

Mama was doing her best to keep the secret of the additional guests from the sisters and Asher. I suppose she wanted them to be surprised, too, but also didn't want them saying anything to Papa or Nana if they called. She and Daddy worked on the guest room. Since it wasn't used that often, Mama said it needed dusting and vacuuming. *Oh no, Mama. You know how much I hate the vacuum cleaner! But—if it is for Nana and Papa, I'll try to keep my mouth shut for once.* Mama also ticked off aloud the other tasks she wanted to complete in the guest room: fluff the comforter and pillows in the dryer, put clean sheets on the bed, provide clean towels and washcloths, and have guest toiletries in the guest bath. *Wow. There sure is a lot to think about when humans come for a visit. None of this 'just put some food and water down' like they do for us dawgs.*

And Mama had decided what she wanted to make for that Thursday evening dinner: her famous Mexican casserole that Mavis always made when Mama was growing up, along with Spanish rice, refried beans, chips and salsa, and banana pudding for dessert, since it was Daddy's favorite—even though it wasn't exactly a Mexican-style dessert. Everybody loves Mexican food, so all that will certainly be a hit, she reasoned aloud. Annika was especially happy that Mama was making a Mexican dinner, since she loves Mexican food better than anyone I know. *I've heard Mama say that she thinks Annika could eat an entire basket of chips with salsa at a Mexican restaurant, along with her meal, too—I think she should have been named 'Mexika' instead of Annika. But that's just my own opinion.*

The days passed, but not fast enough for the children (or for me, either). Every day, Asher asked Mama, "Nana and Papa coming today?" And she would patiently explain how many more days until they came. After about the third day, Mama got the idea of marking the kitchen calendar so the children could see for themselves how many more days until Nana and Papa would arrive. She drew a big red star with a marker on "the day," then she crossed off that day and wrote in how many more days until THE day: eight, seven, six, five, four—and so on. Each night before the children went to bed, she also crossed off that day. They never tired of staring at that calendar, the sisters remarking to each other "five more days," or "four more days," until I was getting tired of hearing it. But Mama was really smart to fix the calendar so they could look at it. Asher even made a point of "checking" the calendar often, and I do believe my smart boy also understood, since he can pretty much count to ten on his own—but sometimes he gets seven and eight mixed up in the order.

That's kinda cute, though.

6
Countdown to Zero Day!

The final days while we were all waiting for Nana and Papa to come did seem to drag by—and I alone, other than Mama and Daddy, knew that Sellars and Renata were also coming to see us in a few days. The children were already thrilled, so I am sure they would have been "over the top" if they had also known who else was coming to see me! *Mum's the word, though, and I do not plan on spoiling the surprise for them.*

The children were also very helpful to Mama as we prepared for our family's visit. Mama had told the sisters that they must keep their room and the playroom "presentable," because she was going to dust and vacuum the entire house before Thursday. On that day, she would be busy in the kitchen, so it was up to them to pick up after themselves, put things away, and generally be helpful where needed. I must admit that they did very well. I even overheard Annika getting after Asher for leaving his toys in the living room. "Asher, do you think I'm your servant? Get these toys and put them away NOW." Asher looked at his sister in surprise, but picked up his toys and carried them to the playroom without a word. His sisters usually didn't say anything at all about toys, shoes, books, and anything else lying around in the living room—since they were often the culprits who left things where they dropped them. But they're a little older now, so I can see that the sisters are getting more mature and responsible. It certainly was humorous to hear one of them getting after their brother for the very thing *they* often did themselves!

Since Wednesday was Mama's busy day (besides Sunday), she made the sisters a list of chores to do when they got home from school every day that week before our company was to arrive. On Wednesday, Mama had ladies'

Bible study which lasted until after lunch, then she would rush home and put Asher down for his nap (he went with Mama to the Bible study since childcare was provided). Then, she'd pick up the sisters from school at 3:00, help with a weekly Bible club after school, and they'd come home for a little while. They would eat dinner at church for the weekly family meal there, go to church, where she directed the children's choir—practice was during the church service. *I get tired just thinking about all that Mama does.*

On Monday when the sisters came home, Mama showed them the chart she had made for them. Each item had a checkbox beside it, and for each chore they completed daily through Thursday, she would place a gold star in its box. If they had a gold star in every box, Mama would take them to get ice cream. She had even made a few chores for Asher: to take his vitamin, to brush his teeth, pick up his toys, and so on. The children loved the idea. *Hey, I barked, I'll help, too, if you'll give me something yummy to eat— how about some of those delicious bacon treats?? I can even pick up toys in my mouth and carry them to the playroom—but I can't reach the shelves. Even half a bacon treat??*

Mama laughed. "Sarge, do you want to help us, too, buddy? What do you think you could do around here?" *Mama, are you serious? I work hard, but you hardly ever notice how I've saved the children's lives several times, prevented catastrophes, and so on.*

"He could help us pick up toys and stuff," answered Alexa. "A lot of times, he grabs a small toy and runs off with it—so, if we could just get him to put the toys in the playroom, that would be helping us."

"Sarge help Asher clean up?" Asher looked at me and smiled. "Sarge pick up Asher's books, too?" *Of course I would, dear boy—if Mama asks me.*

"Mama, you didn't make a chart for Sarge," stated

Annika. "But I don't think he should eat ice cream, anyway."

"Hmmm," said Mama. "Oh, I don't think we can get Sarge in on cleaning up," she said. "You might see if he'll take some toys and put them away, but it isn't exactly his responsibility to pick up after you children, you know." *My thoughts exactly, Mama. But you know I'd do just about anything to get a tasty morsel of food.*

"It might be easier just to do it ourselves than try to make him understand that we want him to put things away," Alexa pointed out. "I love you, Sarge, but you're just a dawg—sometimes you are kinda dumb and don't understand what we want you to do." And she rubbed my ears. *Oh, I'm not dumb at all, my dear sister. I understand exactly what you humans want me to do just about all the time—but I choose not to do it. After all, if I start doing things like cleaning up, I might end up being the maid around here! That sort of thing would cut into my resting time. Nope—believe I'll pass. And if you humans mistakenly think I don't understand, I'll just have to live with that. Besides—I know better. We doxies are smart, so playing dumb sometimes fits in better with our own plans.*

And so it was. The week passed, the children helped keep the house uncluttered, and on Thursday morning Mama made her Mexican casserole and kept it in the refrigerator until time to bake it in the oven. Then she quickly dusted, enlisting Asher's help, such as it was. Daddy called around lunchtime, saying he was coming home in about an hour and would stay and help her finish up everything. Mama was so glad, because she still had to put sheets on the bed in the guest room, finish the rest of the food for dinner, and vacuum. *Oh, how I hate that noisy vacuum cleaner! Maybe Daddy and I can go outside while she vacuums.*

When Daddy got home later, he did help Mama

finish up around the house. I must admit that everything looked so nice. I chose to sit in the chair by the window and stay out of their way. *After all, who am I to hinder you from your work?* She put Asher down for his nap, but he was so excited about who was coming that I didn't think he'd even sleep. In fact, after a long time, Mama went back to his room to check on him like she always does. I trotted along after her because I was also interested to see if he ever went to sleep. We waited outside his door for a moment, listening. I could hear my boy in there talking, singing, and just sounding like he was having a fine time in there.

Mama opened the door: "Asher, have you gone to sleep at all since Mama put you down?"

"No."

"How long have you been lying there, talking and singing?"

"Years." With that, Mama burst out laughing, and I would have, too—if dawgs laughed. She went in and got my boy up, and he was smiling at her. *Little devil! I don't know where you got that "years" comment from—and you didn't even hesitate, either. You sure come out with some funny stuff sometimes, Asher.*

Daddy came to the door: "What were you laughing at?" Mama explained to him that Asher hadn't slept at all, so when she asked him how long he had been talking and singing, he replied with "years." Daddy smiled, taking Asher. "You are something, Asher. We just don't know where you get some of the things you say! For a two-almost-three-year-old, you sure are a smarty pants!" Daddy laughed.

"Asher pants not smart," he retorted. "Asher smart!" Mama and Daddy laughed at that, too. *Hey, you oughta be a comedian when you grow up—you are already a pretty good one now!*

We all headed back into the living room. "Philip,"

asked Mama, "would you mind taking Asher outside—and Sarge, too? I need to vacuum the living room, hallway, and bedrooms, and I just don't want to hear Sarge's 'comments' about the vacuum cleaner today. I mopped the kitchen, dining room, and bathrooms already."

"Sure will," replied Daddy. "Asher, wanna go swing for a little while so Mama can vacuum without us men in her way? And Sarge, you come along too, although I doubt you'll want to swing." *Nope—but I'd like to go outside, Daddy. Thank you, Mama, for sparing me from that dreaded machine. And there's always something interesting to inspect in the yard.*

Asher laughed. "Sarge not swing 'cause him fall off swing." *Exactly, Asher. Besides, I'm just too long to hang onto one of those swing seats. One time Annika put me on the slide, and the sisters thought that was so hilarious when I slid down that slide. I wasn't amused, and Mama scolded them, thankfully. I don't go near that slide when they are out there now!*

It was a bit nippy outside, but sunny, so if I stayed in the sun, I didn't feel cold. Daddy pushed Asher in the swing, but I noticed that he didn't go as high as Annika did. She always wanted the swing to go as high as it could—and so did Alexa. The harder anyone pushed them, the better they liked it. *Asher just isn't big enough to go that high, and I'm glad Daddy knows that.*

I moseyed over to the big oak trees in the front yard, looking for something interesting. I realized there wouldn't be any bugs since it was chilly this time of the year, but it was fun to hunt for stray acorns and crack them open with my teeth. I heard Asher squealing in delight as Daddy pushed him in his swing. After a little while, I heard him say, "Get down now. Go down slide." So Daddy and he went over to the slide, and I watched as Daddy helped him up the ladder in the back, set him down securely, and run to the bottom of the slide before Asher got there. Asher said,

"Again!" So they did that for quite a while. I was ready to go back inside and get on my comfy couch when Mama opened the front door and called, "Okay, men, I'm finished! Come on back in. They'll be here soon!"

Daddy helped Asher down from the slide and we were heading back toward the house when I saw a large motor home pulling into our driveway. *Sellars and Renata!* I barked and started running over to the driveway. *C'mon Daddy! Hurry, Asher! They're here!* I barked to them. *Oh boy oh boy oh boy!*

I reached the driveway as the motor home came to a stop, just as Daddy and Asher came up behind me. Mama came running out with a big smile on her face. "Yay! They're here, and won't Papa and Nana be surprised!" She reached us, and we all stood there smiling as the doors on the vehicle opened. "Oh, we're so glad you came!" shouted Mama, jumping up and down like the sisters. *So that's where they got it from.*

Both Sellars and Renata emerged, smiling and walking a bit funny. "Heh, heh. Me and Renata's kinda stiff after settin' fer so long, Holly," laughed Sellars. "Ain't Robert and Ray-melle here yet?"

Mama hugged them both, commenting that Nana and Papa were due any time now. Renata said, "Look at how big Asher has gotten since we saw him at Christmas! My, what a big boy you are—come give Aunt Renata a hug!" Asher shyly came over to her, and as she bent down, he put his arms around her neck. "Oh, what a cutie. Do you remember us, Asher?" Renata asked him. He nodded yes, smiling.

"Hey, don't this ugly ol 'man git a hug, too?" inquired Sellars. "C'mere, boy, an' give me a bear hug."

Asher laughed, stating the obvious: "Asher not bear!" Sellars laughed, too, reaching down and squeezing Asher, his long arms wrapping all the way around Asher. *I can hardly see you in there, Asher! Hey, remember me,*

Sellars? I may be short, but I'm your favorite here! I barked.

"Lookie there, Renata," laughed Sellars. "That there dawg is sayin' he wants a hug from us, too! Well, git on over here, Sarge, and let's us chow hounds greet one another. I shore am glad to see you, boy. Why, if I didn't have my Bubba at home, I'd fer shore git me a dash-hound jest like you, heh heh. I still might git me one before it's over with, too." *Oh, Sellars! I'm so glad to see you and Renata! And Nana and Papa will be here soon, too! I'm hoping you will give me something good to eat, because they try to starve me around here, you know.* And my tail, which often has a mind of its own, was wagging in double time.

Renata was hugging Daddy. "Philip, I brought you something special to eat, and I know you'll enjoy it, 'cause I baked it 'specially for you," she said as she gave him a hug.

"Thank you. I know I will love whatever it is—by the way, what is it?" Daddy asked about as enthusiastically as I had ever seen him act.

"I made you a gooey, delicious cinnamon bun cake," Renata replied proudly.

"Oh, my goodness," laughed Mama. "He loves cinnamon buns. I doubt he'll even share it with the rest of us!" Daddy just smiled, but said nothing. *I believe you're right, Mama—but not that I would get any of it, anyway. Dawgs can't have sweets, I've been told about a million times. They must really be good, though, the way humans talk about them, eat them, watch commercials about them, and think about ways to get more of them. That's the way I feel about bacon treats, so I understand very well.*

"Can I help you bring in anything?" asked Daddy. "Let's not stand in the driveway any longer—y'all are welcome to come into the house, you know!" Sellars and Renata laughed.

"We ain't really got nuthin' to take in, do we,

Renata? Since we'll be sleeping out here—an' you gotta help me hook her up later—they ain't no need to brang in our nighties."

"Sellars wear nightgown like sisters??" Asher laughed. So did everyone else.

"Aw, naw, Sellars was jest tryin' to be funny," he replied. "Now that would be a sight fer sore eyes, I kin tell ya. But don't y'all worry none—I wear PJ's, not nightgowns."

We all headed for the house, entering by the kitchen door under the carport. "Come on in to our home," said Mama. "It's the church parsonage, and we love it. Lots of room, convenient, and comfortable."

"Oh, Holly," exclaimed Renata as we all entered the kitchen, "I like your large kitchen—and look at all that counter space. My kitchen at home has lots of room, too, since our house is an old farmhouse." Renata's eyes wandered around the kitchen and on into the dining room, which was just behind the counter.

"Sellars, let's go sit down in the living room while the women talk about the kitchen," said Daddy. "I'm sure you're tired. Would you like a glass of iced tea or a cup of coffee? I just made a pot of coffee a little while ago."

"Sounds like a plan, Philip," said Sellars. "I'd love to have a cup of coffee. Asher, you come on with Sellars and set on my lap while yore daddy gits the coffee. I'd like to jest talk to you, anyway." So Sellars led Asher to the couch, and they sat down. I whirled around and went back into the kitchen just as Mama was asking Renata if she would like to see the rest of the house.

"Oh, I'd love to, Holly. I like the way your dining room is connected to the kitchen. And it is so large. You have plenty of room around the table, and I see you have your computer desk over in the corner. Nice."

"Let's see the living room first, since it's right through this door," said Mama. They peered in at Sellars and Asher, who both waved at the women. "This living room is so large that behind the couch here"—she waved her arm—"we have our treadmill and exercise bike. I also keep a little stash of Asher's books and toys back there since he likes to play in here while the girls are at school. Oh, that reminds me—I hope Nana and Papa come soon, because it's almost time to go pick up the girls from school, and they wanted to go with me."

"Oh, they'll be here on time, I'm sure," answered Renata. "Robert and Ramelle wouldn't miss that for the world." They looked over the living room, which contained a couch, loveseat, a recliner, some end tables, the TV and its cabinet, and the decorative tree in the corner. Renata exclaimed again at how large the room was. Mama replied that they did like having all this space. *It usually looks like an obstacle course, though, Renata. The children seem to like leaving their toys, books, and shoes all over the floor. But it looks great right now.*

They headed on down through the living room as I looked back and saw Daddy carrying two steaming cups of coffee. Sellars made some comment about that being just what the doctor ordered. *What doctor? We don't have a doctor here.*

As I trotted along behind Mama and Renata, they came out of the door at the other end of the living room and into the dining room. Just as we entered, in pranced Piper and Aslan, looking for all the world like they were a welcoming committee. They sat down in front of the computer desk, staring, their tails twitching. *Hmmmm. Wonder what you boys are up to? You usually hide when people come, so since you actually came out, something must be up.*

"Awww, look at those pretty kitties," said Renata. "Holly, that black-and-white one is huge! And look at the smaller white one with brown rings around his tail. They're both beautiful." Mama explained that Piper's fur was so

41

thick and fuzzy because he was a Norwegian forest cat, while Aslan was flame-point Siamese. Renata rubbed them both behind the ears. I could hear those cats purring all the way across the room, for heaven's sake. *You two might fool these human ladies, but you don't fool me one bit. You aren't all that innocent, I know. You probably just want something from them, don't you?*

"Let's go on over to this little hallway," said Mama. "Here's the girls' room, which they share. Beside it is the main bathroom, basically the children's," she pointed out. "And across the hall are the playroom and the guest room, or our UNC Tarheel room and guest bath." Renata looked in on all of them, complimenting Mama's decorating abilities. She liked everything.

"Now," said Mama. We'll go down this long hallway to Asher's room and the master bedroom. Several years ago, this section was added onto the parsonage when the pastor at the time had four children. Each room also has a full bath."

"This home has five bedrooms and four baths?" asked Renata. "That's a large parsonage, and it's nice that you can use one of the rooms as a playroom. I saw all those toys and books in there—with three children, you need a playroom."

We headed down the hall and turned right, into Mama and Daddy's room. "And here's our bedroom," said Mama. "We have a full bath through that door over there, and we really like the large closet over here in the corner," Mama pointed out.

"Oh, Holly, I love the colors in here," said Renata. "Your comforter is beautiful—black-and-white arabesque design, but you have teal window sheers and decorative pillows. Nice." She peeked into the bathroom, exclaiming, "And your shower curtain is the same material as your comforter. Your teal towels really set it off in here, too. You certainly have a flair for decorating!"

"Thank you," Mama replied. "I guess I got my creativity from my mom, who loves making her house inviting and colorful, too. Asher's room is right across the hall, so let's go see it." They headed across the hall to Asher's room, which contained his crib, his dresser, his rocking horse, shelves containing his little trucks, and a small Asher-sized chair in the corner.

"What a nice little boy's room," stated Renata. "I love the greens, blues, and yellows in the curtains and crib linens."

"Before long, we'll get him a 'big boy bed,' as he likes to call it," said Mama. "And here's another full bath with a nice shower instead of a tub. When Mom and Dad come for a weekend, they like to use the shower in here. This is where you and Sellars can shower if you want." Renata poked her head in and looked around, saying that they'd probably just use their little shower in the motor home.

"Oh, I love that shower curtain, too," she said. "It looks like chiffon squares in sea green. Very pretty."

Just then I heard my favorite voice in the world, and it sounded like it was in the kitchen. I started barking, whirling around and galloping down the hall and into the kitchen. Mama and Renata hastened after me. *Papa! Is it really you in my house? Nana, too?*

And there, standing in our kitchen were my beloved Nana and Papa Duke. I could hardly contain my excitement, so I just kept barking to tell them how happy I was to see them. Papa laughed that beloved laugh of his when he saw me, and beckoned for me to come to him. I ran over, he picked me up, and I smothered his face with doggie kisses. *Oh, Papa! I've missed you so much, and you've never come here to see me before! I am so glad to see you! I love you, Papa!*

Nana was patting me on the back as Papa said, "Sarge, ol' boy, I shore am glad to see you, too! Why, Ray-melle an' me could hardly wait to git here an' see everbody.

43

And findin' out that Sellars an' Renata wuz here is jest like icin' on the cake!" *Cake? Where? What kind? Bacon, maybe?*

Asher came running out of the living room, followed by Sellars and Daddy. Asher shouted, "Papa! Nana!" Nana reached down and picked him up.

"Oh, look at this sweet boy! Give Nana a big hug, Asher. Look at you, growing like a weed. Robert, look how big he's getting!" *A weed? He's not that skinny, Nana.*

"I see that, Ray-melle. Ever time I see him, he gits so much bigger. Why, he'll be grown before we know it!"

"Duke, who woulda thought we'd all be here together at Holly and Philip's house? Ain't that sumthin'? Me and Renata got real excited when Holly invited us, let me tell ya," boomed Sellars.

Papa put me down and replied, "Yeah, me an' Ray-melle was lookin' forward to gittin' here an' seein' 'em, but we're even more excited to be here now that you an' Renata is here, too. Now that's my kind of surprise!" And the two men clapped each other on the back.

Mama said, "I have to leave in a few minutes to pick up the girls from school. I don't know how they concentrated on anything today, being so thrilled about y'all coming. And we didn't even tell them Sellars and Renata were coming—they will just about faint when they find out y'all are here, too. Does anyone feel like going with me to their school?"

"Why don't Ramelle and Robert go with you, since the girls are expecting them?" stated Renata. "Sellars and I will just stay here, and we can see them when y'all get back. That way, the grandparents can spend a little time with them before y'all come back home."

"Good idea. You two can visit with Philip, Asher, and Sarge until we get back—and the cats, if they don't go hide somewhere. I'll warn you that we'll be longer than usual, because the girls wanted Nana and Papa to see their classrooms and meet their teachers—if y'all feel up to it after driving down here," she said to Nana and Papa.

"Why, of course we'll go see their rooms," Nana insisted. "Who knows when we'll ever get back down here, so we want to see everything we can while we're here. Right, Robert?"

"Right," replied Papa. "Them girls might be glad to see us, but not half as glad as we are to see them. Let's go!" And Papa acted like he was going to run right out the door, much to the amusement of all of us. *Papa, you are so funny. And cute.*

"Let me get my car keys and purse, and we'll go." Mama picked up her purse, fished out her keys, and they headed out the door. Asher acted a little upset that Nana and Papa were leaving already, but Papa reassured him that they were just going to pick up the girls and would be back in a little while. Papa made a silly face at him, causing Asher to laugh. They headed out the door.

The men chatted, but Sellars did most of the talking. Daddy did a good job of carrying the conversation, although he's the quiet one in the family. I would've helped if I could have, but then, they wouldn't have been able to understand what I said, so I mostly just listened. Asher showed Sellars his favorite toy train, and Sellars really acted as though he liked it a lot. He let Asher explain how it went around the track, pretending he didn't know a thing about trains.

At least, I *think* Sellars was pretending.

7
Mexican Fiesta: Olé!

Before long, Mama and the others were back home, the sisters literally dancing into the house. Apparently, they had noticed the motor home out front, so as they burst in, Annika yelled, "Sellars and Renata, where are you?" Both sisters ran into the living room and then just stood there, staring at Sellars and Renata as if they couldn't believe those two were actually here, too.

Alexa came out of her trance first and ran over to hug Renata. "Mama didn't tell us you were coming, too— she really surprised us. Oh, I'm so glad you came!" she exclaimed breathlessly.

Annika ran over to Sellars to hug him. "Wow, this was a fun surprise, too!" she said cheerfully. "It's like having two papas and two nanas here at one time!" Just then, Mama, Nana, and Papa came in from outside. Annika turned to Mama: "Mama, this is so good. First, we knew Nana and Papa were coming, but then to find out that Sellars and Renata were here—"

"You ain't half as happy to see us as we are to see y'all," laughed Sellars. "Why, Renata an' me was talkin' all the way here 'bout how good it would be to see y'all again!"

"That is the truth," added Renata. "And here we all are, together again! Ramelle, we couldn't wait to see you and Robert, too, of course."

Nana laughed. "I was beginning to wonder there for a minute, Renata."

"An' ol' Duke," commented Sellars. *Ahem. What about a certain dawg? Aren't y'all a bit glad to see me, too?* I boofed. They all turned and looked down at me. "Ol' Sarge, you know we came to see the Number One Dawg in Georgia—an' that's you. Heh heh heh," all the while patting me on the head. *That's better.*

Sellars turned to Papa. "How'd you like goin' back to school, huh? Did ya learn anything while you was there today?"

"Oh, I learned that I cain't figger out them computers, that's for sure," replied Papa. "We met the girls' teachers, and they was jest as nice as they could be, but boy, they shore was young lookin'!"

"Heh, heh," laughed Sellars. "Duke, everbody looks young now to us ol' geezers, ya know!"

"That's fer sure, Sellars," replied Papa. "But these girls is learnin' more now than I have ever learned, what with computers, printers, dvd's, and all that stuff. I did good to jest write my name on a piece of paper so's you could read it when I was their age!" Everyone laughed.

"Robert and Ramelle, would y'all like a cup of coffee or a glass of tea?" asked Daddy. Both said they'd love a cup of coffee, so Daddy proceeded to the kitchen to get it, soon returning with their two mugs of coffee.

"Thank you, Philip," said Nana. "This will hit the spot." *What spot, Nana? And why would the coffee 'hit it'??* She took a sip. "Ah. Very good." *No answer for me, I suppose. I don't think I'll figure that one out, either.*

Papa also sipped his and gave the thumbs up sign, indicating that he liked Daddy's coffee-making skills.

"Nana, I've already shown Renata the house, but you didn't have time when y'all got here. Go ahead and finish your coffee, and I'll give you a tour if you like," Mama said.

"Oh, I can walk and carry my coffee—let's go!" said Nana, getting right up. "I love this large living room."

"Oh, trust me," replied Renata. "You'll love the rest of the house, too." Nana smiled as she and Mama left the living room to tour the house.

"Papa see Asher's toys?" the little boy looked up at Papa inquiringly.

"Asher, Papa might be too tired right now," replied Daddy.

"Naw, I ain't too tired to see them toys," he replied. "C'mon and show Papa," he smiled.

"We'll come, too," said Annika. "The playroom has most of our toys and books, too. Wanna come, Alexa?"

So Annika, Alexa, Asher, and Papa headed for the playroom, apparently meeting up with Mama and Nana. I overheard them talking and laughing, so they must have been having fun in there. Daddy, Renata, and Sellars were doing just fine in the living room, and I decided to stay in there with them. *After all, I have seen this house plenty of times.*

Soon, however, everyone came back into the living room. Mama said she needed to get into the kitchen so we could eat dinner on time. Papa perked up at that statement.

"Holly, whatcha havin' fer supper tonight? I know it'll be good."

"We're having my Mexican enchilada casserole, Spanish rice, refried beans, chips and salsa, and banana pudding for dessert! I know everybody likes Mexican, so I made plenty," she smiled. "I just want to go on record to say that I *know* banana pudding isn't Mexican food, but Philip loves it."

"Now that sounds like a winner, don't it, Sellars?" said Papa. "An' I bet they probly eat banana puddin' down in Mexico—if they don't, hit's their loss!"

"It shore does, Holly," added Sellars. "I ain't had me no good Mexican food in a long time, so that will be just fine."

"What's in your Mexican casserole, Holly? It sounds mighty good," said Renata.

"Mom used to make it for us all the time, and I think she just put some things together without a recipe," replied Mama. "You just layer the ingredients like you're making lasagna. Instead of noodles, you use corn tortillas. Then, seasoned enchilada meat, enchilada sauce, white corn, and grated cheese—I use a combination of cheddar and Monterrey jack with jalapeños in it, and continue layering until the pan has about one inch of clearance at the top. I top it with extra cheese right before baking it. I have mine already put together in the fridge, so all I have to do is pop it into a 350-degree oven for about 40 minutes. Vóila— Mexican casserole! I also have the Spanish rice and refried beans ready to heat as well."

"Goodness," replied Renata. "Sounds like you really planned ahead, too. Let me know if I can do anything to help."

"Me, too," said Nana. "What can we do to help you, Holly?"

"Oh, nothing right now. Maybe in a little while you ladies can set the table. I have a tablecloth from Guatemala that I picked up on one of my mission trips in college, so I'll get that out and cover the table now." Mama left the living room. In a short while, I heard that all-too-familiar Spanish music from the dining room. In a moment, Mama appeared in the doorway wearing a *sombrero* covered in bright embroidery and sequins. *"Olé!"*

"Would you look at that!" exclaimed Sellars. "Ain't you a sight fer sore eyes, heh heh."

The others smiled, nodding their heads. *Just so you don't get the brilliant idea that I should be wearing that thing, Mama. I could probably hide under it, you know.*

Mama replied, "I like a little authenticity when I have Mexican food, so I'd better finish everything up." She disappeared back into the kitchen.

Before long, with Renata and Nana's help, dinner was served. The table looked festive, the food smelled heavenly, and everyone hastened to the table. Renata remarked that she really looked forward to eating that meal. Sellars commented that he didn't just look forward to it—he was actually gonna eat it!

Papa and the children hastened in from the living

room, too, and everyone sat where Mama indicated. I watched carefully to see where Papa was going to sit so that I could position myself under his chair—in hopes of getting some of that good food from someone who loved me and liked to share with me. *Unlike everyone else in this family.*

Daddy said grace, and Mama explained that she'd serve the casserole since it was large and so hot. Papa acted like he was going to throw his plate to her like a Frisbee, causing the children to giggle. Asher, in fact, picked up his little plate, all set to do the same thing, but Mama deftly snatched it from him just in time. "Asher, Papa was just joking—he wasn't really going to throw his plate to me, were you, Papa?"

"Naw, I wasn't joking—I'm hongry and I thought that would be the quickest way to git it over there since I'm down at the other end of the table," and he winked at Asher.

The festive meal proceeded with much laughter and exclamations about how delicious it was. Papa did manage to drop me a bite or two of the casserole and an old tortilla chip, but that was all. *I sure am glad you didn't give me any of that hot pepper, Papa. I don't like it when my tongue feels like it's on fire.*

Mama told the sisters to help clear the table so she could serve the banana pudding. I was surprised that they weren't "too tired" to help, but since we had company present, they jumped right up and proceeded to do just that. *Wow. Guess they want to make a good impression. They sure did with me.*

Nana and Renata also started to get up, but Mama shook her head, signaling for them to sit back down. "No, ladies—you're our guests, and it is our pleasure to let you relax. Right, girls?"

"Yes, Mama," they chorused. The sisters came back to the table for another load, carefully picking up the rest of the plates and carrying them to the kitchen and depositing them on the counter.

"Is that all we need to do for now, Mama?" Annika asked.

"Yes, Honey, and thank you," replied Mama. "Come on back and sit down so we can have dessert." Mama had been busy, too, while they were clearing the table: she had gotten out the banana pudding, dessert plates, and Daddy had gotten coffee for everyone except the children. She began serving the banana pudding to Papa and Sellars first, then Nana and Renata, then Daddy, and finally, the children. It was silent for a few minutes as dessert was consumed. Mama mentioned that tomorrow, they could all go fishing at Mr. Cecil's pond, if that was agreeable.

"Agreeable?" hollered Papa. "Me and Sellars shore would love that, now wouldn't we, Sellars?"

"Ain't it the truth," smiled Sellars. "Me an' you gotta redeem ourselves and catch us some fish, don't we? Raymelle an' Renata ain't never gonna let us live it down if we don't!"

Renata laughed. "We're going, too, aren't we, Ramelle? Holly, be sure to bring a camera so we can 'capture the moment' that will surely go down in history!"

"That should be on the evening news, too—IF they catch anything," added Nana.

The friendly bantering went back and forth for a while, with Annika adding that she liked to fish, too. Of course, Alexa said she did, too. *I sure don't. I don't mind watching others, but I'm not much for jumping into that pond and hunting down something to eat. No sir. I'm happy having my food handed to me, thank you.*

Soon, Sellars pushed back his chair and patted his tummy. "Mighty fine meal, Holly—might fine. I enjoyed every mouthful, and I declare I couldn't put one more bite of anything in my mouth right now." He sipped his coffee.

"It was delicious, Holly," added Nana. "You are a wonderful cook, and I enjoyed your food, too!"

Mama replied: "How could I be anything less than a

decent cook in this family?? Food is one of our best friends!" *Except for me, Mama. I don't get enough of it to know if it is my friend or not. I am so mistreated around here.*

They were all now finished, so Daddy helped Asher down from his booster seat, and Mama told the sisters to go into the living room with the men and visit while the ladies finished up in the kitchen. They scampered off happily. I decided to hang around "just in case" any of the ladies accidentally dropped any food.

Apparently, that's about the only way I'm gonna get any more people food tonight.

8
Another Fishing Story

The next day, after a large country breakfast of pancakes, sausage, grits, scrambled eggs, and coffee, we all headed over to Mr. Cecil's pond. Papa did himself proud at breakfast, at least in my eyes—he provided me with a good breakfast to start off my day. *He sent eggs down my way, and I love the way Mama soft scrambles eggs.* Sausage is a bit too spicy for my taste, and since we didn't have bacon, I didn't mind not getting any of that.

Mama said Mr. Cecil had plenty of fishing rods and bait, because a lot of people from church liked to go over there. Papa and Sellars were really excited because they said they'd be sure to catch some fish this time.

Mama let me go, too, because I had plenty of room to run around on their farm. I liked going because there were so many interesting things to see and smell. And, they had a couple of laid back old hound dogs whose company I enjoyed.

As we drove up in front of their large farmhouse, out came Mr. Cecil and his wife, waving to us. As we got out— we had to take two cars, since we couldn't all fit into one— Mama began the introductions. "Mr. Cecil and Miss Penny, this is Papa Duke, Nana Duke, and some good friends, Sellars and Renata. Y'all, meet Mr. Cecil and Miss Penny." They all shook hands or hugged.

"I understand that you men are some famous fishermen, so I'm mighty honored to have y'all with us," said Mr. Cecil with a twinkle in his eye. Mama could hardly keep from laughing.

"I don't know who told you that, but you got some bad information," laughed Papa. "We ain't famous, and we sure ain't been fishermen for a l-o-o-o-n-n-n-g time!"

Mr. Cecil laughed. "Yeah, Holly put me up to saying

53

that. Hope y'all kin take a joke—I ain't much of a fisherman myself, but I shore do like the tryin,' anyhow."

"Then me and you is gonna git along jest fine," added Sellars. "Maybe we'll have us some decent luck this time, though." I heard Nana and Renata snickering, causing the children to laugh, too. *I might as well get in on the act,* and began barking: *Catch some fish, Papa and Sellars!* Of course, they couldn't understand what I was saying.

"Can we fish, too, Mr. Cecil?" asked Alexa.

"Why, shore you can if it's okay with your parents," he replied. "How many of y'all want to fish, so I can git enough poles out?" Mama and Daddy said they did, and of course the children wanted to, and Papa and Sellars. Nana said she and Renata could cook fish, but weren't interested in trying to catch any.

Miss Penny told them to come on into the house and "set awhile" with her—she had made some cookies that morning. How about coffee and cookies to go with some nice conversation? Nana and Renata thought that was a fabulous idea, so the three ladies trooped on toward the house. *What about me? I might want a cookie—but I won't get one.*

"Holly, you let us know if anybody—especially Robert or Sellars—catches anything, all right?" said Nana over her shoulder. Mama nodded, smiling. I didn't particularly want to sit on the grass and watch, so I got up to explore the huge yard.

"Now Sargie, don't you stray too far," called Mama. "Stay within sight, okay?" I barked to let her know I heard her, and moseyed over to a big bush. I could still hear the children's squeals of delight, Papa and Sellars' laughter, and Mr. Cecil's comments as he helped the children put bait on their hooks. I kept exploring, satisfied that everything was under control.

I headed over to the barn where I knew Mr. Cecil

kept a few cows and horses. There were some pretty interesting sounds and smells coming from there, but since the door was closed, I headed on past the barn and over to the fence where I saw several goats. They were nibbling something that appeared to be grass. They watched me and I watched them for a few minutes, but that got boring, so I moved on. Just as I turned around, I heard a faint *meow* on the other side of the barn. Since I live with cats, it was obvious to me that there had to be a cat over there somewhere, so I proceeded to find it. As I rounded the corner of the barn, there it was: an orange tabby cat that looked a lot like Tate, Aunt Bethany and Uncle Kurt's orange cat. The cat saw me, but didn't bother to get up, but just lay there, twitching its tail. It yawned, then laid its head back down, presumably to sleep. I was getting a bit tired myself, and since I usually napped when Asher did, I decided to lie down near the cat, who acted like I was invisible. Fine with me, since I was tired—I wouldn't bother the cat, and I didn't think it would bother me. That's all I remember until Mama came looking for me later.

"S-a-a-a-a-rge! Where are you?" I woke up with a start and shook my head, looking around. *Where am I? Where is Mama? I hear her, but I don't see her. Oh yeah— I'm at Mr. Cecil's, and I guess I fell asleep.* The cat had disappeared—or had I merely dreamed it? I'll never know, because I didn't see the cat again.

"Sargie!" I heard Mama calling me again. I barked in reply, getting up to head toward her voice. Mama and I came around the corner of the barn at the same time, but from different directions. "There you are, boy! I didn't know where you had gotten to. GUESS WHAT, Sarge! Papa, Sellars, and Alexa all caught a fish—in fact, Papa caught three! Can you believe that?" *Wh-a-a-a-t?? I didn't think they knew how!* "We'll be leaving in a little while, but the children were running to the house to tell Nana and Renata the surprising news—bet they'll faint from shock," Mama said with a smile. *I'm a bit shocked myself, Mama. Too bad I had to miss the event of the century!*

We headed back toward the house, and I could see all of them standing on the porch, talking excitedly. Nana and Renata were acting like they were going to faint, fanning themselves, and then sat down in a couple of the rocking chairs on the porch, overcome with the shock of it all. *Y'all are pretending, aren't you? It would make sense if you ladies really were about to faint from shock!* As Mama and I reached the house, Renata, fanning herself, was exclaiming, "Sellars, are you SURE that y'all caught those fish? I just can't believe it."

"Yes, we did, Honey Lamb, so I guess ol' Duke an' me has got our touch back—right, Duke?"

"Yep," replied Papa. "We used to be purty good fishermen in Alaska, but somehow we just lost it—but it's back, now. WE ARE FISHERMEN again, at last!"

"Papa an' Sellars good fishers today!" Asher piped up. "Yay Papa! Yay Sellars!"

Everybody began talking at once, and I could hardly tell what anybody was saying. Mama did one of those loud whistles with her fingers to her mouth, and everyone stopped in midsentence: "This is truly a red-letter day. And Nana, I did take some pictures of Sellars and Papa holding up the fish they caught. I used my cell phone camera, so we'll preserve the moment for posterity!" Everyone clapped. *Wonder if this event really will be on the TV news like Nana said earlier?*

"I caught a fish, too," said Alexa. "Mama took my picture with my fish. So does that mean I'm a fisherman, too?"

"It shore does, Honey," declared Papa. "We're real proud of you, too, but me an' Sellars ain't caught nuthin' in so long that it's about like this was our first catch, too!"

Annika, downcast, commented, "I didn't catch anything at all." Papa told her he would give her one of his, and that seemed to make her happy.

Everyone thanked Mr. Cecil and Miss Penny, and we headed home, satisfied. *Papa and Sellars really can catch fish—I was beginning to wonder if they ever would. But what will we have to eat tonight? I don't think there's enough fish to feed all of us.*

I heard Mama tell Daddy while we were on the way home that she had all the fixings for dinner—all he had to do was just cook the hamburgers and hot dogs on the grill outside.

Mama, how do you always manage to talk about something I just thought? I love anything on the grill, and with Papa here, I'm certain to get something good to eat.

Can't wait—anything on the grill is 'good eatin,' as Papa likes to say.

9

A Hot Dog for the Hot Dawg

We had a wonderful cookout that evening. There was a bit of chill in the air, but everyone wore jackets and sat under the carport while Daddy grilled. However, the children didn't actually sit—they ran around, played with a ball, sat on various laps and got up again, and so on. I sat on Papa's lap so I could smell the meat cooking. My nose went into overdrive since I was so hungry, waiting for that food.

Mama, Nana, and Renata prepared the "fixings" while Daddy grilled, and just when Daddy was putting the hamburgers and hot dogs on a platter, declaring that they were done, Mama opened the kitchen door. She said they had everything ready inside, so with that perfect timing, we all went into the dining room for dinner. Mama told the children to go wash their hands, while the adults all sat down around the table. I couldn't see what was on the kitchen counter—Mama usually lined the food up and let everyone come by and get it—but I could pretty much determine what it was by smelling: potato salad, baked beans, pasta salad, lettuce and tomato, sliced onions, and of course mustard, ketchup, and mayonnaise. There was even some cole slaw and chili, since Mama knew what Papa liked on his burgers and dogs. When the children returned, Papa said grace, and Mama went first to fix the children's plates for them. Then, everyone else filled their plates and sat back down.

I was waiting under Papa's chair, and soon he dropped down some small pieces of hot dog, and next came a little bite of hamburger, my favorite. I was happy. *Hey, Papa: did you know you gave this hot dawg some hot dog?? He didn't seem to notice, so my joke was lost on everyone but me. That's okay, though, because if I bark to draw attention to my joke, Mama will be sure to notice and put a stop to the hot dog/hot dawg thingy immediately.*

Much mirth and conversation accompanied the meal, which ended with the cinnamon bun cake that Renata had brought. That cake caused many oohs and aahs. *My humans love food as much as I do, the supreme chow hound.*

After everything was cleared and put away, we were all in the living room. Mama asked if they'd all like to visit Toccoa Falls the next day—it was one of the tallest waterfalls in the Eastern U.S. *I wasn't sure what "falls" were, but if a dawg listens carefully, he can usually figure out what he wants to know.* Before long I found out that they were talking about water just falling over a cliff. *Really? That's a tourist attraction??* Renata said they'd been there many years ago, and asked how far it was to the falls. Mama replied that it took about 45 minutes to get there.

Mama asked if they'd all like to eat at a restaurant there, too. That met with everyone's agreement, with Papa commenting that no matter what we did, we always made time to eat! So, they all decided to leave midmorning the next day, which was Saturday, spend some time at the falls, located on the campus of Toccoa Falls College, eat lunch, then drive around Toccoa before heading back home. I, of course, wouldn't be accompanying them to the falls, but that was fine with me—I needed to catch up on some much-needed sleep. *I don't usually nap very much when we have company at home—I might miss out on something interesting.*

The rest of the evening was filled with various activities: the sisters sang some songs; Mama, Renata, and Papa also sang some songs, which reminded me of that New Year's open house Nana had so long ago. Asher recited his numbers and a Bible verse he had learned, and in general my humans just enjoyed each other's company. I was content to sit by, watching and listening. Papa, with the children's prodding, told some of his funny stories, which they loved. I especially loved to hear Papa's stories, accompanied by laughter, even if I had heard them before: the first time I went fishing with Papa and Sellars when Sellars "caught" Papa's glasses, the Purple Heart story when Papa had run into a coconut tree in the war, and the Haystack story, also in the war.

I will always have fondness for Papa's funny stories, because I am especially fond of my papa.

10
Toccoa Falls:
Water Falling Over a Cliff

The next morning, I heard voices in the kitchen pretty early. We usually slept a little later on Saturdays since the sisters didn't have to go to school. I also smelled coffee, so that meant to me that bacon and/or other good things to eat couldn't be far behind! I yawned, stretched, and padded down the hall to the kitchen.

Papa, Nana, Sellars, Renata, and Mama were all sitting around the dining table drinking coffee. Mama was probably drinking orange juice, however, since she didn't like coffee. Just as I entered, Mama was getting up and saying she'd put the casserole into the oven before the children got up.

"I love breakfast casseroles, Holly," commented Renata. "There are so many recipes for them—what do you put in yours?"

"I've made several different ones before, but today I fixed Philip and the children's favorite: I use the 'store-bought' croissant dough for the crust—you know, the kind in the refrigerated section in the grocery store, beside the canned biscuits? I spread the dough sheets out in the bottom of the pan and bake them for ten minutes so they won't be too soggy. I already did that last night before I went to bed! Next comes the sausage-egg-cheese mixture. I browned my sausage last night and broke it into small pieces, beat the eggs and combined them with the sausage, and added grated cheddar cheese. I poured all that on top of the 'crust.' Now, all I have to do is put the top crust on—more sheets of croissant dough that I will brush with a beaten egg to make 'em shiny when done. That's it!"

"Sounds mighty good to me," laughed Sellars. "You sure you got enough of that to feed all of us?"

"Oh, I'm also making a big pot of grits," Mama replied. "I knew y'all would want those with the casserole." *That all sounds perfectly yummy to me, Mama. Maybe— just maybe—I'll get some of it.*

Mama got up from the table and I watched as she poured water and grits into a large saucepan, added salt and butter, and turned the burner on. Renata and Nana had gone over to the kitchen with her, but she said there was really nothing else for them to do—they were welcome to watch and talk, if they wished. Both women held their coffee cups, and the ladies chatted as Mama added the top crust to her large casserole, beat a couple of eggs, and brushed the egg over the top of the crust. She popped her casserole into the oven. "Now—all we have to do is wait about 30 minutes, and the grits and the casserole will be ready," declared Mama.

Just then, Annika came into the kitchen, rubbing her eyes. "Mornin,'" said Papa with a smile. Annika smiled back, and went over to hug him. "You ain't exactly awake yet, are you?" he asked. She didn't say anything, just smiled and nodded.

Mama commented, "This is late for you to be up, Annika." She turned to Renata and Nana: "She's the early riser in the family, often up before anyone else. Now Alexa and Asher—I'll probably have to wake them when we're ready to eat."

"What about Philip?" asked Sellars. "Don't he get up early, too?"

"Yes, he does," answered Daddy, who was smiling as he entered the dining room. "I've been up quite a while—I usually have my quiet time with the Lord first thing, then get my shower—before putting in an appearance," he replied.

"That is a good thang to do, then," replied Sellars. "I always say it's best to start your day off with the Lord 'stead of puttin' Him at the end of the day." Daddy nodded.

"Something's smelling really good, too," continued Daddy, rubbing his tummy. "I know we're having Holly's breakfast casserole since I saw her cooking the sausage last night—it's one of my favorites, too."

Mama began placing plates and silverware on the table, with Nana bringing the napkins and placing them beside each plate. Renata brought two jars and set them on the table.

"What's this stuff?" asked Papa, pointing to the jars of *something*.

"Oh, you'll love those," Mama replied. "One of our church members, Miss Savannah, makes her special relish, and she says it goes with just about anything, so I thought y'all might like some with your breakfast."

"Are you talkin' about pickle-lilly?" asked Papa. "Why, Ray-melle, tell 'em how much I like to have that with my breakfast!"

"He's right," nodded Nana. "He made some jars of it himself last summer, since he couldn't seem to find any at Jackson Brothers across the road. His is mighty hot, though, and I don't eat it."

"Miss Savannah's isn't hot at all," added Mama. "She gave us two jars since they are two different kinds of her relish. One is green-pepper based, and the other has corn added to it."

"Me an' Renata have eat that stuff on occasion," added Sellars. "I don't mind if it has a little heat in it, but I don't wanna have to use a fire extinguisher after eatin' it!" he laughed. That made Papa laugh, too, and Annika giggled.

"A fire extinguisher?" she asked. "You mean you have to put out a fire in your mouth??"

"Honey, he's just exaggerating," Renata explained. "He just means he doesn't want to eat something so spicy that his mouth feels like it is on fire!" *Whew. He had me going for a minute, too. I've seen fire extinguishers, and* they just scare me—that noise they make sounds like they're gonna gobble me up, so I steer clear of them.

"You and Papa are so much alike," Mama added. "He loves to say things like that, too."

"Robert made some salsa so hot one year that you *would* need a fire extinguisher if you ate any," said Nana. "He gave some to Clark and Mavis when they visited. She later told us that she took a jar to a woman she worked with, who had commented that she loved hot salsa. The woman wasn't in her office when Mavis brought it to her, so Mavis just left it on her desk with a note."

Papa continued the story: "And I know how hot that stuff was—why, I could hardly even eat much of it myself, and I like it hot. Mavis asked the woman the next time she saw her if the salsa was hot enough for her. The woman told Mavis, 'I thought you were going to bring me some *hot* salsa!' Can you believe that? She musta had a tongue made outa asbestos or somethin'!" That comment made them all laugh. *A tongue made out of asbestos? I don't even know what asbestos is, for heaven's sake, so I guess the joke just didn't make any sense this time. Oh well.*

"Papa, what is ask-best-os?" inquired Annika. *Thank you. Sometimes we need some explaining done around here.*

"It's some hard stuff, kinda like roof shingles, an' it don't burn easy," replied Papa. "That's why I said that lady's tongue was probly made outa asbestos, 'cause I know my salsa jest about melted the jars I put it in!" *Annika seemed satisfied, and so was I—but I am not too sure about those jars actually melting, Papa.*

Mama spoke to Daddy: "Philip, will you go wake up our two sleepyheads? Everything will be ready to eat in a few minutes, and I want them awake enough so they'll eat a good breakfast before we go to Toccoa." Daddy nodded.

"Wait," said Papa. "Let me go wake 'em up." So he and Daddy left the room, heading to Alexa first. I followed them, waiting in the hall outside Alexa's room. Papa boomed in his deep voice, "Rise and shine! Up n' at 'em! Get them feet on the floor NOW!" As I watched, Alexa emerged from her room with her curly hair sticking out in every direction. She was quite a sight to behold. Yawning, she entered the bathroom and closed the door.

"Okay, one down and one to go," Papa commented to Daddy, and they headed down the hall to Asher's room. I loped down the hall just as Daddy turned on the light in Asher's room. Asher was curled up in his crib, still sleeping.

Papa went over to the crib, and in his booming voice, said loudly, "C'mon, soldier! Time for breakfast, an' you gotta git up right now." Asher jumped when Papa yelled, but opened his eyes and started grinning. He sat up.

"Papa scare me!" said Asher, but he looked none the worse from the experience. He held up his arms to Papa, who picked the boy up and held him tightly. "Papa wake Asher up fast!" added the boy.

"Come on over here and let Daddy change your diaper," said Daddy. Papa put Asher down so Asher could walk over to Daddy, who was standing beside the changing table.

"You mean this here big boy still wears a diaper?" asked Papa incredulously. "I figgered he'd be outa that stage by now."

"Oh, we're working on it—he still wears a diaper at night," said Daddy. "Right, Asher? Mama says that one day soon, you're gonna wear regular big boy underwear."

"Asher wear underwear sometimes," Asher replied. "Asher not baby. Asher getting big."

"Yes, you sure are gettin' big," replied Papa. "An' are you gittin' hungry like Papa is? Mama has made us a real good breakfast, so let's hurry up and get back in there before Sellars eats it all!" Asher laughed as Daddy put him down, and he ran out of the room toward the dining room.

65

"Philip, I ain't much on runnin' at my age, but I kin still git a move-on when good food is around!" He and Daddy walked quickly, but I was in front and galloped my way to that good food.

When I got there with Daddy and Papa close behind, everyone was ready to eat. Mama was spooning the steaming casserole into plates, Sellars was spooning the grits, and Renata and Nana were bringing the coffee pot and juice to the table. Daddy and Papa sat down, and so did the ladies. Daddy said grace, which was followed by amens from Papa and Sellars, and they began eating. I made my way to Papa's chair. *Oh, how I love sausage—if it's the mild kind, Papa. And eggs. And cheese.* I didn't dare bark to remind him, because that would also remind Mama. So I kept quiet. But it was hard to do!

Papa commented that the pickle-lilly was wonderful, and it went great with breakfast. Sellars said he liked it, too. Everyone ate in silence for a few minutes. Papa did drop a few morsels my way, and I had a hard time staying quiet because three of my favorites were in that casserole. *Oh my, it is even better than my nose imagined. Wish they'd just let me eat all I want of that dish. That will never happen in this house, though. Mama watches what the children eat, what the cats eat, and what I eat. The only one around here who gets to eat what he wants is Daddy. No fair.*

Various topics of conversation were discussed, but I didn't pay very close attention, because my nose was zeroed in on those heavenly smells from the casserole. I did hear Sellars saying how good Mama's casserole was. They practically talked that to death, in my humble opinion. *Not that anybody actually cares what my opinion is!*

Just then, Nana laughed, asking Papa if he remembered that time in the Army when he was serving eggs to order at breakfast in the mess hall. A young WAC said she wanted her eggs any old way, it didn't matter.

Papa laughed and said he did remember that.

"So what happened, Duke?" asked Sellars. "Why didn't she just tell you she wanted them eggs fried or scrambled?"

"I dunno, Sellars. I'd had to get up mighty early, and I wasn't in no mood to be trifled with that mornin.'"

"Papa, what's a WAC?" asked Annika. *Thank you. I doubt it means what first came to mind: Women Are Clever.*

"Them letters—WAC stood for Women's Army Corps. *Oh. Wrong again.* Back then, they had a separate part of the Army for the women. We just called 'em WACS—most of 'em were nurses."

"I want to be a nurse when I grow up," stated Alexa proudly. "I love to put bandages on my dolls."

"That's a fine thing, too," said Sellars. "But I want to know how your ol' papa fixed them eggs fer that WAC."

Papa smiled. "Like I said, I wasn't in a good mood, so when I asked her how she wanted her eggs, she just said, 'Oh, any ol' way is fine.' She was battin' them eyelashes at me, too, an' I didn't like that, neither. So I just took two eggs an' cracked 'em right on her tray for her!"

"Papa, you gave her raw eggs?" asked Annika, incredulous.

"I shore did, Honey. I tole her, 'There ya go. You said you didn't care how yore eggs was fixed, so move on down the line!'"

"Heh, heh. Leave it to you to think that one up," laughed Sellars. "Did ya git in trouble fer doin' that?"

"Naw. Back then, a lot of them soldiers didn't really like havin' the women comin' through the line at meals anyway, so a bunch of 'em thought that was real funny. Of course, I wasn't a Christian then, either. I wouldn't do something like that now, 'cause I don't think it would be pleasin' to the Lord." He looked at the children: "Y'all don't go doin' stuff like that, ya hear? The Lord wants us to

67

treat our fellow man—and woman—with kindness, and I'm
sorry to say I wasn't too kind to that young lady back then."

"We wouldn't give somebody raw eggs, Papa," said
Alexa. "They are too yucky!"

Papa just laughed. "Good. Y'all are mighty sweet
children, but Papa just had to remind y'all not to do what
he did back then, that's all."

*Papa, you sure aren't mean now. I can't even
imagine you being unkind to anyone now, so whatever
being a Christian means, it really has made you different
from how you said you were before.*

After much commotion, Mama had the children
ready to go, and they finally prepared to leave. I overheard
Daddy say something about their leaving later than they
had wanted to. Papa said that it didn't matter, "cause we
ain't goin' to no fire." Daddy just laughed and agreed. *That
is just silly. Who even thought they were going to a fire?
But I already heard the explanation for that one, so I get it
this time, Papa.*

Before they left, Mama made certain that the cats
and I had food (such as it was, since it was just my usual
cardboard, a.k.a. dog food) and fresh water. She told me to
be a good boy, remarking to no one in particular that the
cats could fend for themselves. *Mama, if you'll leave the
rest of that casserole out where I can reach it, I'd gladly
clean out that serving dish for you! And I plan on
napping, so I hope Piper and Aslan don't get any funny
ideas about annoying me like they sometimes do.*

Each of the children hugged me as they went out the
door. Asher also kissed the top of my head and patted it.
*Good-bye, and have fun watching that water falling over
the cliff. If you think that is worth driving nearly an hour
to see, then go for it. As for myself, I hear my comfy couch
calling me.*

❧   ❧   ❧

They returned home later that afternoon, and they all seemed tired. From what I could figure out from their conversation, they loved the waterfall and took lots of pictures. They ate at a restaurant in Toccoa Falls. They drove around town. They came home. *Glad I stayed here. Sounds kinda boring to me.*

The evening was pretty uneventful, since tomorrow was Sunday and Mama had to get things ready for church, which meant she had to lay out the children's clothes, shoes, and hair bows for the sisters. Then she laid out Asher's church clothes as she called them: a little white shirt, a vest, long pants, and black shoes. Daddy gave them all a bath and tucked them into bed, but not one of them complained. Sellars and Renata headed out to their motor home earlier than usual, with Sellars saying something about getting his beauty sleep so he could listen to Daddy's sermon tomorrow. Papa and Nana stayed up awhile, but said they were tired, too, so they soon headed to the Tarheel room after Sellars and Renata left. That was the end of that day.

The next morning, it was breakfast as usual—this time, Mama had made French toast and bacon for everyone—and then they went to church until lunchtime. For the meal, Papa "rustled up" (his words) some meatloaf, mashed potatoes, green beans, corn on the cob, and biscuits, and it all smelled so good. Nana, Sellars, and Renata helped him, giving Mama a much-needed break. Papa was in charge of the meatloaf, Sellars prepared the green beans, Nana made the mashed potatoes and biscuits, and Renata fixed the corn—and "threw together" a four-layer pudding dessert, which especially pleased the children.

After lunch, everyone wanted to take a nap, a common custom on Sunday afternoons. There would be no church service that particular night, so they just ate a light supper and enjoyed each other's company. Since they were going back home the next day, I suppose they just wanted to spend some time together, laughing and making funny comments. Papa didn't tell any stories this time, but just about anything he talks about turns into a funny story. He and Sellars talked about this and that, which made the children laugh, anyway. Papa and Sellars just have a gift for exaggerating, making even regular experiences seem hilarious. Oh, I almost forgot: Papa did tell about the time a bumblebee chased him through a corn field.

Sellars had been talking about how his uncle liked to keep bees and sell the honey. That must have reminded Papa of something. "Did I ever tell y'all about the time a bumblebee chased me through a corn field?" The children giggled.

"Papa, why did it chase you? Was it mad at you?" laughed Alexa.

"It sure acted like it was mad at me. Me and Ray-melle was visiting her folks one summer when we lived in New Jersey. I had gone out to the corn field to git a few ears of corn fer Grandma Lambert—Ray-melle's mama—to fix fer our dinner. I musta disturbed that mean ol' bumblebee when I reached fer an ear, 'cause the next thang I knew, I heard loud buzzing. An' that ol' bee was a'buzzin' around my head real close, so I decided to move on down the row."

"I don't like to get stung!" exclaimed Alexa. "It hurts, and Mama has to put ice on it."

"Honey, yore ol' papa don't like to git stung neither, so that's why I moseyed on down the row, to git away from that bumblebee. Only hit didn't work—he tore off after me!"

"Duke, I ain't never heard of a bee chasin' anybody 'cept you!" Sellars added.

"Yeah, I know. I'm jest lucky that way, I guess.

Anyhow, I went on down the corn row, an' I heard him a'comin' after me, so I started walkin' faster. But the faster I walked, the faster that thang flew, 'cause he stayed right behind me!"

"Papa, what did you do then, to get away from the bee?" asked Annika.

"I just started flat-out runnin' then. I ran all the way to the end of that row, and that blamed bee was still buzzin' around my head. I had heard that if you suddenly lay down, the bee would just fly on over and go somewheres else, so that's what I did when I got outa that corn field. There was an empty field right beside it, so as I was runnin,' I looked and seen an ol' log layin' over near some trees. I turned left and ran and fast as my legs could carry me over to them trees an' that log. I gotta say that I was young then, and in good shape, so I wasn't jest pokin' along, you know."

"What happened next?" Alexa wanted to know.

"That bee was still right on me, so when I got to that log, I laid down behind it an' waited for that bee to keep goin.' You know what? He didn't keep goin'—like a dive bomber, he zeroed in 'fer his target an' stung me right on the end of my nose! An' that hurt—a lot! I flapped him away then. I don't know if I squashed him, but I didn't hear him buzzin' no more. I went on back to the house a'holdin' my hurtin' nose. When I got there, Ray-melle and Grandma Lambert asked me what happened, an' why was I holdin' my nose? Had I run into a skunk or somethin'?" *Oh, yuck. I hear that skunks reallllly smell awful.*

Nana took over the story: "We saw Robert coming from those trees carrying several ears of corn with his other hand on his nose. He had a scowl on his face, too. I looked at Mom, she looked at me, and we were waiting at the door to find out what happened."

"When I got to the house, they was standin' there with a question mark over their heads, so all I said was: 'A bumblebee chased me outa that corn field and to that log over there. I even laid down and he dove after me, stingin' me on the end of my nose.' Boy, does it hurt!"

Nana added, "Mom told him to come into the kitchen and sit down at the table. She got him some ice to go on it, and he said the hurt finally quit after several minutes."

"An' that, children, is the story of 'Papa and the Bumblebee.' *Oh, Papa. Stuff happens to you that never happens to anyone else: the fence, the palm tree, even the fishing story with Sellars. You are something!*

It was a wonderful evening. I'll always remember Papa's smiling face and deep voice, Sellars' *heh hehs*, and the children's giggles.

I know that bumblebee sting was painful, but leave it to Papa to make it funny for the children. He oughta write a book about his stories.

11
Magnets and Gratitude

One afternoon Mama called the children together in the living room. "Sarge, you come, too." So I trotted along behind Annika as we left the playroom and headed into the living room. "Children—and Sarge—I'm going to play the cd of TWO stories that Grandma Mavis just had published in a couple of magazines! She told me about them a few months ago, but said that magazine articles have a long lead time, meaning that it's a long time from submission to getting something published." She held up a cd: "This is it—one is published in the travel magazine she told me about, and this is a story about all her refrigerator magnets. The other is an article she wrote about gratitude, and it is in a Christian magazine. She recorded herself reading them on a cd—and she gives out copies to friends. After their trip out to see Kurt and Bethany, where she bought several more magnets, she says they are great souvenirs. Magnets are everywhere and don't take up much space in a suitcase. Oh, I am so excited for her! I'm going to sit down right now and play it for you while I cook dinner—I can hear it from the kitchen, even though I've already heard it once myself. Sarge, you'll just have to bear with it—I think you'll enjoy the souvenir story because you were with Mom and Dad when she bought some of her magnets." *Oh yes. I remember them well, and that trip was a doozie.*

"And, the one about gratitude—that's something we can all get more of, no matter what age we are."

"Mama, what is gratitude?" asked Alexa. "I've heard about it, but I'm not sure what it is, exactly." *Oh, I know what it is, and I have plenty of it myself. Of course, I can't tell you.*

"Why don't you listen to the article and see if you can figure it out?" replied Mama. We'll see if you girls can learn

what it is from Grandma Mavis's article, then we can talk
about it after you hear it. " Smiling, Mama inserted the cd
into the player, and Mavis's familiar voice began reading
her magnet article aloud:

NOT JUST SOUVENIRS:
REFRIGERATOR MAGNETS
By Mavis Duke Hinton

Yes, I've enjoyed collecting refrigerator
magnets for many years, and I have hundreds of
these colorful bits of plastic, wood, glass, fabric—
what have you. Do I have one from every place I've
ever visited or lived? In a word, no. Growing up in
a military family and living overseas, there was no
such thing as fridge magnets when I was a child. A
"dear" friend asked the other day, "Oh, did they
even have refrigerators when you were a child??"
He should have been prepared to duck . . . really!
(Duck? You put a duck on your refrigerator??)
More than just colorful bits on our
refrigerator, these magnets represent wonderful
memories of enjoyable trips and fun places we've
visited, as well as the blessings in my life. For
without the Lord in my life, none of the places and
events we have visited really matters at all.
Photographs are merely slices of time revealing
split seconds of life, but magnets represent the
entirety of the experience.

My husband Clark tells people that we'll have
to get a second fridge one of these days if I keep
collecting. He may be right, but I have arranged
my collection in such a way that there's still plenty
of room for more (that is, if you count the other
side and top as space)! In fact, I'll admit that I'm
probably a bit compulsive about my magnets, as I

even have them grouped by particular themes:

U.S. States: a quick glance across the fridge reveals some of the states we have visited in the U.S., in no particular order: NY, NJ, VT, KY, ME, RI, OK, IN, AR, MI, NH, DE, MD, TN, FL, GA, SC, AZ, NM, TX, MA, VA, WV, and IL. *(Hey, I've been to some of those states, too!)*

New York City: *The Phantom of the Opera* at the Majestic Theater, the United Nations, The Empire State Building, The Statue of Liberty, Little Italy, Long Island Ferry, St. Patrick's Cathedral, Twin Towers (we were there in May before Sept. 11 on one of many trips), Central Park, Fulton's Fish Market, Brooklyn, Long Island, Rockefeller Center, Macy's, the Bronx Zoo, Junior's in Brooklyn (the absolute *best* cheesecake), and of course a New York City taxicab. *(I didn't know you visited all of those places.)*

Other Cities/Places: The Biltmore House in Asheville, NC (I cannot imagine maintaining its more than 50 bathrooms); Linville Caverns in the NC mountains; Cape May, NJ; the Chesapeake Bay Bridge/Tunnel (we once lived on MD's Eastern Shore in Pocomoke City); Stone Mountain, GA; The Georgia Aquarium, Atlanta, GA; the Grand Hotel in Mackinac Island, MI (featured in the movie *Somewhere In Time*, starring Jane Seymour and Christopher Reeve--I love that movie!); the Grand Canyon; Niagara Falls; The Continental Divide, NM; PA Dutch Country; Hersey's Chocolate Factory; Sedona, AZ; Myrtle Beach, SC; Disney World in FL; various points of interest around Washington, DC, such as the Jefferson Memorial, the Capitol Building; and the Smithsonian; and of course, Graceland in Memphis, TN. I also have a guitar-shaped magnet emblazoned with the name

ELVIS. **For barbecue lovers, we ate at Interstate Barbecue in Memphis, and trust me, it deserves its rating in the top ten BBQ restaurants in the country.** *(I saw some of those places on our trip! They didn't let me go in, of course, but I was there—and I even ate some of Interstate Barbecue's brisket, too.)*

<u>Countries</u>: **I have a loaf of French bread from Paris, France, and also a miniature sombrero and woven blanket from Mexico. I bought neither one myself, and although I lived in France and visited Paris as a child, my brother brought me the Paris magnet. Clark's sister Alicia gave me the Mexico magnet. And, there's a maple leaf flag, representing our enjoyable car trip across much of beautiful Canada a few years ago.**

<u>Chocolate</u>: **one proclaims that "Families are like fudge: mostly sweet with a few nuts." Another of my favorites is my chocolate chip cookie, which looks so real that someone actually tried to eat it years ago when I placed it on a tray (as a joke) with real cookies! I also have a chocolate candy bar. It looks real, too, and the granddaughters thought it WAS the real thing.**

<u>Old Timey Americana</u>: **an old treadle sewing machine, a wood cook stove, an ironing board/iron, along with a hand-cranked meat grinder, a cast iron skillet containing eggs and bacon, percolator for coffee, egg beater, old radio, carton of eggs, sacks of flour and grain, rolling pin, Coca-Cola memorabilia (remember the polar bears?), Ivory soap, and a milk bottle like those which were once delivered to homes.**

<u>Foods</u>: **a tossed salad, a blueberry pie, a tin of muffins, a stack of pancakes, a bunch of bananas, a cutting board laden cheese and salami, French fries, a hot dog, a hamburger, a basket of**

apples, a basket of fresh veggies.

Cows: ranging from one that moos when a button is pushed to a cow thermometer, along with another proclaiming "Cow Collector"—even a little stuffed animal cow with magnets on its hooves. In fact, my kitchen is decorated with black-and-white cow decor, but that's for another article. *(Oh, I bet Asher loves those!)*

Sayings: my personal favorites, "Grandmas are special" (I didn't buy that—the granddaughters gave it to me); and "A daughter is a forever friend" (because mine are).

Others are terse:
"I express my individuality by collecting mass-produced magnets."
"You can't scare me: I'm a teacher!"
"Lord, grant me patience, but hurry!"
"Never trust a skinny cook."
"I am woman—I am invincible—I am tired."

Miscellaneous: for some inexplicable reason, I also have a trashcan full of trash, a butterfly, a gumball machine, a gingerbread man, an outdoor grill, and a painting by the French artist Monet (Oh yes: that was from the National Gallery of Art in Washington, DC). And, in honor of the dachshunds in our family, of course I have a black-and-tan doxie magnet. *(As you should. And is it front and center, its rightful place on your fridge?)*

Before there were magnets: Although my family and I visited the World's Fair in Brussels, Belgium, when I was a child, there were no magnets back then, so I made one out of a necklace I had depicting The Atomium, a huge silver building shaped like an atom, with concourses connecting the sections representing "neutrons" and "electrons" to the "nucleus" of the building.

Quite imposing. While on this same trip, we experienced the Tulip Festival in Holland, which was breathtaking, with intricate floats made entirely of flowers, mostly tulips and hyacinths. No magnet there, but I do have a pair of decorative wooden shoes. We visited medieval castles in Germany, and I had a mouse souvenir I bought from a little shop. As an adult, I've wondered about the significance of a mouse souvenir from a castle--perhaps because mice were common inhabitants in them? On another trip across Europe, we attended a bull fight in Spain accompanied with much ceremony and flourishes from the bull fighters, but that was not really to my liking—I felt sorry for the bull. No magnet for that, but I do have a handkerchief depicting the event.

My final mention, but perhaps my most important magnet, proclaims: "Seek ye first the kingdom of God and His righteousness, and all these things shall be added unto you" (Matthew 6:33 KJV). This one magnet simply sums up the purpose of life and all of its events, travels, and experiences.

I wouldn't have it any other way.

The story ended, and Annika and Alexa began clapping. Asher followed their lead and joined in, smiling. Mama heard them from the kitchen, stopped what she was doing, and came into the living room. She turned off the cd player. "Girls and Asher, wasn't that interesting? Who would have thought that those magnets that I've looked at over the years—and you children scattered all over Mom and Dad's house—would be turned into such an interesting article?" *I'm sure I don't know, Mama.* "I'll text her right now to let her know we got it, and how much you enjoyed it. I'm so proud of my mama!" *Me, too.*

"Mama, I didn't know that Grandma Mavis's

magnets were from *places* she went to," said Alexa. "I just thought they were cute little toys for us to play with!"

"I didn't know that, either," stated Annika. "My favorite one is the cow that moos!"

Alexa added, after a moment of thought, "She has so many I like, but I think my favorite magnet is the chocolate chip cookie. It looks so real I want to eat it every time I see it!"

Not to be outdone, Asher piped up, "Asher like yellow car magnet!"

Mama and the sisters looked puzzled. "I didn't know she had a yellow car magnet," commented Mama, who stopped for a moment. "Wait!" She began laughing: "He means the New York City taxi magnet!" The sisters joined in the laughter. Mama then hugged Asher for his contribution to the conversation. *Nobody's asked me, but I guess my favorite is the little guitar from Memphis, since I was there when Lester, the Elvis impersonator, stopped by the motor home. Duke and I were by ourselves while Clark and Mavis were shopping at Graceland—he heard us barking and came over. So, I have quite an interest in it myself.*

"Children, let's listen to the *Gratitude* article now. Remember, you'll be trying to find out what it is." *All right, Mama. I'm game, even if I already know what it is.*

"G" IS FOR GRATITUDE

Have you ever had one of those days where things did not go according to plan, or it just went downhill after you managed to crawl out of bed? The dog wouldn't even wag his tail as you walked by--but bared his teeth and snarled? *(Hey, I resent that! Although I'm not really a 'morning dawg,' I don't snarl at humans.)* **People didn't smile at you, even if you smiled at them first? Or, you tried to handle**

some business by phone, but could not get through? I recently got the recorded message, "All our representatives are currently helping other customers. Please remain on the line and the first available representative will take your call. You have a wait time of 45 minutes. Thank you."

If the last item sounds crazy, I did not make it up—I was calling an insurance company, and my wait time was actually 45 minutes. I put the call on speaker and simply worked on the computer until "my turn." Of course, once I got a live person, I was transferred a few times and had to explain myself each time, but I finally accomplished what I needed to do. Whew!

I said all that to say this: oftentimes, it is downright hard to have an attitude of gratitude. Life happens, and it isn't always a bed of roses. By the way, who coined that phrase? Why would a bed of roses represent something comfortable or something that turned out right? Roses have thorns, so how absurd is it to even want a bed of roses? But I'm getting off topic here.

A situation occurred recently that upset me deeply. I just did not understand why those who had promised something had let me down, and then didn't even seem to care that they had broken their promise! I mean, it didn't really seem very important to them at all. (Before I proceed further, I want to make it clear that these people were not family members, thankfully.) *I'm glad to hear that, Mavis. We wouldn't want to upset you.*

It wasn't something trivial, but rather important to me, actually. I knew my attitude was wrong, so I took it to the Lord in prayer. I asked for wisdom, a change of heart, and gratitude that so many other things in my life have gone so right.

As I prayed and asked the Lord for His help in changing my hurt feelings, He brought to my mind all those things for which I am blessed. Going over them in my mind, I could feel my anger and resentment ebbing away. My pity party was over, and I was able to have victory over this difficulty.

Oh, it is so easy to glibly tell people to let go of negative feelings, to pray about them, and to turn them over to the Lord, but it just isn't that easy to DO. I knew my anger and hurt would eventually subside on the surface, but I didn't want buried resentment, either. So, I thanked Him for all the good things in my life, realizing that nothing happens in a Christian's life without God's permission—even so-called bad or negative things.

So: why do such circumstances occur in life? We won't always learn why, but then, God is not obligated to explain Himself to us. We must simply trust Him and His reasons. I did decide that perhaps one reason was to make me take stock of myself. I am sure that there have been times in my life when I have let others down—maybe not intentionally—but rather than casting stones at others, it was better to look inwardly and make certain that my life was what it should be.

I am grateful for my Lord who answers prayer. I could not have gotten rid of the resentful and hurt feelings on my own. I would have been able to go on, of course, but I didn't want to carry around the baggage of those feelings. And they're gone now. He took them away, and for that, I have much gratitude. I can move on, live my life, and not have any resentment toward those who seemed not to care.

The situation is no longer my problem, anyway! *Ouch! I suppose I should stop getting upset*

*when my humans won't give me some of their human food.
Instead, I should be grateful when they do.*

Mama turned off the cd player. "All right, girls, what
is gratitude?" she asked.

"I think it means to be thankful for things we have,"
replied Annika.

"That's a great start," stated Mama. "But do you
think gratitude means to be thankful for just the good
things?"

The sisters thought for a moment. "In the story,
Grandma Mavis had some things happen that she didn't
like, but she thanked God for them, anyway," Alexa replied.
"It would be hard to be thankful for something I don't like,
Mama."

"Oh, I know, Honey. What Grandma was saying is
this: no matter what happens to one of God's children, God
already knows about it, and even allows it. Sometimes
something that seems bad teaches us how to be better—
more like Him. Do you understand what I'm saying?"

"I think so, Mama," commented Annika. "I don't
know if I can do it, though. Maybe that's one of those
grownup things that children don't have to do!" she
laughed.

"Oh, I don't think that is true at all," Mama answered
with a smile. "It's an attitude that all of us—children and
grownups alike—have to work on throughout our lives.
God loves us, would never hurt us, but will allow certain
situations to happen to us so we can learn from them. Do
you think we would be thankful if we always got everything
we wanted? We would never learn how to thank God
because we'd become selfish people," Mama finished.

"Asher thankful for Sarge," my boy said with a smile.
I went over and gave him a doggie kiss. *Believe me, I am so
thankful for you, too, my little man.*

"I get it now, Mama," said Alexa proudly. "I might
not like some things that happen to me, but since God loves

me, He lets some things happen so I can learn to be a good person the way He wants me to. Is that right?" *Wow, Alexa. That's pretty smart for a little girl like you. I'm impressed.*

"Yes, Alexa, that's exactly right. People don't enjoy being around a selfish person, do we? Learning to be grateful for what we have sometimes means that we have to learn a lesson or two along the way before we can do that. *I wonder if the children have really learned about gratitude? They're young, so there's still time for them to learn it. I've been around a lot longer than they have, and I already know what I'm grateful for!*

And Mama took out her cell phone and texted a message to Mavis. Just then, Asher told Mama that he wanted to eat, so Mama decided to get back on the merry-go-round and finish preparing dinner.

That's what I call our whirlwind life around here!

12
Happy Howl-o-wiener!

A week later, I heard the sisters talking about getting costumes for something at school. *Hey, don't you have enough princess dresses around here? Where would Mama put more costumes, since your princess trunk is bursting at the seams now!*

I was in the playroom with them after supper when Mama came in. Annika asked, "Mama, what can I be for Halloween? My teacher said we could dress up for our party at school, but I don't have anything yet to wear."

"Me, too," added Alexa. "Can we get something new and not have to wear one of our old princess dresses? Oh, we like them," she quickly added, "but it would be so fun to have a something different to wear."

"Since you mentioned it, girls, I was planning on getting you new costumes—and Asher, too—but I haven't done so yet. Don't worry—you know I can pick out something you'll like, and I kinda wanted to surprise you. Our church is having that fall festival in a few weeks, too, and everyone in the community is invited. Daddy says that's a good way to reach people for the Lord who don't usually go to church."

"You mean we get to have a party at school AND a party at church?" squealed Alexa, who looked thrilled. "What will we do at the church party?"

"It's a fall festival, not just a party. A festival committee has been planning it for months—Daddy has gone to their meetings, and although I don't know the exact details myself, I've been to many of these over the years. All of you will love it: they'll have lots of things children will enjoy, like a beanbag throw, apple dunking, a cake walk, face painting, a couple of those big inflatable things where you can go inside and jump like you're on a trampoline—"

"Oh boy, I love those trampoline things!" exclaimed Annika. "What else?"

Mama continued: "Hmmm. Let's see—oh yes. A ring toss, face painting, a basketball throw, and there will be prizes at some of the games, too. There will also be prizes for the best costumes, so that's why I want to get y'all something really cute. Several men of the church are also grilling hamburgers and hot dogs, and there will also be corn dogs, French fries, cotton candy, and all those cakes for the cake walk—you can even win a cake. There will be judging for the best costumes, and—" Mama dropped her voice to a mere whisper: "I have heard through the grapevine that there will even be pony rides!" *Grapevine? I didn't know there were any plants that could talk! Oh. That must be one of those dumb ol' 'figures of speech' again. Humans sure say some odd things when they are trying to say something else!*

"Oh, I just love everything you said, Mama. How many days is it until the fall festival??" Annika wanted to know.

"We're having it on a Saturday so more people can attend, so it's three more weeks—that 21 more days, girls. That will give me time to get your costumes, thankfully." *More power to you, Mama. Just don't try to dress me up like you've been known to do in the past. I'll never forget that hat and coat you made me—oh, I appreciated the thought, but I didn't like being paraded around the community while wearing it!*

Then, dropping to a whisper again, Mama added, "And I'm gonna get Sargie a costume, too. Since much of the festival will be held outside, people can bring their doggies if they want. Wouldn't it be fun to dress Sarge up, too?" *NO, IT WOULDN'T. Mama, don't you remember that I have excellent hearing? Oh no—what do you propose to dress me up like—Prince Charming??*

"Yay!" squealed Alexa. "What kind of costume are you getting for Sargie?"

"The pet store in Anderson has lots of doggie costumes there, like all kinds of super heroes, butterflies, men's suits—even a pumpkin one, so I'm just not sure yet which one would be best for Sargie. Wouldn't he look so cute in one of those, IF I can find just the right one?" Mama laughed.

"I think that's a good idea for Sargie," added Annika. "Oh, I can hardly wait for the festival to come!" *Goody for you—but I'm gonna hide so nobody can find me—WAIT. Did I hear right? You said they would have FOOD at the fall festival? Hmmmm. Food vs. costume. Food vs. costume. Okay, food wins. I'll even wear something silly if I get to eat human food. And there will be lots of children there, I hear. They're all suckers for giving dawgs their food. This fall festival thing just might turn into an enjoyable outing for me and a decent method for getting human food after all.*

Mama followed through on her promise to get costumes for Asher, the sisters, and for me. She went shopping later that week, arriving home with a large shopping bag. She pulled out the costumes one by one, asking the children to guess what they were. The sisters automatically guessed what Annika's costume was, because it was so obvious, even to me. She was thrilled, and just had to try it on immediately. Mama said she would help each of them, because she didn't want the costumes torn. Alexa couldn't figure out what her costume was, but she thought it was pretty. Mama said she wanted to save Asher's until she put it on him, because she wanted to see if he knew what it was after he tried it on.

First, Annika was transformed into a bumblebee. She had black tights, a short yellow ballerina-type skirt, and a long-sleeved yellow-and-black striped top with a fitted hood for her head with little antennae on top, and to complete her costume, there were little yellow wings of some kind of sheer fabric. Mama said she could wear her black patent shoes with it, too. Annika kept looking at herself in the mirror and giggling.

Next came Alexa's costume. Mama told Alexa that since she already had naturally curly hair, it wouldn't take much to create tight ringlets. And, with a big red bow on top of her head, she was gonna be Shirley Temple! Now I didn't know who Shirley Temple was, but Alexa sure did. She said she LOVED watching old Shirley Temple movies on TV and knew most of her songs. In fact, Alexa immediately launched into one of them—at the top of her lungs! *Ouch. My sensitive ears.* Mama shushed her and said to try on her dress, which was a soft white material covered with red polka dots. According to Mama, this dress looked just like one in Shirley's movies: it had a short full skirt, the red bodice had sequins on it, and there were short puff sleeves. Alexa would wear white tights she already had, her black patent Sunday shoes, along with that big red bow in her hair. Alexa was thrilled, and kept twirling around because the skirt was so full. She almost fell on me, in fact, so I got myself out of her way!

Then Mama smilingly pulled Asher's costume out of her shopping bag. It was some kind of black-and-white fuzzy material, but I couldn't tell what it was. Mama slipped it on over his other clothes, and it was just one piece, like those footed pajamas. Aha! This wasn't pajamas, though—Asher was gonna be a cow! It had a hood for his head that had cow ears on top, and a tail was attached to the back. Mama guided him over to the mirror on the wall, then asked him if he knew what his costume was. He looked at himself in that getup, began smiling, and then calmly said, "Asher moo moo cow." *Aha! So the young man figured it out.* Annika commented that he sure was a cute cow, and Alexa gave him a hug.

Then, Mama turned to me with a smile. I remembered that same gleam in her eyes from that time she made me that hat and coat—but this time I decided to just take it like a proud dachshund, because I knew I would be going to the festival where they would have lots of good FOOD. Therefore, it was worth looking like an idiot for a few hours in exchange for getting something good to eat.

She was sitting on the floor of the playroom and scooted over to where I was, still smiling, but I stayed put, much to her surprise. My costume consisted of several straps she put around my sides and under my tummy. *Is this some kind of saddle, and I'm going as a horse, Mama?* Then she attached two saddlebag-looking things to my sides, so I was now certain that I was going as a horse. Next, she attached something long, zigzaggy, and yellow on my back, like a stripe but I couldn't see it well, so I had no clue what it was for. *Oh no, Mama—I'm not going as a skunk, am I??* Once she finished, Mama started laughing, and pointed at me, telling the sisters to stop twirling their skirts around and look at Sarge!

Mama, still laughing, guided me over to the mirror, lifted me up on the table beside it, and pointed at my reflection in the mirror. I was speechless! Mama had turned me into a hot dog! Yep, I had a bun half on each of my sides, and that "yellow thing" on my back was a strip of "mustard." *I guess that makes me a hot dog inside a bun. Papa has been calling me his hot dawg for years, but now I really am one.*

What could I say? I was what I was, and I would have to deal with all the attention I would surely get at the festival. Wait—wasn't attention exactly what I wanted? If people thought I was cute, wouldn't they be more likely to give me some of their food? Especially the children—they would just love my cute costume, so after thinking it over, I grew excited and barked at my reflection, wagging my tail.

Annika said that Papa had called me a hot dog lots of times, but now, Sargie really would be a hot dog! Mama misunderstood the reason for my excitement, telling the children that I liked my costume, too.

Oh, I do, Mama—but not for the reason you think!

13
Now That Takes the Cake!

The morning of the festival, Mama was running around the house like crazy, getting children fed and instructing them on the proper behavior at the event. I've noticed that children have to be reminded about their behavior pretty often, because in the excitement of anticipation, they tend to forget and just do what comes to them in the moment. Oh, I suppose humans just take longer than we dawgs do to catch on to most things. For example, I never wore a diaper, I walked on my own in a few days, and fed myself from the beginning. I must admit, though, that when good food is involved, Mama sometimes has to restrain me or remind me (loudly, at times) with her special NO that she reserves for the children and me.

That morning, she was constantly asking Daddy and the sisters to do this and do that before we walked across the road to the church. I had propped myself up on the back of the couch and had a direct view across the road to the church, where there were already several cars. I saw a number of humans setting up booths outside, men getting their grills ready, and ladies taking covered dishes inside the fellowship hall. Children were wearing costumes, but I couldn't really tell what they were from the window. *I'll find out before long, anyway.*

Daddy disappeared into the bedroom for a little while, and when he came back in a few minutes, he inquired, "How do y'all like my costume for the festival?" I looked him over, but I couldn't even tell that he was wearing a costume; the sisters stared at him for a moment, then at each other, and shrugged. He was wearing a shirt, slacks, shoes, and a large sign around his neck. Annika read it aloud: "PHILIP'S HEAD," and there was also a big arrow pointing up toward his face. Annika said, "Daddy, what kind of costume is that? Why do you have an arrow pointing to your face—people already know that's your head!" The sisters looked at each other again, raising their eyebrows. *Good. I'm not the only one around here who doesn't get it.*

"Girls, have you never heard of a Philips head screwdriver?" asked Mama. "Daddy is just wearing a sign that makes a joke about that, since he's already wearing his own 'Philip's head.' Get it?" She began laughing, obviously thinking it was really funny, but I personally thought it fell far short of any scrap of humor. The sisters weren't laughing, either.

"The adults will think it is funny," said Daddy, who seemed a bit annoyed. "Many of the men at church use tools quite often, so I'll probably win the prize for the best costume today!" The sisters protested, making comments like "No, you won't, Daddy! It's not funny!" and "That is not even a costume, anyway, Daddy—you're just wearing a sign!" *I'm with you, girls. It isn't funny at all, Daddy. Sorry, but that so-called joke will fall as flat as a pancake over there.*

Apparently, while we were all engrossed in Daddy's non-costume, Mama had sneaked back to the bedroom and put on her own costume—I didn't know she was also going to dress up for the festival. She came back into the living room wearing a long green dress with sparkles on it and long full sleeves, and a shiny green shawl around her shoulders. She also had silk leaves in her hair and attached to her costume. She twirled around, and although she looked nice, I could not determine what she was. *A plant, maybe?*

"Oh, Mama, that is such a pretty princess dress!" exclaimed Alexa. "I love the green, 'cause it looks like a mermaid, but you're not a mermaid."

"With all those leaves, are you a tree?" giggled Annika. Even Asher went up to Mama and tried to pull off

91

one of the leaves. She shooed him away.

"This ensemble, dear children," said Mama as she twirled around slowly and dramatically, "is my 'Mother Nature' costume. Oh, there's really no such person as Mother Nature, but people are always saying something regarding Mother Nature, so I decided to be her today. Besides, I already had the formal dress and shawl, and the silk leaves were in some of my craft supplies. Do you like it?"

Daddy said, "I think it looks very colorful and nice. Maybe you should wear a sign like me, saying 'Mother Nature' so people will know. Otherwise, they'll just think you're a tree, like Annika said!"

"Oh, I'll just let people decide for themselves who I am," retorted Mama. "I like this costume I came up with, so we'll leave it at that. Is everybody ready to go to the festival??" The sisters squealed, I barked, and Asher clapped. So, out the door we went, leaving the cats looking out the window from my vantage point on the back of the couch. *So, fuzz balls, where were you when we were getting into our costumes? Hmmm. I don't think any cat would even wear a costume, but maybe Piper could go as a fuzzy skunk since he's already black and white—all Mama would have to do is make a white stripe on his back. Aslan could just be himself and go as some kind of evil sidekick. He wouldn't even have to practice that!*

It only took us a few moments to cross the road and join the others, who by now had everything set up. Cars were driving up, and families were walking toward the booths. It would be crowded before long. I trotted along beside Daddy, who was holding my leash. I held my head high, proud of my representation as the noble hot dog. *Representing a food is right down my alley.*

One of the first humans we met was Miss Janet, who was dressed like a pirate, complete with a patch over one eye.

"Ahoy, mates!" she greeted us. "Would you look at Sarge! My, my, my. I love all your costumes, but I'm afraid that Pastor Philip and Sarge will steal the thunder today!" Daddy smiled triumphantly at the sisters, who turned away, pretending not hear what Miss Janet said. *Thunder? Oh, I hope it doesn't rain and ruin everything. I want something to eat before we go home.*

"Are you all set up?" Mama asked her.

Before Miss Janet could reply, Annika asked, "What kind of booth do you have, Miss Janet?"

"I'm doing face painting for the children," she replied. "Would y'all like to have a small design painted on your face? I can do a pumpkin, a black cat, a Cross, a star or a heart—look at these pictures here on my table. If Mama and Daddy say it is okay, that is."

"Oh, that's fine," replied Daddy. He looked at the children: "Do y'all want Miss Janet to paint your face now, or would you rather look around and come back later?"

"Later!" said the sisters. "Oh, we really want you to paint something on our faces, Miss Janet," said Annika, "but first we want to see what else is here. You don't mind if we come back later, do you?"

"Of course not, sillies. I see that I already have a few children waiting for me, so I'll go ahead and do them now. See y'all later, and have fun!"

Just then, I heard another voice exclaim: "Say, would y'all look at that purty family! My, my, and all of y'all are wearin' costumes!" I knew that voice, and from behind a nearby booth came a smiling Miss Savannah. She was dressed in a shimmery blue and silver formal gown with a full skirt, white shawl, lace gloves, and a fan in her hand that she kept snapping open and closed, while batting her eyelashes at everyone. *Is something wrong with your eyes today, Miss Savannah?* On her head was a big fancy hat sporting a peacock feather. "Why, Asher punkin,' what are you dressed up as, young man?" inquired Miss

Savannah.

"Asher Moo Moo," he responded proudly. "Ears!" he yelled, pointing to them on top of his hood. "Tail!" he yelled, while trying to show that to her, too. She patted him on the head and then gave him a hug.

"And girls, I know exactly what y'all are," she exclaimed. "Miss Annika, you are shore the purtiest bumblebee I ever saw—and Miss Alexa, you got to be Shirley Temple—why, you look just like her, too!" The sisters beamed, twirling around so Miss Savannah could admire them from all angles.

Miss Savannah took one look at Daddy's "costume," did a double take, then burst out laughing. "Haw haw. Pastor, leave it to you to have the funniest costume I've seen around here today. Philips head, haw haw. That's a good one!" Daddy looked at the sisters and gave them a triumphant grin with an "I-told-you-so" expression. They made faces at him, but giggled.

Then Miss Savannah looked at Mama. "Why, Miss Holly, you are truly a vision in that beautiful green costume—only you could come up with a Mother Nature costume that looks so purty! And putting leaves in your hair is a nice touch. Why, if I did that, folks would ask me if I'd been a 'layin' down on the ground—but you can pull that off real fine!"

"Thank you, Savannah," replied Mama. "Oh, I won't twirl around for you like the girls did, though. You look mighty fine today, too. Where did you find such a beautiful gown?"

Miss Savannah explained that she had several trunks of antique clothing up in her attic, and this particular dress and hat had once been worn by her great grandmother when she had attended a fancy ball in Atlanta. It was indeed a beautiful gown, and the blue and silver shiny material made her eyes even more blue today.

Just then, several others came up to speak to Mama

and Daddy. One older couple, wearing huge foam squares, explained to the sisters that they were a pair of dice. *Why, who would have thought to dress up in something like that? I like it, and I know what dice are, since the girls have them with a couple of their board games.* Their grandson Jason, who was probably about nine, proudly told the sisters that he was an astronaut. His costume was mostly shiny silver and a big clear globe on his head.

Two other gentlemen of the church had sauntered over to our family and were talking to Daddy. They slapped their knees and had a big laugh over Daddy's costume. *People, I just do not understand what is so humorous about a sign with an arrow on it. Like I've thought many times, humans make no sense to me sometimes.*

The sisters were jumping up and down to go see everything, so Mama took Asher's hand and led them over toward some of the booths. Daddy took my leash and told me that we'd head over toward the other side where other people had some dogs. So, he strolled over there and I trotted along beside him in my hot dog contraption. Several children saw me and pointed, exclaiming "Look at that hot dog!" and "Hey, Dawg, did ya know you're wearin' a hot dog bun?" and such. *Of course. I'm not stupid, you know.*

I kept trotting along, but I rather enjoyed the attention, I must admit. I could smell the grills close by, so I knew they meant FOOD. Therefore, I was happy to trot along toward them. Daddy must have been hungry, too, because he headed straight for those grills where several men were working over them. I heard a couple of dogs barking, and I saw two large dogs tied to a couple of trees near the grills. *I sincerely hope that Daddy doesn't tie me to a tree like I'm a dawg, too.*

As he approached the first grill, a few men greeted Daddy and began laughing and pointing at his "costume." One called to the others, "Hey, y'all take a gander at what

Pastor Philip is dressed up as!" Several came over to where we were, and they all enjoyed his sign, too. They thought I was "quite a dawg," too, and offered to fix Daddy a big juicy burger, which he immediately accepted. I was sure he was hungry now. They asked if he wanted any fries and a soft drink, and of course he did—Daddy just loves cheeseburgers and fries. *If I'm lucky, maybe he'll drop me a bite or two—but I'm not going hold my breath. He isn't Papa, after all.*

We strolled over to some picnic tables where humans were already eating: families with children, older couples, and teenagers, all dressed in various types of costumes. I saw that one was wearing a box on his head that looked a little like a computer screen. Another was dressed as a super hero, with a flowing cape. And one of the girls was a gigantic butterfly, wearing a black costume and shiny golden wings. They all smiled at Daddy, laughing at pointing at his "costume" as he spoke to everyone and shook hands with them. Apparently most of the people attended Daddy's church, because he seemed to know everyone.

A gentleman named Otis brought Daddy his food, and Daddy thanked him, then bowed his head a moment, silently saying grace like I've seen him do many times, before he took that first bite of his cheeseburger. He called over to the men who had prepared the food, "Now that's a cheeseburger! Juicy, cooked just right, and it really hits the spot! Thank you!" I boofed softly, and Daddy looked down at me: "Sarge, this is sort of a special occasion, so if you don't tell Mama, I'll give you some of my burger." And he proceeded to break off a piece of it and drop it my way. Never a slouch in the catching department, I caught the bite in midair. He dropped two or three more bites my way, which to my taste buds, were excellent. He was almost finished when we saw Mama and the children making their way to us. I saw Mama pick up Asher and continue walking, and the sisters were skipping toward us, holding hands.

"Daddy, guess what I won!" exclaimed Alexa breathlessly. Not giving him a chance to reply, she held up a small doll. "I threw some beanbags into a hole on a game board over there. The man said if I got three in there, I could win a doll, and I did it! See? Isn't this little dolly cute?"

Daddy agreed that it was indeed a cute "dolly." Annika was bursting with her news as well. "And I played basketball and got enough balls in the basket to win this!" She produced a small teddy bear with a big red bow around its neck. "See how soft he is, Daddy!" She held it up in front of his face. Daddy squeezed it and also commented that the bear was probably the softest little bear he had ever seen in his life. *I'm impressed—both of you won something!*

Asher was hungry, so Mama said she wanted to get him something to eat. Daddy offered to hold him while Mama got Asher and the sisters some food, and motioned for the sisters to sit down across from him. Alexa saw some of her friends, so being the social butterfly, she was off to several other tables to talk with children and grownups alike. Alexa returned as soon as she saw Mama with food: a hot dog, baked beans, and potato salad for Asher, and Daddy said he would help him with his food so he wouldn't "wear it" on his cow costume. Mama had corn dogs, French fries, and baked beans for the sisters, who said they were starving. Annika said their grace, and they started wolfing down their food. They didn't actually say much because they were so hungry, and they managed to eat their food without spilling anything on their costumes, no mean feat. *That has to be a first—I suppose my sisters are growing up!*

Daddy held Asher's corn dog for him, allowing the little man to take bites as he wished.

Mama mentioned that Asher could hold that himself, but Daddy replied that he didn't want Asher to drop it. I saw that Daddy had also placed a few French fries on a napkin for Asher, who also ate those on his own. Mama had gotten herself a cheeseburger, too, and much to my surprise, she dropped a couple of bites my way. I almost missed the first bite from sheer astonishment, but I recovered quickly. Several humans came and sat down at our table near us, and everyone was having a great time eating, talking, and laughing. One of the families, the Hatleys, had two children. One was a little cowboy who kept coming over and patting me on the head. I think he really liked me, or at least liked my costume.

"Now Mather," cautioned Mama Hatley, "don't you hurt that cute little hot dog!"

"No, Mama, I won't," Mather replied. "I just never saw a doggie dressed up for Halloween before." I licked his hand and wagged my tail to indicate that I liked him, too. I also gave him my best doggie smile for good measure.

"Look, Mama, Sarge really likes me, don't you, Sarge?" *Of course I do! I like all children if they don't pull my ears, but especially if they give me some good FOOD,* I barked.

"Mama, can we go play some more games now?" begged Annika. "We're finished with our food."

"I'm not quite finished," said Mama, with her mouth full. She chewed for a moment. "Tell you what. See Miss Marlene over there in the green and white checkered dress? She's in charge of the cake walk. You and Alexa go over there and tell her you want to be in the next cake walk, and she'll help you."

"But Mama, what will we do in a cake walk? We've never been in one before," added Alexa.

"Everybody stands around the big table where the cakes are arranged. In front of each cake is a small sign with a number on it. When the music starts, you will walk around the table while the music is playing, but when they stop the music, you are supposed to stop immediately. Miss Marlene or one of her helpers will draw a number out of a bowl on the other table, and if the number in the drawing matches the number on the cake you are standing in front of, you win that cake!"

"Oh, boy! I love homemade cakes, and I see one over there with chocolate frosting!" yelled Annika as she scampered over to Miss Marlene.

"Hey, wait for me!" shouted Alexa, who ran after her. I saw Annika talking to Miss Marlene, who directed both girls to their places around the table. There were probably about twenty other humans—children, adults of all ages— who were also hoping to win a cake. Mama and Daddy were watching the progress of the cake walk, and so was I. Other families were standing back away from the table, apparently watching their loved ones and hoping for a win, too. *C'mon, Sisters! Be alert now. I want you to win a delicious cake!*

Mama had finished eating, so Daddy kept Asher with him as she and I made our way over to the cake walk table. We stood back a little so we could see without getting in the way. I was glad that Mama decided to pick me up. *It's hard for me to see through a sea of legs, Mama.* Before long, the music stopped, and the participants stopped where they were. Miss Marlene called out a number, but nobody said anything or acted excited. Apparently, nobody had stopped in front of the right cake—there were twice as many cakes as there were humans participating, so they started the music again. Annika looked over at Mama with her fingers crossed, and Mama gave her the thumbs-up sign. Everyone continued around the table as the music played, but suddenly, it stopped again. Several children were giggling, while one older boy dressed as a clown tried to stand between two cakes in case one of those numbers was called. Miss Marlene saw him and pointed for him to move, so he sheepishly took a couple of steps in order to stand squarely in front of a yellow cake. Miss Marlene was drawing a number out of the bowl. She peered at the slip of paper and announced, "Number 24 is the winner! Who is standing in front of a cake that has number 24?" She paused a moment, waiting for the winner to indicate who had won. I saw Alexa look at her number, then at her sister's. She then nudged Annika and said something to her. Annika looked down at the chocolate cake in front of her and started screaming, "It's me! I won! My cake is Number 24!!!" Both girls were jumping up and down as Miss Marlene came over to where Annika was standing.

"You are absolutely right, Annika. This delicious chocolate cake is, in fact, Number 24! Congratulations, Missy. And do you know who made this delicious buttery chocolate cake?" Annika shook her head no. "Miss Savannah made this cake, and she's about the best cook around here!"

Mama, still holding me, headed over to Annika. I was glad to be held, because I wanted to hear everything clearly. "Annika, you won a cake! How about that!"

"Yeah, and Miss Savannah made it, too, Mama!" exclaimed Alexa. "We know it will be so yummy!"

"Holly, if y'all are going to be staying awhile, I can put your cake back in the fellowship hall with your name on it. That way, you can pick it up when you get ready to go home," Miss Marlene called over to Mama.

"Oh, thank you. No, we're not going home yet, although Asher is getting a little tired. I better find him something interesting to do to keep him occupied. Girls, let's go find something else to do before we go home." They skipped along behind Mama as we went back over to the table where Daddy and Asher were.

"Daddy, I won Miss Savannah's butter chocolate cake!" shouted Annika. "We'll get it when we get ready to go home, Miss Marlene said!"

100

"Chocolate?? You mean you didn't win me that delicious banana split cake I saw over there?" Daddy chided jokingly, since he didn't like chocolate.

"Sorry, Daddy," replied Alexa. "Sissy won chocolate, and all of us but you like it a lot. Guess you'll just have to do without!"

Daddy just retorted, "Oh, I'll find me something around here to munch on," he replied. "Miss Mary has made some of her oatmeal raisin cookies, so I'm going to eat some of those in a minute. But I also saw Miss Jean's butterscotch brownies, and since I don't want to hurt anybody's feelings, I'll probably force down one of those, too," he finished, with a twinkle in his eye.

"It's a good quality for a pastor to be so careful of everyone's feelings," Mama joked. "Enjoy yourself." She turned to the sisters. "C'mon, girls. Asher's getting tired of just sitting here, and I saw Mr. Cecil giving rides on his horse cart over there in the field beside the church. Who wants a ride on the horse cart?" Both girls squealed, and Asher smiled. Maybe he didn't know what a horse cart was, but he did know the words *horse* and *ride*. Daddy took my leash and said we'd come along, too.

Good. I've always wanted to ride in a horse cart myself.

14
And the Winner Is . . .

It took us only a couple of minutes to reach the horse cart site, and since nobody else was waiting, Mama said that meant we were up next. Mr. Cecil soon returned with three smiling children. He helped them out of the cart as they called their thanks to him over their shoulders and scampered off in search of more fun. Mr. Cecil, the older gentleman who had the pond where Sellars and Papa had fished, was about as wide as he was tall, but had a friendly expression and a big smile under his white curly beard. He was dressed in bib overalls and a red-and-black plaid shirt, a wide-brimmed straw hat and boots, and had a cane he used for walking. I also noted a friendly twinkle in his clear blue eyes. "Well, lookie here. Pastor, I must say that's about the funniest idear fer a costume I ever seen!" he exclaimed to Daddy. "And Miss Annika, ain't you the purtiest bumblebee. And lookie here at Shirley Temple, Miss Alexa! I always loved Shirley Temple. In fact, I saw her once when me and my brother went to California back when we was real young. I ain't never forgot it—" he stopped. "I do git carried away sometimes. And look at that little man all dressed up like a cow." He directed his next comment to Asher: "Son, what does a cow say?"

Asher put his head down like he was shy, but softly said, "Moooooo." Mr. Cecil slapped his knee and laughed. "Ain't that exactly right. What a smart youngin' you got there, Pastor. Why, Miss Holly, that shore is a purty outfit you got on, too. *I bet he doesn't know what Mama's supposed to be.* I s'pose y'all wanna go fer a ride in my horse cart?"

"YES!" shouted the sisters together. They started jumping up and down again. I barked to make my presence known.

"Well, well. Even the dawg has got into the act—a bona fide hot dawg, heh heh. Ain't you sumthin,' Pup." He patted me on the head. *My head is gonna be sore on top if people keep patting it!*

"Yes, the children want a ride," said Mama. Do you have room for all three, and what about seating? I don't want anyone falling out of the cart, Mr. Cecil."

Hey I want to ride, too, I barked. All looked down at me, so I wagged my tail and barked again to make my wishes known. *Humans are sometimes a bit slow on the uptake, so I remind 'em when I think it is necessary.*

"It sounds to me like the dawg wants to ride, too," said Mr. Cecil. Mama started to say something, but he held up his hand. "Miss Holly, I got plenty of room on the cart, so don't you worry none. The girls can sit on the floor in the back, Asher can sit up front beside me, and I can hold the dawg on my lap real secure so he won't jump down while we're movin' along. Whadya say to that?"

Mama replied that it sounded like he had all the bases covered, so she helped the girls into the back. Daddy put Asher into the front seat beside Mr. Cecil, who picked me up as he climbed in to the driver's seat. And we were off! I saw the two horses' heads bobbing up and down, and could hear the *clop clop* of their hooves across the hard ground. As we "whizzed" by, the sisters were laughing and waving at Mama and Daddy. Asher was clapping and smiling. And my ears were flapping in the breeze. *Hey, this is a lot of fun!* I saw an ol' cat sleeping in the sun, so even though I couldn't get down and run it off, I did manage to tell it what I thought. It woke up, looked startled, and scampered off into the woods. *There. I've done my duty for the day.* Mr. Cecil laughed as he maneuvered the horses and cart around behind a barn.

"Say, dawg, you tole that cat what for! Hey, Asher, there's some cows over there behind that fence! See 'em?" There were, in fact, about fifteen black-and-white cows in the fenced-in field. Asher kept saying, "Moo moos, moo moos!" He was pointing, looking at the cows, and obviously thrilled.

Annika and Alexa also liked seeing the cows, and I heard Alexa counting them: " . . . Nine, ten, eleven, twelve, thirteen, fourteen. See, Sissy? There are fourteen cows over there!" *I "guesstimated" pretty well, didn't I?*

We continued down the country lane, passing by a couple of farmhouses, some chickens, a couple of goats, and horses. With each new discovery, the sisters and Asher grew more and more excited. *For heaven's sake, haven't you ever seen animals before? Oh, maybe not in person, now that I recall. Y'all should have been with us when I visited Sellars and Renata with Nana and Papa last year. He had some animals, and it is more exciting than seeing them in books, I know.*

"Mr. Cecil, this is so fun! Who did those horses belong to?" asked Annika.

"Well, now, young lady, those beauties belong to my brother, and he just might be persuaded to let y'all ride 'em sometime. How would you like that?"

"Could we?" exclaimed Alexa. "We would love to ride a horse, wouldn't we?" she asked Annika, who shook her head *yes* enthusiastically.

"We'll talk to your mama and daddy first, of course, but sometime we'll see about lettin' y'all ride them horses," Mr. Cecil added. "It's about time to head on back to the church, so y'all look hard at everything as we go by." *I am looking as hard as I can—if there are any other cats around, I'll make certain to run them off,* I barked to him.

Soon, we were back at the starting point, and there were Mama and Daddy waiting and smiling. As Daddy lifted Asher out of the cart, the little man excitedly said, "I saw moo moo cows! And one of them said 'Moooooo!'" as the sisters also shared their adventures with Mama: "And we saw horses, chickens, cows, and goats," exclaimed

Annika.

"Sarge saw a cat sleeping, and he barked and scared it off," stated Alexa. "He seemed to like the ride, too."

"The children were well behaved, I'll say," reported Mr. Cecil. "I told 'em mebbe they could ride a horse at my brother's farm sometime, if that was all right with their parents," he commented as he winked at Mama and Daddy. Mama replied that riding a horse just might be a possibility sometime. She also added that since it was getting to be late afternoon, it was about time to take Asher home. Daddy said he'd take Asher home if Mama and the girls wanted to stay a little while longer.

"Mama, we haven't even let Miss Janet paint something on our faces—and they haven't even judged the costumes yet!" cried Alexa. "We can't go home until we see Miss Janet and find out who has the best costume!"

"That's right. Philip, you need to stay around in case your costume wins," smiled Mama.

"You've got an excellent point," replied Daddy. "Girls, you want me to be here since I'll probably win for the best costume, right?" He so enjoyed picking on them in a fun way.

"Daddy, how in the world could YOU win? You're just wearing a silly old sign!" retorted Annika.

"I want you to stay, Daddy," added Alexa. "You won't win, so then you'll know that your costume isn't funny at all!" Daddy just laughed, stating that he'd try to keep Asher from falling apart since he was a tired little boy. Asher was rubbing his eyes, I noticed.

As we walked back to where all the booths were, the sisters ran on ahead to Miss Janet's. Asher was too tired to get his face painted, but Daddy told the sisters we'd wait over by the costume judging for them. We headed on over there, and when we arrived, we saw many humans standing around. A gentleman began speaking into a microphone.

"I'm Macon Gentry, the chairman of our deacon

board, and we welcome all of you to our church fall festival. Visitors, we are so glad y'all came today. I did meet a few of you as I walked around the premises, and we want to invite you to visit our church services—tomorrow being the Lord's Day, y'all come on out and join us in the morning. We'd all love to have you. Bible classes for all ages start at 10:00, and the preaching service starts at 11:00."

Mama whispered to Daddy, "I hope the girls get back here soon because they might miss the costume contest!"

"Oh, Janet knows that. She'll probably paint pretty fast so they won't be late," Daddy whispered back. *Now don't be rude, Mama and Daddy. Somebody else is talking.*

"Now, ladies and gentlemen, we have three well-experienced judges here who will decide on the winning costumes for today's festival. Those who are entering the contest, make your way over to this area," and he pointed to a place that was marked by three or four orange traffic cones. He instructed them to walk past the three judges in single file at his signal. Speaking into the microphone once again, he continued: "Let me introduce the judges. All the way from Lavonia, Georgia—let's give a round of applause to Mr. Claude Van Camp, a local farmer who don't miss a thing!" Clapping ensued as Mr. Van Camp took off his baseball cap and bowed. He was dressed as a farmer, but I don't think that it was a costume. "Next, I want to introduce Miz Ella Roundtree from Commerce—her family has owned Fine's Apparel there for over twenty-five years, and she knows fashion when she sees it." Mrs. Roundtree, who was indeed dressed in a smart business suit, smiled and waved. "And last but not least, another deacon of our church, Mr. Dan Brandt, who lives right over yonder and runs Brandt's Hardware here in town." Mr. Brandt, dressed in a short-sleeved shirt and jeans, stood straight and saluted as everyone applauded.

The sisters came running back just then, breathless.

106

"Did we get here in time?" whispered Alexa. Daddy nodded *yes*. They acted relieved and got in the costume line with us.

"Now, folks," Mr. Macon Gentry directed those to be judged, "we want y'all to walk slowly in front of the judges, single file, and if one of 'em asks you a question about your costume, well, just answer it. All right, start walkin' NOW." Mama and Daddy were in line, and Daddy held my leash. *Oh no! You mean I'm going to walk by the judges, too, Daddy?* I was not prepared for this, but since I wasn't the only one who looked ridiculous, I supposed I would live through the humiliation. I looked around at the other costumes: I saw the cowboy from before, the butterfly, the pair of dice, a Southern belle, two other dogs dressed as clowns—*and I'm sure they feel like clowns, too.*

I also saw Moses carrying two stone tablets, a deck of cards, and a ballerina. I really didn't have time to look further, because Mr. Brandt, one of the judges, had just bent down and spoke to me: "Hey, little hot dawg, you sure are all dressed up today! And you look like you know exactly what to do, too! Where did you find such a humorous costume?" *You talking to me? I didn't exactly buy it myself, you know, but I do realize I am supposed to be a hot dog—I'm a dachshund, and I am smart,* I barked to him. He just laughed as we continued on by.

The judges said something to many of the participants, and I noticed that the lady judge seemed to really like Mama and Alexa's costumes. Both Mr. Brandt and Mr. Van Camp said something to Daddy, and just kept laughing, even after Daddy had gone past them. Both of them wrote something down on their clipboards as well.

As everyone had filed by once, Mr. Gentry spoke once again: "The judges have requested that you make one more quick pass in front of them—they've about decided on the three winners for first, second, and third place. They also have a special prize for the most unusual costume, and they will announce that one before the other three." So, we walked by the judges again, feeling all eyes on us as those in the crowd who didn't participate looked us all over and discussed who they thought the winners should be. I could hear the murmuring and commenting as we paraded by.

We stood together in the prescribed area as the judges conferred and came to their decisions. Mr. Brandt, one of the judges, motioned for the microphone. Someone handed it to him, and with much enthusiasm, announced to the eagerly waiting crowd:

"Folks, it was a tough decision, but we've made our choices for first, second, and third place. The hardest choice today was for the most unusual costume, because there were several which fit into that category. In fact, we could not come to a consensus on just one, so we have THREE costumes we'd like to declare as 'most unusual.' As I call you, please come up front so we can all congratulate you. Each winner gets a gift certificate to Miz Roundtree's store, Fine's Apparel." There was much more excited murmuring as Mrs. Roundtree handed Mr. Brandt a slip of paper. "The first costume to win in the category of 'most unusual' is the pair of dice! Come on up, Brother James and Miz Lily!" That older couple came up, red-faced, but looked thrilled to have won. Mrs. Roundtree gave them an envelope as everyone clapped and cheered.

"Next, after much discussion, we decided that a costume ain't just for humans. If anybody is in costume, why, they oughta have just as good a chance to win as anybody else! With that said, we have chosen Sarge the Hot Dog as the next 'most unusual' costume!" Mama screamed and clapped. *WHAT? My costume won a prize? Wow!* Mama led me up front to much applause. She picked me up as carefully as she could so she wouldn't crush my hot dog bun halves. Mr. Brandt handed Mama an envelope while several people patted me on the head. I was thrilled, since I had never won anything before. Mr. Brandt cleared his throat, taking the microphone once again. "I ask: have y'all ever seen a nicer hot dog than Sarge?" Applause erupted once again, and I reveled in the attention. *This makes up for all those times I've felt ignored, even though I probably won't find anything to wear at that store. I don't care—I'll let Mama have it.* I wagged my tail and barked, and everyone laughed.

"Moving right along, our final 'most unusual' costume took the most discussion. In fact, it is so understated that it far outshines anything else we've seen here today, folks. Preacher Philip, come on up here! You are our third winner!" I could see the sisters' mouths falling open in sheer shock. *I don't get it, either, sisters. These people must know something that we don't.*

I heard Miss Savannah exclaim, "Way to go, Pastor Philip! You stole the show today for sure!" Sheepishly, Daddy made his way to the front. Mr. Brandt handed him the microphone. Daddy cleared his throat and looked out at the crowd of smiling faces.

"I must admit that my wife, Holly, thought up my costume. I wasn't even going to wear a costume—in fact, our daughters declared that it was the worst costume they had ever seen, and I'd be sure to not win anything today just wearing an ol' sign. Of course, they just don't get the subtle humor because they're children, but our judges here are very discerning individuals with great intelligence!" The crowd roared in appreciation of his statement. Once the laughter settled down, he continued: "And, since my dear wife thought up AND created my illustrious costume, I suppose it would only be fair to hand over the gift certificate to her. So—Holly, this one's for you!" Daddy handed the envelope over to Mama, who smilingly took it and held it up, as in triumph. The crowd loved it, clapping and cheering.

Daddy handed the microphone back to Mr. Brandt. "Folks, we'd better get a move on and announce our other

winners. Each of these will receive a gift card to one of our
fine restaurants in nearby Commerce. Now that is a good
deal, because all of 'em are good places to eat—I know,
because I've tried 'em all! Okay, the third place costume
goes to Moses and his stone tablets. Come on up, Jethro,
and git your certificate!" The man dressed as Moses came
bounding up to the front of the crowd, wearing a big smile
on his face. He accepted the gift certificate and thanked the
judges. I noticed that his beard was a bit lopsided now, but
nobody seemed to mind that at all.

Mr. Brandt continued: "And now, our second place
winner won because his costume was not only a good one,
but because it ain't store bought! Yep, he made his costume
himself, and we judges got a kick outa seein' it today.
Jimmy Ray Jones, who came dressed as a truck, come on
up here right now!" I was interested in seeing that one,
because I had somehow missed seeing it before. *A truck?
How can somebody dress up as a truck?* But there he was:
Jimmy Ray had a huge cardboard box painted red to
resemble a pickup truck complete with "lights" and "tires."
It was on his body like he was in the driver's seat, and as he
came forward, he "drove" the real steering wheel that he
had somehow attached to the body of his truck. As he
reached the judges, he even blew the horn on his truck!
The crowd loved it, and accompanied by applause and
catcalls, Jimmy Ray accepted his gift certificate by saluting
to the crowd. Mr. Brandt asked, "Jimmy Ray, how long did
it take you to create this fine masterpiece of a costume?"

Beaming, the young man replied, "Y'all know I work
as a mechanic at my uncle Waylon's shop. We have all
kinds of car parts just layin' around over there, so when I
saw that big empty box in his storeroom in the back, the
idea hit me to make me a truck. I found the steerin' wheel,
headlights, and horn back there, too. I got me some red
paint, black paint, an' silver paint—and the next thing you
know, I had me a red truck!" *I personally think he did*

great. In fact, I bet Asher would love to play with it, too!

"You sure did a fine job on it, my boy. Congratulations," smiled Mr. Brant. As Jimmy Ray moved away, I knew it was time to announce the first place winner for best costume of the day. Anticipation building, it seemed to run through the crowd as people were murmuring and smiling, looking around as if to see if they could pick the winner themselves. Mr. Brant waited a moment to build the suspense, then speaking into the microphone, jubilantly proclaimed: "Without further ado, our first place winner for best costume at our fall festival goes to . . ." It was suddenly completely silent. The only sound was traffic on the highway beside our churchyard. *Well, man, get on with it!* I barked. The crowd erupted in laughter and clapping.

I overheard someone in the crowd yell out, "That dawg is right! We been waitin' long enough, Mr. Brandt! Tell us who the winner is!" Mama, red-faced, picked me up and shushed me, but I didn't know why. I merely said what everyone else had been thinking. I saw several humans smiling at me and nodding their heads. *Maybe I won't get into trouble with Mama later since so many here seemed to think what I said was appropriate.*

Mr. Brandt, chuckling, commented, "I know Charlie, and I agree. Dawgs know what's goin' on more n' we give 'em credit for sometimes, ain't that right! All right, then. The first place winner for best costume today is . . . Miss Savannah Butler—she's wearin' an authentic formal gown from about a century ago, and it shore is purty! Come on up, Miss Savannah."

Mama put me down so she could clap for Miss Savannah. *Rats! It's hard for me to see her down here, Mama!* But I couldn't exactly jump up on Mama, so I stayed put and stretched my neck. Before long, Miss Savannah regally glided forward, and as she reached Mr. Brandt, she snapped opened her decorative fan and covered her face, except for her eyes. She blinked at the crowd several times. They loved it. "Miss Savannah is a fine example of a Southern belle, and we are happy to declare her our winner for the day," exclaimed Mr. Brandt. He handed her the gift certificate, as a young man ran up with a camera, asking if all the winners would stand together so he could take a picture for the town newspaper. Of course, that meant that Daddy and I would also be in the picture, so Daddy picked me up and carried me up front. We were quite a sight: a Philips head, a hot dog, a pair of dice, a truck, Moses, and a Southern belle. I felt certain that our unusual picture would land on the front page of the little weekly. I found out I was right when Daddy brought home the newspaper several days later to show me.

Since the costume judging signaled the end of the festival, I saw people getting into their vehicles, calling good-byes to their friends. Ladies began to clear tables, while men started removing equipment and booths. All in all, I had had a great time. Mama spoke to several of the people, and all said they had a wonderful time, too. There was another new family with three little children, and the father said they had just moved to the area. They had been invited to come by one of their neighbors, a church member named Mr. John Taylor. Mama introduced them to Daddy, who also invited them to attend church in the morning. The father smiled and said they'd love to.

Daddy told Mama he would stay and help get everything cleared out if she wanted to take the children and me home. I noticed that the sisters had said very little for a while, and that they looked tired. Asher had gone to sleep in his stroller. I was not only a "hot dog," but a dog-tired dawg, too. I was ready to go home and rest on the comfy couch. I suppose Piper and Aslan would be wondering where we were, although they could see the church from their perches on the back of the couch.

I thought the festival was lots of fun. I met new

112

people, enjoyed the bites of good food I managed to scrounge up, and even won a prize for best costume.

I actually enjoyed being a hot dog, but it made me miss my papa, who was the first human to ever call me a hot dog.

Maybe I'll get to see him soon.

15
Daddy Preaches a Revival

After the fall festival, my family stayed on the go that next week. One of the new families who had come to the festival, the Sherwoods, did visit church the following Sunday. In fact, I heard Mama telling Mavis on the phone that they had been coming regularly ever since, and she hoped they would join our church soon. Daddy had already visited their home, and he told Mama that he had come away assured that the parents were already Christians, having accepted the Lord as their Savior several years ago. Their little children were still a bit young just yet to understand, however. *I'm not a young pup any longer, but I still don't have a clue about church, Christians, and prayer. Daddy does not even try to explain those to me, but I guess these are just things for the human mind to understand, not for us dawgs. That's okay; humans don't understand a lot of things about us, either, and I don't think they ever will. So, I am content, knowing that I won't always understand everything they do.*

That Sunday after the fall festival also kicked off the church fall revival, with nightly services all week until Friday night. Daddy had been spending much more time preparing for this "revival." I don't quite get what a revival is for, but Mama and Daddy sure were excited about having one. Daddy and another pastor friend from Southeastern Baptist Theological Seminary in Wake Forest (where Daddy graduated) alternated preaching every night, and both Mama and Daddy seemed pleased at the turnout. Several humans joined the church, which pleased Daddy very much. He said something about being glad to have more sheep in the fold. *Where are the sheep? I wanted to see them up close, but I looked all over the house and yard, even across the street at the church, and never could find them. Daddy, were you just fooling me?*

There was even special music at the nightly services, with Mama singing a couple of solos, and several duets and trios also sang specials. I like music myself for the most part, as long as it doesn't get too screechy for my sensitive ears. Mama has a beautiful voice, but some of her songs have such high notes in them that I have to hide my head under a pillow a bit to muffle the sound now and then when she's practicing at home. *She takes a dim view of my singing—which she calls howling—so I no longer don't try to sing along with her like did when I was a puppy.*

On Friday night, it was Daddy's turn to preach, and Mama was supposed to sing. She had been practicing with the sisters so they could sing with her that night. They were excited to be doing so, since they love to sing like Mama does. When I heard them practicing their song here at home, my ears didn't hurt at all—I guess Mama had chosen a song that wouldn't be too hard for their young voices to sing. Judging from the phone calls Mama received from church members after their song that night, I supposed that they sounded really good. Several even stopped by here the next day, giving the sisters hugs and praising their singing. Mama said she was glad they liked to sing, and reminded the sisters that the praise they received only meant that they were using their talents that the Lord had given them. She told them that she hoped they'd always use their talents to glorify God in whatever occupation the Lord led them to choose when they grew up.

Alexa declared that she wanted to be a missionary someday so that she could live in another country far away and tell people about Jesus. Annika said she didn't really want to be a missionary, but maybe a doctor or a cheerleader instead. After all, she reasoned, doctors and cheerleaders could tell people about Jesus, too, even without moving far away. Mama laughed, saying something about how very much alike those two professions were, winking at me. *Hmmm. I've always thought a doctor and a cheerleader are very, very different types of jobs. Oh well. What do I know?*

Daddy's seminary friend, Pastor Gene Miller, came and ate dinner at our house one night. He was a little older than Daddy, with dark brown hair graying at the temples, but he wore glasses like Daddy does. He was also taller and a little wider than Daddy. He was a really nice man because he held me before dinner, even rubbing my ears while he and Daddy talked about the Bible, salvation by grace, eternity, and other topics I didn't understand. *I always say that you can tell if humans are nice by the way they treat us dawgs. If I am well treated, then the human is nice. If not, then the human is not nice. And I've never been wrong in my assessment of humans.*

The revival ended, with Daddy declaring that the church members had done a fine job of inviting their friends and neighbors to the services. Several people had "accepted the Lord," according to Daddy (which makes no sense to me), and I even overheard Daddy thanking God in prayer for the souls that had come into the Kingdom that week. There would be a baptismal service at church the next Sunday. Daddy was really excited about that; I know this because he spoke of it often. He told Mama that his messages would always be geared on behalf of the lost, because people accepting Christ was important to his heart as a pastor. *Whatever he means, I know it is good.*

Daddy is a good man. He loves all of us, and I love him so much, too. He might be the quiet type, but we definitely need *somebody* in this family who doesn't talk all the time.

16
Preparing for Turkey Day

They say time flies as one grows older, so that must be the case for me. Oh, I'm still a youthful-looking and handsome specimen of a dachshund, but it truly seemed like hardly any time had passed since the fall festival when I won a prize for my costume—but now it was already mid-November. This month was full of birthdays in our family: Daddy's is on the 19th, Alexa's is on the 21st, and Mavis's is on the 27th.

I had also been longing to see Papa Duke. I was really worried when he had been in the hospital that time, and although Mama had talked to Nana a few times since then, we hadn't been to visit them because so much had been going on around here.

Aunt Bethany and Uncle Kurt had been at the cookout back then, and so had Uncle Steve and Aunt Dorothy, but it just seemed like a long time to me. Mama told Daddy the other day that her mom had emailed that Sellars and Renata had called Papa a couple of times to check on him since they visited us here. How nice—but unless somebody around here keeps me informed, I usually just have to guess what's going on in this family. *Thankfully, I was within earshot, or I wouldn't even know that tidbit of information!* Humans don't realize that their pets just might be interested in the family doings; after all, aren't we part of the family, too? *It's a good thing I have excellent hearing, or I'd be totally in the dark about things around here.*

I keep my wits about me, pay attention, and I can usually piece together enough information to keep myself from being totally ignorant. I sometimes wonder if the cats think about the rest of the family like I do. They don't seem to be interested in anything or anyone unless something

117

relates to *them*, meaning that they are mostly concerned only about things that affect their well-being. We dawgs, on the other hand, crave human companionship and attention, and I miss Papa and everybody else when I don't see them often.

My ears perked up one evening after the children were in bed; Mama and Daddy started talking about Nana and Papa. Mama said she wanted the entire family together over Thanksgiving, especially since Papa had not been as strong since his surgery. *He seemed fine to me when y'all went to see that water going over the cliff and he and Sellars actually caught some fish, as I recall. But I do seem to remember that he did rest more after he did things.*

Daddy commented, "Why don't you and your mom talk about it and organize a Thanksgiving meal? You'd better do it quickly so Kurt and Bethany can book their flight home, and if you want Sellars and Renata to come, they need to be notified in advance so they can make plans, too."

"Oh, Philip, it just seems so long since we've all been together. Papa and Nana, and Sellars and Renata came to see us, but that was nearly two months ago, and we all need to be together for Thanksgiving, especially. I'll call Mom tomorrow, and see if we can get this show on the road." *Now you're talking—this is a "show" I can definitely get excited about!*

I know that Thanksgiving represents some of the best food I've ever tasted—next to the Christmas meal, of course. Wondering if Papa would be doing some of his delicious cooking this year, I began to worry about my special papa. I went over to Mama, put my paws up on the side of the couch, and barked to her: *Mama, is Papa going to be okay? When will we get to see him again? I wanna go see Papa NOW,* I barked and whined.

Mama lifted me up onto her lap. "Philip, I believe

Sarge knows we're talking about Papa, don't you?" *Of course I know that, Mama. I'm not a dumb dawg, you know.* She continued, "Sarge, I'm calling Mom tomorrow, and we're going to plan a fabulous Thanksgiving feast, as only our family can do. You just wait—it will be like old times—and we're all going to Papa Duke's house for Turkey Day if Nana thinks all of us won't be too much for him!" *Oh boy oh boy oh boy—Papa and me together again!*

Daddy commented: "Your mom's birthday is coming up, too. Couldn't we celebrate it then, also since it is on the day after Thanksgiving this year. We've got a lot to plan here!"

"Oh, that's right," exclaimed Mama. "In the back of my mind, I've been thinking about what to do on her birthday, but wouldn't it be wonderful for all of us to celebrate it at Papa's house? I just know she'd love having all of us together again. By the way," Mama continued, "since your birthday is on the 19th and Alexa's is on the 21st, why don't we just celebrate both of them along with Mom's? With all these parties, that's all we'll be doing if we don't just combine 'em into one—besides, we'll all be together on Thanksgiving, anyway!" I could see that Mama was thrilled at the idea, and as she sat looking thoughtful, I knew those wheels in her mind were turning, too.

Daddy replied, "That's fine by me, but do you think your papa is up for everybody descending on their house this year? He's recovered, of course, but Nana has been saying that he's just not up to his former strength."

"I agree, but Mom and I will work it all out tomorrow when I call her. In fact, I'll text Bethany right now!" She picked up her cell phone to do so. "Okay. I'm just sending her a brief text, but she'll know what I mean." She read aloud as she was texting: "CAN Y'ALL COME TO PAPA'S FOR THANKSGIVING? WE'RE GONNA CELEBRATE PHILIP, ALEXA, AND MOM'S BDAYS THEN, TOO! IF YES, LET ME KNOW & BOOK A FLIGHT ASAP.

"We just have to invite Sellars and Renata, because they're family, too. I'll go send an email to Steve and Dorothy in a little while. I'd call, but they're on the go so much that I probably won't be able to reach them, and I don't like to call anyone after 9:30 or 10:00 at night." She looked at her watch. "Why, it's 9:20 already!"

"I doubt that they've already gone to bed," said Daddy. "But perhaps an email is better. They usually respond to them pretty quickly."

Mama's phone beeped, and she looked at it. "Oh good. Bethany has replied to my text message already." She read the message aloud to Daddy: "WE WOULD LOVE TO COME! WILL BOOK FLIGHT ONLINE RIGHT NOW. WILL MAKE PECAN PIES WHEN I COME, TOO. CAN'T WAIT! WILL CALL TOMORROW. XOX." *What, my dear aunt, does XOX mean??*

"Oh, I'm so glad they're coming!" Mama exclaimed. "Kurt gets a couple of days off for Thanksgiving, anyway, so I hope it's not too late for them to get a decent flight." *I suppose I won't get an answer, since Annika is in bed and can't ask about XOX.* She continued, "We won't shoot for making it a surprise birthday party for Mom—and you already know about this, too. I'll make cupcakes to take to school for Alexa's class; this time of year there just isn't time to fit in a big party. I'll see if her teacher will let me do it right after school by decorating the conference room and making it a princess party—she'll love that. Maybe I can contact all the parents and try to keep that a surprise for her. I just don't want to complicate things, and she knows her birthday is coming up, of course. Let's just pray that everything can be worked out so that it is best for all concerned."

So that was exactly what Mama and Daddy did—right then. They held hands and prayed for their family members by name, offered thanks for the recent church revival, and asked for wisdom and guidance for the

Thanksgiving dinner/birthday celebration. Afterwards, they went to bed.

I went to bed, too, in my special doggie bed from Papa, but I was too thrilled about Thanksgiving to sleep right away. I was thinking of my papa and all those good times we've had together. I recalled that Christmas when Papa made me wait until last to open my doggie bed present from him. Nana came to my rescue by telling Papa to help me open it—or I would have never managed to chew that box open!

I also thought about the time when I was staying with him and Nana, and Papa got trapped in that barbed-wire fence, or "tied up tight," as he tells the story. I got Mr. Vance to come and help Papa get loose—that was the day when Papa told me I was his special granddawg.

And what a great trip we had when I visited Sellars and Renata with Nana and Papa. Sellars made me feel right at home, but his mama pig Tenderloin sure didn't like me very much! I hoped that he and Renata could come for Thanksgiving, because Sellars was like another papa to our family. The time I went fishing with Papa and Sellars is one of my all-time favorite memories, and although they didn't catch any fish that day, Sellars sure caught a big surprise when he hooked Papa's glasses on his fishing line! Our family still enjoys talking about "the fishing story."

Finally growing drowsy, I thought about Papa's friendly and smiling face the first time I ever saw him when I was a little pup. I remembered once more his welcoming laugh as he came out to the car and saw me in the back seat—I knew he loved me right then. His big hand patted me gently, and one of the first things he mentioned was food! We've been good buddies ever since.

Good-night, my special Papa. I can hardly wait until I see you again.

17
Thanksgiving/Birthday Celebration

Mama called Mavis the next day after she had put Asher down for his morning nap. The sisters had gone to school a couple of hours before, so it was just Mama, Daddy, and me in the living room. Although I couldn't hear both sides of their conversation, judging from Mama's comments, I think that Mavis had already thought about the Thanksgiving gathering at Papa's. "Mom, we know your birthday is the day after, but we want to celebrate it with you on Thanksgiving Day—and how about also celebrating Philip's and Alexa's, too? None of us has time for three different birthday celebrations—plus Thanksgiving—this month! I know that the girls and Asher would especially love being in on a BIG birthday celebration!"

Daddy, sitting on the couch, cupped his ear: "Holly, put her on speaker so I can hear what she says," he whispered to Mama. "That way, you won't have to repeat everything to me later." *That is a great idea, Daddy. I have good ears, but even I can't hear what most people (except Papa) say on the phone without the speaker. I want to know what's going on around here, anyway. I usually just have to adopt a 'wait and see' approach, which creates far too many scheduling problems for me, too. I can't plan a thing in advance!*

Mama nodded. "Wait, Mom. Philip is here, too, so I'm gonna put you on speaker, okay?" Mama pushed a button. "Now—say something, Mom, so I know I have the volume adjusted properly."

"All righty. Am I loud enough?" Mavis's voice boomed out. *Ouch!* I barked. *That is loud enough to be heard a block away!*

Mama laughed. "Oh, you're loud enough! I need to 'turn you down' a little, so wait a sec." Mama adjusted the volume, then continued, "Okay, that should do it now." *Whew. I was gonna have to dig up some ear plugs, Mama.*

Mavis inquired, "I heard Sarge speaking. Hi, Boy! Hi, Philip. How are you doing today?" *Oh, I'm as fine as can be.*

"Fine, my favorite mother-in-law. I've got to leave for the church in a few minutes, but Holly said she was going to call you and plan everything, so I wanted to be here. Sounds like Thanksgiving is going to be a big bash this year," replied Daddy.

"Yes—I'm really looking forward to it, and I know Clark is," answered Mavis. "Does it seem to you guys that it's been a long time since we were all together? We had the cookout at Mom and Dad's in late September, so it hasn't even been two months."

Mama replied, "And that was not too long after Papa went to the hospital. We were there then to visit him, and so were you and Dad, but not all of us. I hope Papa is doing okay now, don't you?"

"Oh, Mom says he's better, just slower. After all, at his age, he isn't able to do everything like he used to—in fact, neither can I!" Mavis laughed.

They continued talking and planning for several minutes. Daddy listened, even suggesting an idea or two, then said he'd have to go on to the church. Before going out the door, he said to make sure that somebody brought a banana pudding for Thanksgiving—or at least some butterscotch brownies. Mama assured him that his favorites would be included on the menu, and with a wave, he was out the door.

I continued listening closely because I wanted to know what we were going to eat on Thanksgiving, too—one of my favorite family meals. I didn't bother keeping up with who was bringing what—just so they showed up with good food was all that mattered to me, of course. It sounded like the meal would have the traditional turkey and dressing, cranberry sauce, mashed potatoes and gravy, green bean casserole *(oh, yummy!)*, candied yams, yeast rolls, corn pudding casserole, and lots of desserts: banana pudding, a red velvet cake, pecan pie, a batch of fudge, and a lemon meringue pie. Mama said that Dorothy might make those Czechoslovakian Christmas cookies that Daddy always loves, and Renata would probably make something good, too. *Why so many desserts, especially since I don't get to taste any of them?*

With the meal all planned, Mavis was going to call Nana and Papa as well as Sellars and Renata. Mama said she had already contacted Bethany and Kurt. Mama told Mavis she had also emailed Steve and Dorothy. *Oh, this will be a wonderful time. The food will be so good like it always is, and Papa will make sure I get my fair share.*

During the next week, Mama had talked to Aunt Bethany on the phone, as well as Uncle Steve. From what I could gather by my usual method of eavesdropping, Kurt and Bethany would arrive at Raleigh/Durham on Wednesday, the day before Thanksgiving, with their flight arriving at 3:30 in the afternoon. Like last time, they'd rent a car and drive to Sanford, a trip of about an hour. She would make her pecan pies that evening.

Uncle Steve and Aunt Dorothy would be bringing Zoe and Charlie, much to my delight. *They might not have much to say, but they're still my doggie "cousins" and I enjoy seeing them.* They would drive from Cary early Thanksgiving morning, since it only took them about forty-five minutes to get to Sanford. Clark and Mavis would also drive from Garner on Thanksgiving morning, bringing Duke along, of course. I believe Dorothy was going to bring Daddy's favorite cookies, but the other food she said was a surprise. *Hey, maybe she's made some special doggie bacon treats for me! That would be a wonderful surprise.*

♣ ♣ ♣

Mama did much planning and phone calling to prepare for Alexa's princess birthday party at school, too. First, she called Miss Farmer, Alexa's teacher, to find out if the school conference room would be available for Mama to have Alexa's party right after school on the 21st, explaining about all the other things going on in our family—thus the need for having the party at school. Apparently, Miss Farmer checked with the school office, and called Mama right back, saying that would be fine.

Next, Mama got the phone numbers of all of Alexa's classmates and called their parents to invite the children to the party, to take place at 3:00 and lasting until 4:30. Most of them told Mama right then that their child would be coming. *I suppose it's a lot easier since the children will already be at school, anyway, and the parents can just pick them up later.* Mama stressed that the party was supposed to be a surprise, so she didn't even mention it to Annika, in case she couldn't keep from telling Alexa about it.

Mama went to the store and got the party decorations, favors, and the food she'd need for Alexa's party. She accomplished all this while the sisters were at school, and of course Asher was too young to spill the beans, according to Mama. *Is that what you're going to have to eat at the party, Mama? I've never heard of birthday beans! Oh, that's right. It means keeping a secret. Geez. I must be slipping in my old age.*

On the day of the 21st, Mama sent the sisters off to school with Daddy as usual, then went into overdrive making the birthday cake, decorating it, and getting everything ready. She wrapped Alexa's presents while the cake was in the oven. Daddy was also going to get off work early and go with Mama to the school and help her get the party ready. I wished I could go, but I consoled myself with the fact that I would be able to join in the big birthday celebration at Papa's on Thanksgiving. *That will be better. I'd much rather eat all that Thanksgiving yummy food, and they won't give me any cake, anyway!*

Mama made Alexa a princess doll cake. She had bought a special doll to put in the middle of the cake, and the doll's "dress" was special fondant frosting. Mama colored the frosting a light blue, and wrote Alexa's name on it in frosting, too. Oh, it was so pretty, and I just knew Alexa would love it. She also made cupcakes for the children, decorating each with blue frosting and putting little gold crowns on them like princesses wear.

Asher woke up from his nap, Mama gave him his lunch, and shortly after, Daddy came home. He watched Asher while Mama got ready for the party. When she came back into the living room, she was all dressed up and looked really pretty. Daddy thought so, too. Soon, Daddy began carrying the party things out to the van for Mama, and Asher was getting excited. He understood about birthday parties, and was thrilled it was for his "sissie," whom he loved so much. Soon, Mama told me to be a good boy while they were at the party, and Asher hugged me before they left. I settled down for a nap, while keeping one eye open to watch the cats batting around a bottle cap like it was the best toy in the world. *Cats. They'll play with anything!*

Later that afternoon, they all came home with much excitement and downright exhilaration. Alexa had been very surprised and couldn't stop talking about her party. Annika was pleased for her sister, and Asher kept clapping and smiling, constantly saying "Cake! Cake!" Alexa loved the princess cake, the cupcakes, the decorations, the favors, and of course, the presents from her classmates.

"Oh, Mama!" exclaimed Alexa. "That was the best birthday party! I thought I'd have to wait until Thanksgiving for my party, but now I get another one then, too!" she sighed happily.

"We're so glad you liked it, Honey," said Daddy. "Mama did a lot of work to get it all ready, spending a long time making and decorating your cake and the cupcakes. I hope you are very thankful to have such a nice mama, young lady!"

Alexa ran over and gave Mama a big hug. "Oh, I am! Thank you so much, Mama! You knew how much I love princess stuff, and all my friends liked the party, too! I can't believe I am now SEVEN YEARS OLD." *Neither can I, little Alexa, neither can I—because I remember when Mama and Daddy brought you home from the hospital as a newborn baby. Boy, I must be getting old.*

The children were hyped up for the rest of the evening, obviously on a "sugar high," according to Mama, but Mama and Daddy got them settled down and had a family devotion before putting them to bed. I was worn out, just watching them laughing, running around, and being in high spirits. Even the cats noticed, sitting like statues and watching the children running back and forth through the house. *Hey, you cats look like you're watching a tennis match, 'cause you're turning your heads back and forth, back and forth. Jumpin' dog biscuits! If sugar causes that much happiness and energy, I really need to see about getting it into my diet.*

🐾　　🐾　　🐾

"Okay, everybody, we're headed to the big cruise ship in a few minutes!" I heard Mama saying from the kitchen. *What? When? Where? Cruise ship?* "Annika and Alexa, help Asher get his roller skates on—he's too little to do it by himself. Philip, have you packed the polar bears? We don't want to forget the polar bears!" *Wha-a-a-t?? I do not understand. This is really weird, Mama.*

I didn't realize that it was already time to go to Papa's house. *Wait—we don't go on a cruise ship to Sanford. Roller skates? Polar bears?* I jumped down from my comfy spot on the couch and trotted into the kitchen to find out what was going on. Only Mama was in there, and she was dressed in a fur coat, roller skates, and a big straw hat—in the house! *Mama, why are you dressed that way? You look funny.*

To investigate further, I whirled around to go find the rest of the family. Ah—there were Piper and Aslan sitting on the computer chair together—but they had big chocolate doughnuts on their heads! *Hey, don't you cats notice anything odd at all??* Staying as far away from them as possible, I hurriedly got past them and trotted on to find Daddy and the children. I heard voices in the playroom, so I went to the door and looked in. There they were all right: Daddy and Annika were tossing a pork chop back and forth, and it smelled heavenly. As if that weren't strange enough, I looked further and saw Alexa and Asher—and they were trying to place strips of bacon on their heads! Daddy saw me and said, "C'mon in, Sarge—we have all these yummy foods here for you, but you were sleeping, so we decided to use them as toys until you got in here!"

Something was definitely not right. I decided I had to straighten everyone out, so I began barking: *You guys have lost it for sure! I've never seen you do anything this outrageous, even if humans ARE crazy most of the time!* I heard Mama singing at the top of her lungs as she skated down the hall toward where we were. As she entered the playroom, she came over to me and began patting me on the head, then rubbing my shoulders and back, telling me to wake up. *Mama, I don't need to wake up—I am already awake! I just don't understand what has come over all of you. I'm getting scared now, because I'm wide awake and all of you are acting wacky—*

Mama spoke again, sounding as if she were far away: "C'mon, Sarge, wake up! You must have been having a humdinger of a dream, buddy! You were barking like mad, but you wouldn't open your eyes. Are you all right?" I opened my eyes and looked around. We were all in our van; Daddy was driving, the children and Mama were looking at me with concern on their faces, and I was astounded. *You mean I was sleeping so soundly I didn't even know we were in the van? Oh my—thank goodness all that was only a dream!* I shook myself, stretched, and yawned.

Daddy was looking at me from the rearview mirror: "You okay now, Sarge? Holly tried to wake you up, but all you did was bark—LOUDLY. That must have been some dream you were having. We're almost to Nana and Papa Duke's house, so you need to wake up and be ready to see them!" *You don't even know the half of it, Daddy. I'm glad it was only a dream, because everybody was acting weird. I can't seem to stop thinking about Alexa and Asher putting those bacon slices on their heads. Whew!* I shook my ears and stretched.

Annika stated, "I didn't know that doggies had dreams—I thought only people did. Wish you could tell us about it, Sargie. I had a dream once that I was a doggie," she giggled. *Oh my goodness, Annika. As much as you love food, you'd be a doggie chow hound like me, I'm sure.*

Alexa piped up, "I dreamed I was a princess in a dream one time. I had servants, and lived in a beautiful palace, and wore fancy dresses—" *Hey, that's not a dream— you dress up like one all the time!*

Mama interrupted, "Daddy just took the exit off Highway 421, so we'll be at Papa and Nana's in about ten minutes. Let me see if your hair is okay," as she turned around and inspected their hairstyles from the front seat. "Yes, you look nice, ladies."

"Asher hair nice, too?" the boy inquired from his car

seat. *Your hair can't get messed up, Asher—like mine, it's too short!*

"Of course," Mama replied, smiling. "Your blond hair looks very nice. Now girls, when we get there, I might want you to carry in some things that aren't too heavy, because we have a lot of things: suitcases, tote bags, toys, food, Sarge's food and bed—"

"Yes, Mama," said the girls in unison. *How do they do that? I guess the old saying, "Great minds think alike" is true, especially for the sisters.*

Shortly, we arrived at that familiar and beloved home. There was Nana's green car, Papa's truck, Clark and Mavis's red van, and the chain-link fence around the yard. *I bet Papa is in the kitchen getting the food ready.*

"There's a little car I don't recognize," said Mama, "so it must be the rental car that Kurt and Bethany drove from the Raleigh/Durham Airport yesterday. Steve and Dorothy should already be here, and so should Sellars and Renata. Hmmmm."

On cue, the front door burst open and spilled out our family. Smiling, out they came to greet us: Kurt and Bethany, Sellars and Papa, and Clark and Uncle Steve. *Oh boy oh boy oh boy! There's my family coming out to see me! I am so happy to see them!* I barked. The children were just as excited as I was. Annika and Alexa were wiggling out of their booster seats, and Asher was clapping and saying "Papa!" Mama and Daddy had already opened their doors, and were in the process of opening the side doors for us when the crew reached us.

"Well, there's my dash-hound! Hey, Sarge! C'mon out and see yore ol' Papa!" He was smiling, wearing a white apron over his clothes, and I couldn't wait to get to him. I jumped against Annika, pushing her with my front paws.

"Hey, don't knock me down, Sarge!" she exclaimed. *But you don't understand—that's my papa out there! Lemme outa here!* The sisters jumped down from the van, and I followed them, running straight to Papa. *Oh, Papa, am I glad to see you! And you smell so good, like turkey, dressing, gravy, candied yams, and all that other good food. I can't wait for Thanksgiving dinner!* Papa laughed that big robust laugh and patted me on the head.

"Ray-melle, Mavis, Renata, and Dorothy stayed in the house getting everything finished up," said Sellars. "We shore are glad to see y'all, but them children have grown so much since last time. Why, girls, y'all are gonna be as tall as me the next time I see you!" They giggled and hugged Sellars, who peered at them, smiling. "An' y'all is jest gittin' uglier and uglier ever time I see you, too. I don't know how any boys are ever gonna be able to stand lookin' at such awful girls when y'all git older!" By now, although Sellars had said the same thing to them recently, the sisters were giggling harder.

"Where are the other cars?" asked Mama. "I thought nobody else was here but Mom and Dad, Kurt and Bethany."

"Oh, they parked 'em around back," replied Kurt. "They had to unload stuff, and it just gave you guys more room out here, anyway."

"Group hug!" yelled Clark. "Let's get the hugging out of the way so we can help y'all bring in your things. Uh, I'll be happy to carry in the food for you," he smiled sweetly. They all gathered around for one big hug, but I couldn't get up there to hug, so I barked to remind them that I was underfoot. Steve picked me up and I licked all the faces I could reach before they separated: Mama and the children heading to the house, and the men staying to help Daddy carry in our things. I decided to go with Mama, since being in the house was closer to Papa's kitchen, a.k.a. food.

As we entered the house with Mama carrying Asher, and the sisters right behind her—I brought up the end of our procession—I heard Nana, Mavis, Dorothy, and Renata exclaiming in happy tones: "Look at that big boy! Where are Annika and Alexa—these girls are too big to be them! Holly, you look great!" and so on. *Well, what about me?? Don't any of you see me?* Just then I heard Duke barking from the back of the house. *Buddy, you mean you didn't even come out to say hello to me? Humph,* I barked to no one in particular.

"I hear Duke, but I don't see him," commented Alexa. "Where is he?"

"Oh, we put the three dawgs in the back bedroom and shut the door," replied Nana. "We figured it would be easier for y'all to get into the house with everything without trying to keep up with them, too."

"Nana, can we let them out after Daddy and the other men bring in our stuff?" inquired Annika.

"Of course, Honey," answered Nana. "It won't be very long, because the men are coming in right now. Let's go over here and sit down so we won't be in their way." So, Nana, Renata, and Mavis sat down on the couch, each holding a child. Mama and Bethany sat in the chairs across the room, and Dorothy sat in Papa's recliner, so I jumped up into her lap. I didn't want to get stepped on, either.

The men entered, laden with suitcases, bags, my stuff, and the food that Mama had brought for the meal. "Somebody direct us so we'll know where to put everything," Steve said. "Of course, we are smart enough to figure out that the food goes in the kitchen—right? But where do you want the rest of their things, Mom?"

Nana replied, "Put everything else in the guest room where Holly and Philip usually sleep, and she can arrange it like she wants later. Is that okay with you, Holly?"

"Of course. We're just so glad to be here, and thankful to have some help bringing in our 'moving van' worth of stuff! I tell you, it takes a lot of suitcases and other odds and ends when traveling with three children and a dog!" *Now, don't blame me, Mama. All I had to bring was my food, my dish, my leash, and my doggie bed.*

"What did you do with your kitties?" asked Renata. "Did you get somebody to check on them for you?"

"Oh yes," replied Mama. "A lady from our church always looks in on them every day when we're out of town. She has cats of her own, and both of our cats know her now and always come out to greet her. At first, she asked me if we even had any cats, 'cause they'd stay in hiding the first time or two we were out of town. But now, they come out and greet her right away." *I'm so glad that Piper and Aslan didn't come with us! I can't imagine having to deal with them in the van, too. And they might have run off at one of our stops.*

"That's nice of her," Renata commented. "You're only going to be away for a few days, but even kitties need to be checked on, don't they?"

Papa looked at his watch: "My goodness, it's already eleven o'clock! Are we gonna eat Thanksgiving dinner or not? And I'm gettin' mighty hongry, too. Why, I been up since four o'clock cookin' the turkey and the other stuff. I couldn't go back to sleep, so I figgered I should just go ahead and git this show on the road!"

"I'm glad you did," said Daddy. "I'm getting kinda hungry myself, 'cause we left early to get here on time. Anytime you want to eat, Robert, is fine with me."

"Yeah, me, too," said Sellars. "We had us a nice big breakfast like we always do, but that was purty early, and my stomach thinks it's got some room in it now—so that means it's time to pack it in again! Heh heh." *Oh Sellars, you probably oughta be an honorary dawg, too, 'cause you love to eat like the rest of us dawgs—and Papa, of course.*

Speaking of dawgs, just then Duke charged into the living room like a bullet fired from a gun. Zoe and Charlie were right behind him, but they were in no hurry. Duke was barking, wagging his tail, running around and licking any hands he could reach, and eventually came over to greet me. *Hiya, Duke! We'll have us a good meal today, won't we, my fellow chow hound?* I jumped down from Dorothy's lap so I could greet Duke properly. Annika, Alexa, and Asher came over to Duke, patting all of us dogs, saying nice things, so we really put on the dog—no pun intended. Duke and I licked faces, pulled hair, jumped up and licked noses, causing all kinds of commotion. Zoe and Charlie just watched, but no matter. The children were laughing, Duke and I were barking, and the grownups were looking on indulgently.

In a moment, Papa drawled, "Ray-melle, is everthang ready for Thanksgiving dinner? I'm HONGRY."

"Yes, Robert, I just took the biscuits out of the oven, Bethany has put ice in the glasses, and Dorothy had already set the table. Renata has just finished arranging all the food along the kitchen counter, so as soon as someone says the blessing, we can EAT." *All right! EAT is one of my key words: Battle stations! I'm reporting for duty!* And Duke was standing at attention, too, ready to compete for food. "Who's gonna do the honors? Clark, why don't you say grace this time?" Nana asked.

"I'd be glad to," replied Clark.

"Before you do," declared Papa, "I'd like to say thanks to all of y'all for your prayers, cards, love, and caring while I was in the hospital and after I got home. God is mighty good, and he took an ol' sinner like me and gave me eternal life all those years ago. I especially want to thank Him fer that." The sisters, Mama, and Bethany all went over and hugged our beloved Papa. *We love you, too, Papa.*

"We're all thankful you're doing better, too," said Clark. "You seem to back to your old self now, and I'm glad."

"I'm 'fit as a fiddle.' Well—maybe an ol' beat-up fiddle that's seen better days—but I'm in purty good shape fer the shape I'm in!" Papa laughed.

Clark began his prayer: "Heavenly Father, we are so thankful for our many blessings on this wonderful Thanksgiving Day. As we share our delicious meal, we thank You for the food, and we also thank You for this family and all the love we have for each other. We're thankful that Robert is doing better, we're blessed to have Sellars and Renata with us once again, and we can never thank You enough for Your gift of eternal life. Thank You, Lord, for loving us, watching over us, and guiding us. In Jesus' name I pray, Amen." It was quiet for a moment, but then bedlam broke out as everyone began scurrying around to get in line to load up their plates.

Nana instructed, "Holly, go first so you can get the children's plates ready. I bet they're hungry, too—aren't you, babies?"

"Yes, we are!" said the sisters together. *They did it again. Weird how they can do that.* "But we're not babies!" Annika exclaimed.

"Hungry! Asher wanna eat Papa food!" piped up Asher. Everyone laughed. *Yep, my boy, that just about sums it up. Trust me—we all wanna eat Papa food.*

"Mama's getting your plate ready, Asher," said Mama. "And Daddy's gonna put you in your booster chair right now," so taking the hint, Daddy did just that. I watched as Mama got Asher's food: turkey and dressing, mashed potatoes, candied yams, corn pudding, green bean casserole. Of course, she put small portions, but that boy could eat when he had a mind to.

"Mama, make sure I get some of everything," Annika called over to her. "I don't see anything I don't like, so give me everything!"

"Me, either," added Alexa. "Oh, this food is going to be so good!" And the sisters started clapping and jumping up and down.

"Hey, no jumping in here," admonished Mama. "Nana's kitchen is not a gym, you know. Y'all go sit down, and I'll bring your plates in just a moment. Alexa, you want some of everything, too?" Alexa nodded in an exaggerated fashion. *So do I, but what I get is contingent on what Papa's willing to share with me. That's fine—he's generous, thankfully.*

Everyone got their plates filled to the brim, then came and sat at the table. Keeping a close eye on Papa, I waited to find my "place" under the chair so I could get my usual bounty from above. I saw that Duke was watching everyone, too, and I wondered who he planned to sit under. *Aha. He's watching Sellars, a brilliant choice. That dawg catches on fast. I'd even pick Sellars myself if Papa wasn't here!*

Quiet prevailed in the dining room for a little while, with only the sounds of silverware clinking on plates, small talk, and so on. Papa sent all my favorites down: green bean casserole, mashed potatoes, turkey, dressing—oh my. I had almost forgotten how good all this tasted. *Keep it up, Papa! And you don't have to worry about making a mess, either—I'm catching it in midair!*

As the meal continued, they must have been slowing down, because conversation picked up. I overheard Mama and Bethany whispering about something, catching the word "birthday" and "cake" in the middle of it. *Oh, that's right! We're also celebrating the three birthdays today, too.*

Steve inquired, "Hey, what are y'all whispering about over there? We wanna hear, too!"

"Oh, nothing, Uncle Steve, nothing at all," answered Bethany sweetly.

"Yeah. It jest ain't polite to whisper in front of all of us," added Sellars. "If y'all are talkin' about more food or sumthin,' then it's only fittin' fer you to share what you know with the rest of us, right, everbody?"

"Okay, okay," Mama replied. "Since all of you know that we are celebrating not one, but THREE birthdays today, we were just making sure that everything was ready. But finish your meal, people. We have the rest of the day to do this, you know."

"Uh, I'm already finished for now," said Renata. "There's something out in our motor home that I need to bring in here, but I'll get it in a little while. Holly and Bethany, will you help me? Oh, and Dorothy, too?" They all replied that they would, but it was quiet again for a minute or two. *I'm puzzled. I guess that's why it is so quiet—the men and the children are trying to figure out what's going on, just like I am.*

In a few minutes, Papa pushed his chair back from the table, forcing me to scramble out of his way. "Man, that was some good food." He patted himself on the back. "Ol' Duke, you might not have fixed the whole meal, but you done real good on the turkey, dressing, gravy, and candied yams. Yessir, you done real good," and he patted his tummy. That must have been some kind of signal, because immediately, Renata, Mama, Bethany, and Dorothy got up.

"We'll be right back," stated Renata. "Ramelle, is the coffee ready?"

"Oh yes. I turned it on before we started eating, so it's ready," replied Nana.

"Where are you going?" asked Alexa. "Are you coming right back?"

"Girls, you come, too," answered Renata. And they all marched out the kitchen door, leaving the men sitting there looking puzzled. Nana and Mavis, however, didn't seem bothered by their exit. *Of course, I've noticed that men often look puzzled when women do unexpected things. It's not all that unusual for men to be confused about women, in my experience.*

"Where are they going?" asked Sellars. "Why, we ain't even had our dessert yet! I looked over the dessert table, and I don't know if I can decide which one I want, 'cause they all look mighty good—"

"Just do like I do, Sellars," said Steve. "Get some of each one!"

"Okay, Booey, I believe I'll do just that. No sense in hurtin' somebody's feelins' by not trying their dessert, now is there? Heh heh." *Booey? I've never heard Steve called that.*

As if reading my mind, Kurt piped up, "Booey? Is that what you called Steve, Sellars? I've never heard that one."

"Yep, Kurt, that's what I called him. Been calling him that since he was a young fella when we was all up in Alaska together."

Daddy pointed out, "I couldn't help but notice that my favorite sister-in-law, Dorothy, made me some of her famous Czechoslovakian cookies—those must have been the surprise food she was telling Holly about a few days ago." And he smiled, looking satisfied.

Just then, the kitchen door opened, and in walked the women. Mama and Bethany were carrying a huge cake with lots of lighted candles on it, and the women began singing the birthday song. Everyone joined in as Mama and Bethany gingerly placed the big cake in the middle of the table, while Dorothy, Renata, and the sisters put all the presents over in the corner of the room. The song ended with clapping and cheering.

"Happy birthday to Mom, Philip, and Alexa!" shouted Mama. "There's so many candles on this cake that y'all had better hurry up and make a wish and blow them out, or the fire department will be showing up!"

"Oh, I had my wish all decided before I even got here," stated Mavis. Philip nodded, saying that he had his, and Alexa did, too.

"All right, then," said Dorothy. "On the count of three, y'all blow out the candles! One, two, THREE!" Mavis, Philip, and Alexa, standing beside the cake, took big breaths and blew as hard as they could. Alexa took a second breath before all the candles were out.

"Hey, Sissie," Annika informed Alexa, "You're only supposed to take one breath, and you took two!"

"I know," said a breathless Alexa. "But there's so many candles, I didn't have enough air to blow them all out!"

"That's just fine," said Nana. "I want to add that we have all these desserts, I know, but Renata made this beautiful crunch cake herself yesterday afternoon. She also decorated it with her special buttercream frosting."

"Did you say crunch cake?" inquired Daddy with a big smile. "Oh, that is one of my favorites! I want a great big piece of that!"

"Do you want ice cream with it?" asked Dorothy from the kitchen.

"No. That cake is sufficient unto itself, and I know I will enjoy it with my coffee. And I just happened to see those cookies you made, too, Dorothy. I'll be sure to eat some of those later."

"Oh, you're quite welcome, Philip. I love to make things that people like to eat!"

Mama, Bethany, Renata, and Dorothy began serving the cake to everyone, finding out who wanted ice cream with theirs, and passing out steaming cups of coffee as well. Once again, quietness reigned in the dining room for the space of a few minutes. Since I knew that we dawgs wouldn't get any dessert, I retreated into the living room, but I could still hear everything. Duke trotted along after me, but of course, Zoe and Charlie were already in there, snoozing. Besides, my belly was quite full, and I just wanted to laze around and listen to the conversation—Papa just might tell another funny story or two. Duke jumped up on the couch, and I jumped into Papa's recliner, which afforded me a better view—it was closer to the dining room.

"Ladies, what are we gonna do with the rest of them delicious desserts?" asked Sellars. "Now, Renata Honey

Lamb, this crunch cake is mighty fine, but I shore don't want none of them other desserts jest settin' there and goin' bad, you know."

"That's real noble of you, Sellars," piped up Steve. "We'll all be here the rest of the day, right? And some of you are staying a couple more days. I doubt that any of the desserts—or the leftover food—will go bad around here."

"I always said that if a cake lasted for longer than twenty-four hours around this house, then there was something wrong with it," said Nana.

"Hey, Mom, that reminds me," Mavis cut in. "Remember that time when Steve and I were little and you made an angel food cake? Oh, you made lots of them over the years, but this time, you weren't taking that cake to anybody, so you and Dad cut it in fourths and we ate the whole thing??"

"Oh, don't tell everything you know!" exclaimed Nana, laughing. "But it's true—we did just that."

"Duke, you mean jest the four of y'all ate a whole cake at one sittin'?" asked Sellars incredulously. "That's an awful lot of cake, even for y'all."

"Well," Papa retorted, "think about angel food cake, Sellars. If you mash all the air out of it, there ain't much left but about one or two bites of cake, you know. So even eatin' that whole cake, we was mostly eatin' just air

"Hey, I never actually thought of it that way," added Kurt. "I'll have to remember that one the next time we have angel food cake. I always felt like I hadn't eaten any afterwards, so now I can eat several pieces without fear of overeating—all that air in there, you know."

"Works for me, too," said Daddy. "I will say, though, that I sure can't eat but one piece of this crunch cake—not because it isn't good, because it's delicious—but it is very dense."

"Oh, any pound cake is pretty heavy," added Dorothy. "All that butter, cream, sugar, eggs, flavorings, shortening—but all of it is so yummy!"

"Before I forget, I gotta tell something on Dad—I forgot the last time or two we were together until I got home," declared Steve. "Of course, Mom, Mavis, and I were kinda in the same boat with Dad this time."

"Let's have it," Mama said, "since we've just about talked cake to death."

"Son, what else could you dig up? I cain't think of nuthin' else that anybody would want to hear about," inserted Papa.

"Oh, this one's pretty funny, Dad," replied Steve. "Remember when your tour of duty in Alaska was up? Where did the U.S. Army proudly send you—in the summer?" Steve let that tidbit sink in. *Where? And why is that important?*

"Oh, I remember all too well," said Mavis. "It was so cold in Alaska, even in summer—compared to down here—so Dad kept saying he wanted to go someplace warm 'so he could sweat.'"

Nana added: "That's right, Robert. Remember you said over and over that you were glad the Army was going to send us to Florida because you wanted to sweat! And boy, did we!"

Papa looked sheepish. "I know I said that several times, but I had forgot how hot it would be in Miami! Man, after three and a half years in Alaska, they sent us to Homestead, which is below Miami—and I had to report for duty in July!"

"The strongest memory I have of our arrival," stated Mavis, "was when we got on base and waited in the car for you while you went in and reported. It was July, the sun was beating down on us, and in that car, we really thought we were all going to melt—and we had no AC in our car back then. Oh, you parked near a scraggly little tree, trying to park in the shade—"

"Yeah," added Nana. We had those plastic seat

covers then, too. I was wearing shorts, and I think the backs of my thighs were blistered from those hot seat covers!"

Steve affirmed her statement: "It wasn't just in the car. The whole time we lived in Homestead, we kept reminding Dad every time he complained about the heat and humidity: 'You wanted to get somewhere so you could sweat, so you've gotten your wish!' Our house didn't have AC, either. Mavis and I took cold showers, ran under the water hose in the backyard—even went shopping with Mom to stores that had air conditioning!"

"We just weren't used to that kind of heat," Nana declared. "Why, it rained several times a day while we were there, and the sidewalks would be dry five minutes later. We had several fans in the house, and we argued about where to put them, because we all wanted one blowing on us ALL THE TIME!"

"Best I recall," said Sellars, "y'all didn't stay down there that long. We wuz stationed in Alabama after Alaska, and that was bad enough, but it was northern Alabama, and it wasn't like bein' in the tropics like y'all were."

"That's when I decided to retire from the military," replied Papa. "We was all just dyin' in that heat. I guess it was the high humidity that really got us. Ray-melle had to put these little 'mildew bags' in our closets so our clothes wouldn't mildew! I had a nice pair of leather shoes, and when I went to put 'em on one Sunday fer church, them shoes was covered with mildew! I had to scrub 'em down, and that got kinda tiresome after a while."

"How long did y'all stay in Homestead?" asked Kurt. "I mean, if it was that miserable, then you must have gotten out of there pretty soon."

"Let's see," mused Papa. "We arrived there in July, school started in late August—"

Mavis finished his thought for him: "We left in November. The air was just starting to get comfortable for us. Goodness! Kids at the bus stop were wearing coats, if you can believe that! Steve and I were still wearing our summer clothes because it was finally becoming bearable to us. People looked at us like we were insane, since temperatures in the sixties seemed cold to them. But not to us!"

"So how did you just leave?" asked Kurt. "Doesn't the Army have some type of regulations about such things?"

"Oh, yes, they do," replied Papa. But I already had in my twenty years—twenty-two and a half, to be exact," he added. "All I had to do was put in my retirement papers in October, and we were outa there in November. I had come up here to Sanford to look for us a place to live—I had it all planned out. I found us an apartment, and then Ray-melle an' me bought a lot and had this house built. So that's the story of my retirement from the U.S. Army."

"I want to add that even after we moved to Sanford in November—and it was quite cold that winter—none of us wore a coat anywhere," said Mavis. "It even snowed, but we just laughed. After Alaska, it just didn't feel cold to us at all. We weren't trying to be funny—we were more comfortable without coats. Oh, how I enjoyed the cool air after a Miami summer!"

Mama said, "Wow. As one who prefers summer, I just don't understand leaving sunny Florida at all, but I think it's time for our birthday trio to open their presents, don't you? Nana, how about we all go into the living room, and some of us will clean up the table really quickly? Then the birthday people can open their gifts."

"Wait—I have one more part of all that to tell y'all," laughed Steve. "We were so miserable that Mavis and I talked Mom into walking to the mall where it was air conditioned. We only had the one car, and Dad used it for work. We were out of school in summer, and we didn't really know anyone. I know we were driving Mom nuts complaining about the heat. So, we thought it was a good idea to go to the mall for a few hours to cool off."

"Oh, and don't forget to tell them how far the mall was," laughed Nana. "By car, it only took a few minutes, but it was at least two miles away. I practically had to drag them the last half of the walk, because they were so hot, tired, and miserable. Well, so was I, but I wasn't going to allow them to quit. We'd have had to walk a mile back home, anyway, and it was only that same distance to get to the mall, so I made 'em keep going."

"We were glad you did, once we got there," added Mavis. "But it was some tough going for what seemed like hours across a desert. Once we got there, we sat down in a restaurant, ordered the largest soft drinks they had, and just sat for a while. I still hate hot weather to this day! After a few hours, we managed to crawl back home," she laughed. "It's funny now, but it certainly wasn't then!"

"Oh, we know that," laughed Clark.

"But I didn't even mention anything about having to take my P.E. class outside, did I? I was a senior, and I had to take it because in Alaska, P.E. only counted a fourth of a credit—so I didn't bother. We had to run laps, do all sorts of exercise OUTSIDE in that heat. My P.E. teacher took pity on me, though, once she realized where I had come from."

"That explains a lot, Mom," said Mama. "I guess it helps me, the summer girl, understand why you dislike summer, since you explained that dreaded trip to the 'oasis.' Are y'all ready for the gifts now?"

"I'll help you, Holly," Dorothy said. So the two women began removing plates, cups, and forks.

"Renata and I will carry the gifts into the living room," said Bethany. "C'mon, everybody! Mom, Philip, and Alexa—y'all sit on the couch together, and the rest of us will sit wherever we can find a seat, okay?" I saw the "herd" heading into the living room, so I jumped down so Papa could have his recliner.

"Why, thank you, Sarge, fer warmin' up my recliner fer me. Now, why don't you jest jump up here on my lap? An' Duke, you come on up here, too." So Duke and I sat with Papa, the best seat in the house, while everyone else found theirs.

In a few minutes, Mama and Dorothy joined us in the living room, and it was decided that Alexa could open her gifts first, much to the little girl's delight. I wanted to help her, because I just love opening presents, but Mama told Papa, "Now hold on to Sargie, Papa. He'll go over there and try to help her open her gifts, because he doesn't care whose gifts they are, as long as he can rip into 'em." *What's wrong with being helpful, Mama?* But Papa did as she asked, and I couldn't have gotten down if I had wanted to. *I forgot how strong your hands are, Papa.*

So Alexa opened her gifts: she got a new princess doll from Sellars and Renata (an instant hit), a pretty pink dress from Steve and Dorothy, and a nice locket necklace from Kurt and Bethany. Clark and Mavis gave her an entire set of play dishes. Mama and Daddy had already given their present to her at home, but they did have a small present for her today: a topaz birthstone ring. Mama said that topaz is the birthstone for the month of November. *I don't know what topaz is, but I can see that it is a sparkling yellow jewel.* Alexa was thrilled with everything.

Next, Daddy was prompted to open his gifts from everyone. He seemed a bit uncomfortable opening his presents with all eyes upon him. *I don't know why, Daddy. Doesn't everybody stare at you when you preach at church?? And this crowd is a lot smaller, too.*

The first present Mama handed him was from Nana and Papa, according to the tag he read aloud. As he opened the box, his face was wreathed in smiles: he lifted out a beautiful black leather Bible cover. He thanked them several times, so I know he liked it. Next, he opened his gift from Mama, a gift certificate to his favorite Christian

145

bookstore. Once again, he smiled broadly. Mama commented that she believe he liked books almost as much as food! Everyone laughed.

Daddy next opened his gift from Kurt and Bethany, a set of gold cuff links engraved with his initials. He liked those, too, and thanked them. Clark said something about wanting to borrow them if the initials had been the right.

Clark and Mavis's gift was small and flat, and turned out to be a music cd set of Daddy's favorite songs. And finally, Steve and Dorothy gave Daddy a light blue sweater emblazoned with "The University of North Carolina, Chapel Hill, NC" in dark blue across the front. That brought a big smile from Daddy, a UNC Tarheel fan, and so was Steve, who had graduated from there himself. Mama said she'd just have to borrow that sometime, because she also liked UNC.

It was finally Mavis's turn, but the children were getting fidgety. She commented that one of the problems with being last was that everybody was tired by then, but Papa said to go ahead and enjoy opening her gifts.

Mama and Daddy gave her a silver necklace and earrings, which she loved and said she would enjoy wearing. Nana and Papa gave her a matched kitchen set of dish towels, potholders, apron, and trivets. Mavis loved the pattern on them, commenting that some of her dishtowels had definitely seen better days. Sellars and Renata gave her a book, which Mavis said she couldn't wait to read. Steve and Dorothy gave her a hot pink scarf and earrings to match, which Mavis said would look great with her new black dress. And finally, she opened her gift from Clark, which turned out to be a large makeup case, filled with every kind of makeup imaginable: lipstick, blush, eye shadow, mascara, foundation, eyeliner pencils, and whatever else it was that ladies put on their faces. Of course, I didn't really have a clue about all that, but the women certainly thought that was a fabulous gift. She asked Clark if he thought she needed some "sprucing up," which brought a laugh. *Does that have anything to do with a spruce tree??*

"Why no, my dear," Clark replied. "I just happen to know how much you love makeup. After all, you have a desk in the bedroom with every drawer full of 'war paint,' so I thought that would be one thing you'd be sure to love. Am I right?"

"Since you put it that way, then yes!" Mavis answered. "You know the old saying: 'The older the barn, the more paint it needs.' So that's why I have so much 'war paint,' as you put it."

"Mom, you always look nice, and you don't look old to us," said Bethany sweetly.

"Thanks. Now THAT was the absolute right thing to say!" Mavis laughed.

Now that all the gifts were opened, Mama told the children it was time to take a little nap. The sisters said they weren't sleepy, but being a wise mama, she replied that they didn't have to sleep, but they had to lie down to rest and be quiet. So they trudged back to their room, but when Mama checked on them in a few minutes, they were sleeping. Asher went to the crib without a peep, but then he was much younger and probably needed that nap.

As Mama returned to the living room and sat down, Steve commented, "You know, I'm not quite ready to leave the subject of Florida alone for today. There are just so many more 'jewels' to share with everyone about our tortured imprisonment when we lived there!"

"I know," added Mavis. "Florida is a beautiful state, but it just seemed like a tropical sauna to us 'Eskimos.' Clark and I have visited there when his sister Alicia lived in St. Petersburg, and we liked it just fine then. But I do want to mention the fact that I really felt like an outsider at the high school I attended there in Miami. My lil' ol' high school in Ft. Greely, a small Army base, only had about a hundred students, but Miami Palmetto High had three thousand! I had to run from one class to the next because they were so spread out and in different buildings and different floors! I don't even know why we had to take P.E.—I know I got enough exercise just trying to get to class on time!"

Steve was smiling: "What I wanted to add was about that hurricane that came through while we lived there. Oh, we didn't have much damage, but I do know that Mom got really mad at us when we were supposed to be preparing for the hurricane. Remember that, Mom?"

"Do I remember?? Robert had to work, and the weatherman said to board up all windows in preparation for the hurricane, put away outdoor furniture, and so on. I tried to get y'all to help me board up the windows, and all you wanted to do was laugh about it."

"I remember, Mom. I guess I would have choked me if I had been you back then," commented Mavis. "We just didn't see that an ol' storm was that big of a deal, and thankfully, it turned out to be weaker than it was predicted." *I've never been in a hurricane, but I'm afraid I'd just blow away unless they tied me up inside a closet!*

"Yeah," said Nana. "All we had were some palm trees messed up, limbs in our yard—from trees, not people, ha ha—and y'all thought that was funny, too. I guess it was just a 'phase' you two were going through at the time. It's a good thing I had some restraint, though!"

"I didn't have to work all the time, did I?" asked Papa. "I don't remember any of this, fer some reason. Y'all know I woulda put them boards on the winders. Ray-melle, why didn't you jest wait 'til I got home from work?"

"You were working double shifts for some reason, but that was a long time ago, Robert. All I know is that you just weren't home much for a while."

"Oh, we knew it was a hurricane, but for some reason, that was just funny to us, as I recall," replied Steve.

"I don't know why now, exactly." They all just sat around, thinking for a few minutes. *I guess humans tend to forget things from many years ago. I already do that myself, and I am not nearly as old as they are.*

Soon, Sellars said he thought he could do with a nap himself, so he and Renata headed out to their motor home, and I jumped down to join Zoe and Charlie beside the fireplace. I couldn't attest to what anybody else did the rest of the afternoon, because I fell asleep myself, to the sound of Papa and Steve laughing.

What a wonderful time, to be with all those I love.

Sometime later that afternoon, something woke me up. I yawned and stretched, overhearing the sound of dishes in the kitchen—I'm certain that hearing the sounds coming from the kitchen woke me, as it usually does. I looked around, and apparently Steve and Dorothy, Clark and Mavis had already gone home. What I can't understand is how they managed to sneak out without my hearing them. I must have been more tired than I realized! That left my family, Kurt and Bethany, and Sellars and Renata with Nana and Papa.

As I trotted into the kitchen to observe what was happening, Papa and Sellars were in the process of filling their plates and heating their food in the microwave. Mama had already gotten the children's plates, as they were sitting at the table eating once again. I saw Daddy bite into one of Dorothy's cookies, and he looked happy. *Hmmmm. Eating sure seems like a major occupation here at Nana and Papa's house—maybe that's one of the reasons why we all love to come here. That's fine with me.*

Bethany was telling Mama that she and Kurt had also taken a long nap, saying that there was just something about the air at this house: it made you want to eat or sleep. *I can agree with that myself.* Mama laughed, saying that when they were little and used to visit here, did Bethany remember how sleepy they would always get after eating? Papa commented that was because all the blood left their brains and traveled to their stomachs! *Oh, Papa. You have a funny answer for everything, don't you?*

Nana and Renata were putting ice in glasses and pouring tea or soda for everyone, then filled their plates, too. All in all, it was a casual meal, with everyone just coming and going as they wished. In fact, Mama and Bethany took their plates into the living room and sat on the couch to eat. Nana, Renata, Daddy, Papa, and Sellars sat at the table with the children, and there was much laughter and fun. Mama and Bethany laughed too, reminiscing over their childhood and various incidents that made them smile.

The evening wore on, with Kurt suggesting a game of some kind. Mama asked how about the men against the women, so they decided to play charades. I thought that must have been a weird game, because they laughed more than they played. Mama would get up there and act silly, and the women would yell out what they thought she was doing. They had a hard time guessing, and the timer went off before they guessed. Since the men had chosen their topic, Mama asked how anybody could act out foam rubber alphabet letters. The women groaned, but then it was the men's turn.

Sellars was to act out the topic that the women had given him, and he just stood there for a minute trying to figure out what to do. He looked ridiculous flailing his arms around, running in circles, and generally making a fool out of himself, but they were all laughing so hard that the men almost forgot to guess what he was doing. Kurt yelled out "a sick buffalo!" causing the women to dissolve into near hysteria.

Daddy then blurted out, "a drowning man!" The women showed annoyance because Daddy had guessed the topic they provided. This foolishness went on for a long time, with even Papa getting up and dancing around like a crazy man, causing much mirth. The men didn't guess what he was doing either. Papa wondered aloud how anybody could act out bacon frying in a pan, which caused loud chuckling and knee slapping from Sellars and giggling from the women and children. Daddy, Clark, Kurt, and Steve just rolled their eyes and shrugged. Kurt said he was glad he hadn't gotten that topic to act out!

Next, Mama was to act out what was on the little piece of paper that Steve handed to her with a wicked grin. He winked back at the men, saying something about Holly never being able to act out that topic.

Mama, being up to any challenge, stared at the paper for a moment. "Steve," she said, "I will win—just you wait and see!" And she proceeded to flap her arms around like *she* was drowning, too.

"A drowning girl!" yelled Annika. Mama shook her head.

"Nope. Let me try again," Mama replied. She then moved her arms slowly up and down, walking around on her tiptoes, but then squinted her eyes, acting like something was in them. She even wiped her arms and legs off, then moved her arms up and down again, walking around on her tiptoes.

"You might as well give up, ladies," yelled Steve. "I thought up this topic, and I really don't think you'll figure it out!"

"A ballerina in a rainstorm!" yelled Dorothy suddenly. All the women started clapping, sure that they had gotten it right.

I looked over at Steve and the men. They looked very glum. "How did you know that?" he asked Dorothy in an annoyed voice.

"I dunno. It just came to me, I guess. That means that the LADIES WIN! Woo hoo!" The sisters jumped up and down, and the women laughed and made faces at the men. The *men aren't very good losers, are they?*

I was relieved when the evening was over, because I just could not have taken any more silly human "humor"—but I was delighted that they had such a good time. Annika, Alexa, and Asher were a bit confused by it all—as was I—but they still laughed a lot.

I love to see and hear my humans laughing. We dogs don't laugh like they do, but that doesn't mean we don't smile or find nothing to laugh about.

Nope—not in this family!

18
Decorating for Christmas!

Mama put up the Christmas tree and decorated the house right after we got home from the Thanksgiving/birthday bash. *You mean it's already been a year since last Christmas? Wow.*

The sisters and Asher were so excited that she was allowing them to help her this year. Daddy brought in the tree box from the storage room outside, and said he would put it together, but then he would just get out of their way while they did the decorating. Some people have real trees, but Mama prefers our artificial one since she leaves it up so long. She said a real tree would get too dry and so many needles would fall off— and are hard to get out of the carpet. *A tree covered with needles? Ouch. It would be hard for all of us to walk without stepping on them, too.*

I watched closely, this tradition of decorating for Christmas. I didn't quite understand what all the hoopla was about, but as Mama told the children while they opened boxes and took out ornaments—*carefully*—Christmas was the celebration of Christ's birth, the most important holiday in the year. She handed Alexa an ornament, admonishing the little girl to be careful with it. "Honey, this ornament was given to Daddy and me by Nana on our first Christmas together—it's a wedding cake."

"Oh, Mama, it's so pretty. Can I hang it right in front? 'Cause everybody ought to see it when they look at our tree," stated Alexa.

"Of course, Honey. Just make sure the ornament hook is securely fastened to the branch of the tree, because it's a little heavier than some of the other ornaments—we don't want it to fall and break, do we?" Mama watched as Alexa carefully hung the ornament, then stood back, looking at it with satisfaction. "Perfect! That is just the right spot for my wedding cake," laughed Mama.

Next, she unwrapped a clear glass globe and handed it to Annika. "Here you go. Where do you want your ornament to go?" Mama asked her.

Annika narrowed her eyes as she inspected the tree, then pointed to a spot on a branch a little lower than the wedding cake ornament. "How about there, Mama? I want to hang it right in front of a tree light so the light will shine through it." Mama nodded, so Annika carefully placed the glass globe right in front of a light. *Wow. It does look pretty with the light behind it.*

"Now, little man," said Mama to Asher, "Mama is going to show you three ornaments, and you get to pick the one that you want to put on the tree first." Mama reached into the box and drew out a small snowman, a golden jingle bell, and a crocheted white snowflake. "These are all pretty, and you will get to hang all three, but which one do you want to hang on the tree first?"

"Ummmmm," said Asher, apparently mulling over his choices. He picked up one, then the other, finally choosing the snowman. "Dis one, Mama. Snowman." So Mama handed it to him, directing his little hand to just the right spot on the tree. He stepped back, beaming. "Asher make tree pretty! Snowman smiling." I looked closely, and he was right: that snowman did have a smile on his face. *What an observant boy you are, Asher.*

"Now Sarge, you get back so we can finish putting the ornaments on the tree," said Mama. "Sorry, but I won't be able to use your help, Sargie." *Mama, I didn't expect to help—besides, I'd have to use my mouth to hold the ornament, and I know you'd be unhappy with me if I broke one!*

I was fascinated with all the various ornaments Mama brought out of the Christmas boxes. Next, there was a red ice skate (not a real one, but a small ceramic one), which she gave to Alexa. Annika hung an angel made of yarn, with lace wings, which was made by Nana, Mama told the children. Asher next hung the golden jingle bell, which jingled when he placed it on the tree, causing him to smile. "Bell make music," he laughed. The children continued hanging the ornaments as Mama passed them out and directed them to the proper spots for placement on the tree. There were beautiful gingerbread men, more angels, red apples, red velvet bows, glow-in-the-dark icicles, gold and silver balls, tiny sleds, knit stockings, candy canes, as well as all sorts of old-fashioned tiny teacups, little hats and dresses, teddy bears and mice, lace fans, strands of pearls and ceramic cranberries to wind around the tree, and ruby-red silk poinsettias to place here and there on the branches. When they finally finished, Mama took out the treetop angel in a white satin robe, holding a candle. She had white wings covered with tiny sparkles. "I need to attach the electrical cord to the outlet on the tree, and we'll have sparkly lights all over our treetop angel," commented Mama, as she stood on a chair and deftly placed the angel atop the tree. She carefully spread out the robe so all the lights would be visible, then plugged in the small cord behind the angel. The tiny white lights glowed, and so did the angel's candle. The children gasped, smiling and clapping.

"Oh, Mama, she is so pretty!" exclaimed Alexa. "She is like the angel of the Lord who appeared to the shepherds in the field when Baby Jesus was born!"

"And she told them 'Lo, I bring you good tidings of great joy,'" quoted Annika. "For unto you is born this day, in the city of David, a Savior, Who is Christ the Lord.' That's from the book of Luke," stated Annika, clearly pleased that she recalled the verses.

"Yes, it is," replied Mama. "And you remembered the verses very well, young lady!" Mama hugged her.

"Baby Jesus born yet?" asked Asher innocently. "Where Baby Jesus?" he asked, looking around the room.

"No, Asher. Baby Jesus was born a *long* time ago in a manger. Shepherds were out in the field watching their sheep, and angels told them about Baby Jesus being born. There was a big star in the sky, too!" Alexa informed him.

"Asher want to see Baby Jesus," the young boy stated seriously. Annika and Alexa looked at each other, shrugging.

Mama said, "I have a Bible story book right here, Honey. There is a picture of Baby Jesus in the manger, with his mother Mary and his daddy Joseph." Mama got the Bible story book off the shelf and sat down on the floor. She motioned for Asher to come sit in her lap, which he did. "Now, let's see—" Mama flipped through a few pages. "Here we are! See, Asher? There's Baby Jesus lying in the manger, which is in a building like a barn—see the donkey, the cow, and the sheep all looking at Him sleeping? And there's His mama Mary and His daddy Joseph, too." Asher looked at the picture intently, taking his little pointer finger and tracing around it slowly.

"Baby Jesus cute," he pronounced judiciously. Mama and the sisters smiled. He then added: "Asher loves Baby Jesus."

"When you are old enough to understand," said Mama, "I hope you will always love Jesus, and accept Him as your Savior, too," she said softly, kissing the top of Asher's blond hair. "Jesus loves you, too, sweet boy. Now—we'd better get back to our decorating, or we'll still be sitting here with nothing done. Who wants to help me set up the nativity scene?" The sisters jumped right up.

"Where are we gonna put it, Mama?" asked Annika. "I think the activity scene is my favorite Christmas decoration!"

Mama laughed gently. "No, honey—*nativity* scene. Let's put it on the fireplace mantel, where it will be beautiful with the figures glowing." So, they all carefully unwrapped the figurines while Mama placed the wooden roof up on the mantel. The sisters handed her the figurines, which were all white trimmed in gold, and Mama placed them: Baby Jesus in the manger, Joseph, Mary, a donkey, a cow, and lamb, and the three Wise Men. *How do they know that those three men are smart? I guess that's just what they called them back then.* Mama connected the cords, then plugged them into the outlet. Each figurine glowed with a soft white inner light. "There. Isn't that pretty?" asked Mama.

"Oh, yes, Mama. I love it. What are we going to decorate next?" Annika asked.

Mama looked at her watch. "Okay, we still have time to finish. Why don't we hang our Christmas stockings over the fireplace now? I have some of those press-on hooks for hanging them, so I'll attach those first so we can hang our stockings." Mama got a package out of the box, and carefully pressed the hooks on the mantel, spacing the eight hooks evenly apart. *Eight? How did you come up with eight? There are only six of us.*

Apparently, Alexa was thinking the same thing. "Mama, why did you hang eight hooks? She began counting on her fingers: Daddy, Mama, Annika, me, and Asher. Mama, there's only five of us, so why do you have eight hooks?"

Mama smiled. "Don't you children know why I put eight??" She paused, allowing them time to think.

In a moment, Annika shouted, "I know! You have stockings for the animals, too!" She laughed, pleased with her deduction. "Sargie, Piper, and Aslan—that's three, plus our five, making eight stockings!"

"That's exactly right," replied Mama. "We all have a stocking with our name on it, so let's hang them, shall we?" So Mama unpacked the stockings, which were dark red velvet with the names in gold lettering. "Here's the one for Daddy, so it has 'Philip' on it—so I'll hang his," she said. Next, she got out hers: "And here's my name, 'Holly,' so I'll hang it right beside Daddy's. Annika, I'll let you hang yours," so she handed Annika the next stocking, and Mama showed her how to hang it on the hook. "Alexa, can you reach the hook okay?"

"Yes, Mama," answered Alexa, who did manage to hang her stocking by standing on her tiptoes.

"Asher, Mama will hold you up high enough to let you hang your stocking," said Mama, lifting the little boy up and guiding his hand. He smiled as he placed his stocking beside Alexa's. Putting him back down, Mama said, "Now we have Sarge, Piper, and Aslan's stockings. I bought these at the pet store last year after Christmas, so I don't think you children even saw them. They are so cute!" Mama drew out a long, skinny stocking that looked like me. It had a doggie face and long, floppy ears, too. On its side was my name, SARGIE. *Oh, good grief. What will they think of next??*

The children giggled. "That looks just like Sargie, Mama!" exclaimed Annika. "How do you like your Christmas stocking, Sargie?" she asked. I barked to indicate how thrilled I was to have my own Christmas stocking. *What are stockings for? I certainly won't wear mine.*

Mama said, "Y'all will receive small gifts in your stockings, so I suppose Sargie will get some treats or little toys in his." *TREAT? Did you say TREAT? Now you're talking!* And I began running around and barking, trying to find my treats. "Oh, not now, silly," laughed Mama. "You'll get your 'surprises' on Christmas—not now!" *Rats. Why do you torture me so?* "And here are Piper and Aslan's stockings," continued Mama. "The black cat stocking is for Piper, of course, and the white cat stocking is for Aslan. How do y'all like them?"

"Kitty cat stocking," laughed Asher. "Doggie stocking with floppy ears, too! Funny!" The sisters laughed indulgently with Asher.

"He's so cute, Mama!" said Alexa. "I hope he'll always stay this cute and sweet when he grows up!"

"Asher cute?" he asked innocently, blinking those big blue eyes. That comment set off another round of laughter. *Yes, dear boy, even a dawg can see that Asher is indeed cute.*

"Yes, Asher is cute," replied Mama, "but we need to finish up our decorating. "Girls, I want to put that lighted garland around the edge of the mantel, and while I'm doing that, you can be 'fluffing up' the green wreaths to go on the windows. They were flattened in the box, but just bend up each piece of greenery so that it looks like a tree branch instead of a pancake, and you'll have it right." The sisters laughed, and began working on their "pancakes." *Mama, you say some of the silliest things sometimes, but you make life so much fun. If dawgs laughed, I sure would laugh at some of the things said around here!*

"By the way, children—did I tell you we aren't going to Papa and Nana's for Christmas this year?" Mama allowed that to sink in.

"Oh, Mama, why not? Oh no! Christmas won't be any fun at all without Papa and Nana! You mean we won't get to see everybody at Christmas? What are we going to do, then?"

After the protests died down a bit, Mama announced: "That's because we're all going to my parents' house in Garner this year: Grandpa Clark's and Grandma Mavis's! Yep—Nana and Papa, our family, Steve and Dorothy, Kurt and Bethany, and—Sellars and Renata, too! How 'bout that!" There was a stunned silence for a moment, then the sisters recovered and started jumping up and down. And so did Asher. *My, he's growing up—he can jump up and down like his sisters!*

"Yay, we get to see everybody for Christmas!" yelled the sisters in singsong fashion. "We get to see everybody for Christmas!"

Mama laughed. "We just saw everybody a few days ago for Thanksgiving, my dear children."

Annika answered, "We know, Mama. But Christmas just isn't Christmas without the whole family, is it?"

And that, my dear girl, is the nitty-gritty, in this dawg's way of thinking: Christmas just isn't Christmas without family. And I wholeheartedly agree. When Papa got sick and ended up in the hospital, I was so worried that something would happen to him. I decided right then that I would never take my family for granted again.

I'm not as young as I used to be, you know. And neither is my special papa. I want to spend every chance I can enjoying his wide grin, listening to his stories, and sitting in his lap. And yes, he gives me food, but that's not why I love him: it's because he thinks like I do—he understands me.

He's my honorary dawg.

19
Our Christmas Gathering

After the house was fully decorated, next there was the wrapping of gifts that seemed to go on every night for days and days. Mama went shopping a number of times, taking the children with her on some of her shopping trips, then Daddy went with her a couple of times, leaving the children with Miss Savannah. She even went shopping by herself one day when she declared that she had forgotten something.

They all stayed so busy, since the children's choir at church, which Mama directed and the sisters sang in, had a Christmas program coming up, so there were extra practice times at church for them. Daddy stayed busy preparing sermons, as usual, but he was asked to speak at various Christmas gatherings around our community, too. He and Mama also took the time to visit the two local nursing homes, along with some of the church ladies, who had wrapped small gifts for all the residents there. Mama also did a lot of baking, as there was a special holiday luncheon at church, which was hosted by the ladies of the church. They were all in a whirlwind of activity. People came to our house, dropping off gifts, invited our family to their homes, so the cats and I just sat back and watched as they came and went, came and went. It was mind boggling. *Jumpin' dawg biscuits! They're never home these days. How can they keep up this pace? They make me tired just watching all they do!* And the cats seemed confused by all the comings and goings, too. They stayed on the back of the couch for hours on end, it seemed, just watching the world outside that window. I believe they were just waiting for everyone to come home each time. *But who really knows what cats are thinking?*

By and by, the time for our Christmas family

161

gathering at Clark and Mavis's was fast approaching. The women had everything under control, with the menu planned, what each family was bringing, and so on. *I guess they've had enough practice—a get together in our family will almost plan itself now. We've had cookouts, family reunions, birthday parties, other holidays—they should know what they're doing!*

Since Clark and Mavis were hosting this year, they would provide the turkey, dressing, rolls, and beverages. Mavis said she'd also make a dessert as well—probably a pig picking cake. *Wh-a-a-a-t? That sounds awful. How could anybody eat that,* I thought, with visions of Sellars' pig Tenderloin running through my head. But as I listened closely (one can learn a lot by just waiting and listening), I found out that it was a moist pineapple cake with a creamy whipped frosting. *Ahhh. Much better sounding, although nobody will give me any sweets, as usual.*

Speaking of Sellars, I was looking forward to seeing him and Renata again, too, although I had seen them at Thanksgiving a few short weeks ago. Sellars and Papa together were just the life of the party. They kept everybody laughing with their crazy comments, exaggerations, and hearty laughter. I just love to hear both of them laugh—especially Papa. When he laughs, it seems that everyone else just has to laugh, too. *It won't be long, my Papa-and-Sellars comedy team. I can hardly wait!*

A few days before we left for Garner, Mama and Daddy told the children they could open gifts from them before we left. That, of course, brought forth a round of squealing and clapping from all three of them! I had overheard Mama and Daddy talking about it a few days before: those gifts would make fewer things to pack and take with us on our trip. *Smart, Mama and Daddy, very smart.* And they even had a gift for me: a new sweater to keep me warm. It was a UNC Tarheel sweater! *I know Uncle Steve will think I'm really something when I wear* this beautiful blue doggie sweater at Christmas. Both he, Daddy, and Mama love anything to do with UNC.

❧ ❧ ❧

"Lookie there," said Sellars as he opened the back door to our van. We had just arrived at Clark and Mavis' house in Garner. "We been waitin' fer y'all, and I just told Renata that I hoped y'all would be here soon! Sarge, c'mon out of that prison and stretch yore legs now." *You better believe I'm as glad to be here as you are to see me, Sellars. This van is packed to the hilt! Mama said if we had one more thing to stuff in it, I might have to be a hood ornament! I remember what that is—they talked about me being one when I was a little pup.* I willingly jumped down, yawned, and stretched.

"Heh, heh, what a dawg you are, Sarge. If we didn't have Bubba on our farm, I do believe I'd get us a dash-hound." *Hey, you keep saying that—what's wrong with having two dawgs, Sellars? You certainly have enough room down there for all those other animals.*

Just then, I heard Duke barking from inside the house. I guess Mavis didn't let him come out because he would get in the way when the men brought in the luggage, presents, and so on. Papa had picked up Asher. "Sellars, look at this little man. Seems like he's grown more, even since Thanksgiving. You gonna give yore ol' Papa a kiss?" Asher shyly hugged and kissed Papa. *He obviously loves Papa just like I do.*

"And there's them ugly girls again," laughed Sellars, causing the sisters to start giggling.

"Sellars, we are NOT ugly!" laughed Alexa. "People tell me I'm pretty all the time," she declared, tossing her curly hair.

"And I'm not ugly, either," stated Annika. "Miss Savannah at church always says 'Pretty is as pretty does,' so she said us girls must be beautiful. I'm not sure what she means, but I think she means we're NOT ugly, Sellars!" He laughed again, realizing they had gotten the better of him this time. The sisters skipped into the house.

Mama looked at Papa: "Asher gets kinda heavy after a while, Papa. Go ahead and put him down, and he can walk on into the house."

"Yeah, he's gittin' kinda heavy," Papa conceded. "Okay, little man—yore mama said for you to go on into the house now." Asher hugged Papa's legs, then ran along after his sisters.

Daddy had already gone to the porch with a load, and as he reached the door, out came Kurt and Steve. Clark followed. "Hey, we're here to help you get the rest of the stuff!" yelled Kurt. Mama nodded, pointing to the back of the van, which was open.

"Help yourself!" she replied. "We've got enough for everybody! One of these days, we're gonna have to rent a trailer when we come up here for Christmas—seriously. Or, maybe we'll just rent a fifteen-passenger van. That way, we can fit in everything and not feel like we're sardines." *Sardines? Where? I want some! Oh. Just another figure of speech again. Just stop using those food-related examples, Mama!*

It had been a long time since I had been here. This brick house was called a split level, meaning it had three floors: the basement had the large family room with the TV, a laundry room, and storage room for Clark's tools; the main floor had the living room, dining room, and kitchen; and the third level had three bedrooms and two bathrooms. There was plenty of room for exploring, and I meant to do just that again when I got the chance.

I headed to the porch with Papa and Sellars, who were not allowed to carry much. Mama had said they had carried enough heavy stuff in their lives, so they ought to leave the rest of our things to the younger men. Sellars said that carrying his belly was probably enough for him to lift, and Papa agreed, laughing. Steve came running out just as we reached the porch, saying he'd had a phone call, and what could he bring in? Mama told him there were a few more suitcases and two boxes full of presents, so he managed to get all the luggage into the house. Daddy came back out and got the rest of the stuff, including my doggie bed. I decided to go on inside, too. I was getting cold, and it was a cloudy Christmas Eve afternoon. Besides, I wanted to see Duke, my buddy. We could play fight all we wanted. But most of all, I just might be persuaded to taste any morsels of food that hopefully would be offered my way.

Steve set down the suitcases and opened the front door, causing a blast of warm air to envelop me. As I trotted into the living room, I spied Duke, who made a beeline for me, and we greeted each other. *Hey, buddy, I'm glad to see you, too! You look healthy, bright-eyed, and shiny. You'll make a formidable opponent if anybody decides to throw a ball for us!*

I spied Zoe and Charlie lying on the floor beside Dorothy's feet. She was sitting on the couch with Renata, Bethany, and Mama, who was holding Asher. Papa and Sellars had just sat down on the loveseat across from the couch, and Annika was sitting on Sellars' lap, Alexa on Papa's. Daddy was just entering the living room, saying he believed everything was where it should be. Kurt was in one of the recliners. I didn't know where Mavis and Nana were—probably in the kitchen or in one of the other rooms getting something ready for everyone.

Just at that moment, Nana and Mavis came down the stairs from the bedrooms. "Hello everybody!" greeted Mavis. "Did y'all have a good trip from Georgia, Holly?" She walked over and began hugging the children. Asher started smiling, because he especially loved his Grandma Mavis.

"Yes, we did, Mom," replied Mama. "No traffic jams, no emotional meltdowns, no problems at all. Am I dreaming? If I am, don't anybody pinch me and wake me up!" she laughed.

"Everything looks so nice, Mavis," commented Dorothy. "I love your tree over there in the corner of the room. This is a big living room, but I was wondering where you'd put the tree, since the front door is over there and the dining room door is over there—and the steps to the basement are here by the kitchen door. And you didn't really have to rearrange the furniture, either."

"Thanks," replied Mavis. "As you know, we don't have a fireplace in this house, so I was trying to decide where to hang our stockings—there are only three, of course, so I came up with the crafty idea to hang them on that antique sewing machine over here. I keep it covered with a lace tablecloth, so I just pinned 'em on the front of it—I put our nativity scene on the top, placed some silk greenery around that, and voilá—instant Christmas," she laughed.

"Well, I like them," said Renata. "Where did you get them? They are each different."

"Mom made those years ago," Mavis replied. "One Christmas when Holly and Bethany were little, when we came home, she had a handmade stocking for each of us hanging on their fireplace. She said to keep them, so I did. I gave Holly and Bethany their stockings years ago, but I kept ours. Of course, I had to buy a stocking for Duke: I glued the shiny letters on his."

"When are we gonna eat our Christmas Eve dinner?" Papa piped up. "It's gittin' on toward four o'clock, and I just might git hungry any minute. I want everything ready in case I do!"

Mavis replied, "All the food is ready and either in the fridge, the oven, or on the counter in there. We'll eat before long, but let's all visit for a little while, shall we?"

Papa nodded. "That sounds good. Ray-melle, don't it seem funny for us to be jest settin' here and not in the kitchen cookin'?"

"It does, but it's kinda nice, too," she answered. "Oh, I did cook the food we brought, but that's all I had to do. It seemed really odd to come here for Christmas—not that I didn't want to," she quickly added. "It's just that we all usually meet at our house during Christmas."

"We thought that having it here makes it a little easier on you and Dad," Mavis said. "We'll all have fun, even if we only have three bedrooms. The children can sleep on air mattresses in the family room downstairs, or wherever you want them to sleep, Holly. Steve and Dorothy only live thirty minutes away, so they won't need a bedroom. Sellars and Renata have their motor home, so that leaves you and Dad in a bedroom, Holly and Philip in a bedroom, and Kurt and Bethany in a bedroom. Clark and I are gonna sleep in the motor home with Sellars and Renata! Won't that be fun!"

"Aw, man, I wanted to sleep in the motor home," protested Annika. "I never got to yet."

"Me, too," added Alexa. "Mama, puleeze can we sleep in the motor home?"

"I don't know," replied Mama. If y'all sleep out there, where are Papa Clark and Grandma Mavis gonna sleep? On the porch??" The sisters giggled, but looked at Sellars.

"Let's see here now," he said, rubbing his chin. "We can figger something out so's everbody is happy. Okay. How 'bout the girls sleep in the motor home with us, Holly? This is Clark and Mavis' house, so shouldn't they have their own room to sleep in?"

Daddy joined in: "I vote for letting Clark and Mavis have their own bedroom. Kurt and Bethany can have one of the guest rooms, and Robert and Ramelle can have the other guest room. Holly, Asher, and I can sleep downstairs in the family room together. The girls can sleep in the motor home with Sellars and Renata—if that's all right with you guys. Does that take care of everybody's sleeping arrangements?"

"Sounds like a good plan to me," Clark replied. "We have a nice queen-size air mattress with a foam topper for y'all, and we have a special bed frame for it, so you'll hardly even know you're on an air mattress," he added. "Don't y'all have Asher's fold–up crib with you?"

"Yes, we do," responded Mama. "Since the family room downstairs is big, there will be plenty of room for our bed plus Asher's crib, if we put it over beside that big closet down there."

"Oh, goody! We get to sleep in the motor home!" sang Annika.

"Girls, just remember that Sellars snores, so did y'all bring some earplugs?" asked Renata, winking at them. *I guess she means it's a joke. That's what winking means when humans do that—unless, of course, they have something in that eye.*

"Hold on there a minute," retorted Sellars. "I ain't that loud, girls. Y'all won't even notice once you git to sleep." The girls giggled again.

"The key phrase is 'git to sleep,'" replied Renata. "Girls, just hurry up and go to sleep quickly tonight, then you probably won't hear him sawing logs." *My goodness. Why would Sellars saw logs at bedtime, and inside the motor home?? I'd think he'd be too tired to do that. Wait— I remember now. "Sawing logs" is just another human way of saying he snores.*

"Mavis, is there anything I can help you do?" asked Dorothy. "I'm getting kinda hungry myself. What time is it?" She looked around the living room in vain for a clock. The antique grandfather clock was in the corner, but it wasn't working.

"It's time to eat!" exclaimed Papa. "We've been talkin' about where we're all gonna sleep, an' it looks like that's all settled, right? Well then, by the time y'all have everthang lined up, I'll be starving!" At that, the women all jumped up and headed into the kitchen. I heard Mavis tell them that the table was already set, the appropriate foods were warming in the oven, and the cold foods were in the fridge. All they had to do was set the food out and arrange it, put ice in the glasses, and then chow down. *Chow down? I know you must have gotten that from Papa. He says that a lot.*

Before long, Mavis reappeared in the kitchen doorway. "Okay, folks. We'll eat in a few, but to save you time, here's what we have: turkey and dressing, mashed potatoes and gravy, candied yams, corn pudding, wild rice salad, green bean casserole, pasta salad, cranberry sauce, baked ham—she looked back toward the kitchen: "Hey, what did I leave out, ladies?" I heard them say something to her. "Oh yes. We also have a congealed cranberry salad, yeast rolls, and corn muffins. I won't mention the desserts for now. Let's all join hands, and Clark will bless the food." They all got up, joining hands throughout the living room. With Mavis in the kitchen doorway, she took Clark's hand in the living room and her other hand was clasped with Bethany, who was standing in the kitchen. Clark said a nice blessing, and they all got in line, preparing to fill their plates. I, of course, was watching Papa like a hawk so I could see where he would be sitting—he looked at me, winked, and proceeded to fill his plate. *Yes, Papa. I'm waiting for you to sit down.* A few feet away, I noticed that Duke had his eyes fastened on Sellars, too. *Looks like Duke is gonna keep Sellars as his own personal food dispenser at these family gatherings. Smart dawg.*

Mama helped the sisters with their plates, since they insisted that they were big now and could get their own food. Under Mama's watchful eye, they took out appropriate portions of food, with Mama making sure they didn't just eat mashed potatoes and candied yams. Asher, of course, was sitting in his booster chair where Daddy had placed him, but he was eager to eat, too: "Asher ready to eat! Asher hungry!" And he banged his little fork on the table. Papa laughed, saying something about Asher being a chip off the old block. Mama said he'd *have* to be, since his great grandparents, grandparents, and parents all loved good food! *What's wrong with that? I must be a chip, too, since I love good food as much as anybody else. And so does Duke. I wonder sometimes if Zoe and Charlie are real dogs—they don't seem to care if anybody is eating or not, and they don't even try to sniff it! I bet if Dorothy put a plate of just meat down in front of them, they'd just stand there and look at it!*

Papa had finally finished filling his plate and had chosen his seat at the table, so I sauntered over there to sit under his chair. Sellars was right behind him, and I noted that Duke knew what to do: he sat underneath Sellars' chair, and we two doxies were all set to eat. Of course, I knew from past experience that Papa would eat some of his food before sending any my way—I think he wanted to taste everything to see what was best before giving me any.

"Mavis, your table is beautiful," exclaimed Renata. "I love that tablecloth with the colorful holly berries and leaves all over it. And you have red and green napkins to go with it, too."

"Thank you. Mom made those for me several years ago, and we've enjoyed using them every Christmas," Mavis replied. "She has always loved to sew, and I have been a willing recipient of her creations, let me tell you."

"Yes, I remember that Ramelle made many of your clothes when we all lived in Alaska and you were a teenager," Renata added. "Didn't she make you that emerald green formal you wore one year?"

Nana answered: "Actually, Sylvia Henderson—who happened to be Steve's third grade teacher—and I made it together. She even saw to it that Mavis had matching shoes. Remember, Mavis? You had white satin high heels, but she went with us to Fairbanks to have them dyed to match the dress. I recall that we took a swatch of that satin with us."

"Yes, I remember, and I was the 'belle of the ball,' so to speak. Boy, we really dressed up for school functions back then. I also had elbow-length white gloves, and Sylvia loaned me her emerald-and-diamond earrings to wear. They weren't real, of course, but to a sixteen-year-old girl, they were fabulous."

Dorothy asked, "I know Ramelle loves to sew, but Mavis, I've never seen you sew anything. Don't you sew, too?"

"I've done some crocheting," Mavis answered. "I've crocheted several baby blankets, afghans, winter scarves, and so on, and in my twenties, I got on an embroidery kick, doing a number of crewel embroidery pictures. But sewing with a sewing machine?? Nope! I never could get the hang of it, and I just didn't enjoy cutting out pieces of fabric and trying to fit them together to resemble clothing!"

"Yeah, I know that," laughed Nana. "One time I helped you with a school sewing project back when girls took home economics, and it was quite a chore for both of us! Somehow you always managed to get the bobbin thread tangled up in the machine, but I couldn't figure out how you did that."

"Me, either. I'd use the machine exactly like you did, but even with you standing over me and watching, that ol' bobbin thread would tangle up and I'd have a mess. Trying to use a sewing machine marred me for life—so I don't use the hateful things."

"I'm not an excellent seamstress," added Renata, "but I manage to sew a few things I need for the house."

"I'm not much on sewing, either," Dorothy said. "If I need something, stores have everything I want, in any color, size, or fabric!"

"This shore is fascinatin,'" laughed Sellars, "but I

don't reckon I've ever sewed a blamed thang myself—not even a button that came off. I just ain't the type. Besides, that's stuff fer women to do. Us ol' codgers never did any of that stuff in our generation, and we ain't gonna learn how to do it now, are we, Duke?" *Duke? Oh—you mean Papa, not the dawg.*

"Naw, I ain't never sewed nuthin,' either, Sellars," Papa replied. "Cookin' is more my style—an' eatin'!" Sellars and the others laughed. "An' seein' how all of y'all are puttin' away all this food, I believe eatin' is somethin' we're *all* good at!" *Humans might be fairly good at eating, but if we dawgs were given the chance, I believe we could outdo you on that score. I wonder just how much human food I could eat if I had an unlimited supply?*

"Oh, Papa, you always say the funniest things," commented Mama, her mouth full. She finished chewing. "Your gift of exaggeration just cracks me up. I love it!"

"Who's exaggeratin'?" replied Papa in mock alarm. "I'm tellin' it like it is. Jes' look around at everbody shovelin' it in, and you'll see what I mean!" *Works for me, Papa.*

Nana asked, "Robert, that reminds me: do you remember that time when we were invited over to the Buchanans' house to eat when Mavis and Steve were little? I believe it was when we lived in Germany, and they were another military family. Anyway, rather than passing around the bowls of food so we could all fill our own plates, the wife had all the plates stacked in front of her, and she placed the food for each of us on our plates herself! Why, she didn't—"

Papa interrupted: "Yeah, I shore do remember! She didn't put nuthin' on them plates! She put about three green peas, a teaspoon of mashed potatoes, and a small meatball on my plate. On MY plate. Oh yeah—she did give me a biscuit, but it was about the size of a quarter." He shook his head at the memory. Papa sent a bite of turkey down my way, which I snapped up in midair. *Yummy. More, Papa, more!*

"I was only nine or ten at the time," added Mavis, "but I remember thinking that she sure was stingy with the food! I might have gotten four peas on my plate, though," she laughed.

Nana added, "I was afraid Robert was going to say something embarrassing, like 'That's a nice snack, but where's our dinner?' or something like that. I could see the disgust in his face all during the meal."

Sellars piped up: "I know ol' Duke musta been mad. He don't like nobody regulatin' what he wants to eat, and I don't, neither! What did y'all do?"

"Well," Papa stated, "I managed to use my manners an' nibble on that food like there really was somethin' on my plate. I thought about askin' fer seconds, but she mighta jest doled out three more peas, one more meatball, and another spoonful of taters. So, I jest kept quiet. Them people was real skinny. You can see why! Oh—an' it wasn't 'cause they didn't have money—they jest didn't eat much of nuthin.' I don't know why they invited us to their house, 'cause they had to figger that we all shore ate a lot, since we was all real—er—healthy lookin.'"

"I don't remember much about that," added Steve, "but I was probably only three or four then."

"Son, there ain't nuthin' to remember about it—we didn't git nuthin' to eat, that's fer shore!" Papa replied. *At least he's making sure I get something to eat,* as he sent down a bite of green bean casserole and one of ham. *Wow. Those are good.*

"I could see that Robert was getting madder and madder when we finished 'eating,'" Nana declared, "so I told 'em we had another place to be, and we soon left. When we got out to the car and were driving away, Robert said, 'Let's go somewhere and get us something to eat!' And we did, too—we stopped by a burger joint there on base and had hamburgers and French fries before we went home!"

"That's right," replied Papa. "I was about to starve to death when we left there. I just don't understand people who don't like good food, do y'all?"

"Papa," giggled Annika, "it was so funny when you said that lady only gave you three peas to eat!" and she kept giggling. "I could've eaten all the food on your plate with one bite!"

"You bet you could. Three peas was all I got. It's kinda hard to cut peas into several bites and try to git 'em on your fork, you know!" Papa joked.

Alexa was also giggling. "Papa, how many bites did it take for you to eat that little meatball?"

I could see that Papa noticed he had a built-in audience, so he hammed it up: "Oh, I took my knife and fork, and cut that lil' ol' meatball into paper thin slices. It was right purty, too, the way I arranged them slices on my plate. Next, I ate one slice at a time, so I was able to stretch out that meatball long enough to make it seem to that lady that I had me somethin' to eat!"

"Heh, heh," laughed Sellars. "I shore woulda liked to have seen that. It would make a mighty funny movie or TV show, wouldn't it?"

"Life in this family would make a good TV show or movie for sure," laughed Nana, "but nobody would believe that most of it really happened!"

"I'm learning more and more about all of you," added Kurt. "Boy, other people are kinda boring compared to you guys!"

"Yeah, they lead normal lives," Steve retorted. "Nobody else gets knocked out by running into a tree, or tied up by a fence!" *Oh, he's talking about some of the things Papa has done.*

"An' don't fergit me and Robert's fishin' story!" exclaimed Sellars. "Never in a million years would I be able to get his glasses off his face again with my fish hook and not scratch him!" Sellars just shook his head at the memory.

"You know," Papa added, "this family enjoys life, though. I thank the Lord for gittin' me through all my troubles, 'cause most of 'em weren't very funny at the time," he smiled. "But we all know Him and will have an eternity together. While we're on the subject of memories—what's your favorite memory in this family?" Comments of approval went around the table. *I sure wish I could talk so you could understand me, Papa. My favorite memory is meeting you the first time. I knew right away that you were just like me!*

"Aw, Papa, we only get to tell one?" asked Bethany. "That's gonna be hard to do!"

"Just keep 'em short, but each one of us can share something—tomorrow is Christmas, and that's one of my favorite times for us all to be together."

"Wait," interjected Mavis. "How about we all get our dessert and coffee, and then we can sit around and listen to everyone's favorite memory? That way, we won't have to hurry through them." Mavis and Dorothy got up and made sure the desserts were placed just so on the dessert table. As they got various dishes out of the fridge and opened the lids of the others Mavis reeled off what they had: "Okay, folks. Here's what we have for dessert today, and I thank all of you for contributing to our 'fathood'! I made a pig-pickin' cake, Dorothy made homemade peanut butter cups, frosted oatmeal cookies, and Philip's Christmas cookies. Mom made her fresh coconut cake, Holly made a banana pudding and a red velvet cake, and Bethany made her famous pecan pies, as well as a chocolate fudge pie, too. Wow. Let's see—oh yes! How could I forget Renata's blueberry cobbler and everyone's favorite crunch cake. We also have vanilla ice cream for any of you who want it with your other desserts. Come and get it!" I ducked way under

Papa's chair as everyone hastily headed over toward the dessert table.

Mama told the sisters that she would get their desserts for them, so they told her which ones they wanted. I noticed that since they each wanted several, Mama put small portions on their dessert plates, but they were happy. She picked out three small portions of dessert for Asher: a small piece of crunch cake, a peanut butter cup, and an oatmeal cookie. I suspected she made those choices because it would be easier for Asher to eat them.

Sellars said, "Hmmm. So many desserts. Mavis, I ain't had any pig pickin' cake for years. Yores is a pineapple cake, ain't it? My mama used to make those, and I always loved 'em."

"That's right, Sellars. Clark's mother, Grandma Alice, used to make them, so after she passed away, I found her recipe box and started making them. She also made the best carrot cake in the world. Oh, this cake: it's a yellow cake with crushed pineapple in the cream cheese frosting. After the cake cools and before frosting it, I spoon pineapple juice over it. Makes the cake very moist and sweet."

"Ain't nuthin' wrong with sweet," replied Sellars. "Guess I'll have me a piece of that, and some of that blueberry cobbler. Renata makes a real mean cobbler, you know."

"A mean cobbler?" Alexa inquired. "How can something to eat be mean??" She thought that comment was so funny. In fact, the sisters started giggling over Sellars' comment.

"Girls, sayin' a food is *mean* jes' means it's the best cobbler you'll ever stick a tooth in," replied Sellars with a smile.

Since I knew that we dawgs wouldn't get any dessert, I decided to go on into the living room and join the two phony dawgs in there. I was getting sleepy after all that good food, and as I headed that way, Duke was right behind me. We could hear everything that was said. I wanted to hear their favorite memories. Papa, especially, would say something else funny, I was sure.

After everyone got settled, Papa announced: "Let's do our memories now, and I'll start. I been thinkin' 'bout 'em, and I guess one of my favorite ones has to be that time when Holly an' Bethany stayed with us for a week when they were little. Y'all usually lived in other states back then, so we didn't git to see y'all that much, so when you came and stayed with me and Ray-melle for a week one summer, we had us a real good time." Papa stopped, apparently thinking of that time. "Y'all helped me in my garden, pickin' vegetables, an' you helped Ray-melle shell peas, butter beans, and snap some green beans, too. So, that week when y'all stayed here was a good time."

Next was Nana. "I remember how filthy you girls got after being outside most of each day," she said. "Robert had a little trailer on the back of his garden tractor, and do y'all remember he drove you around the neighborhood in that trailer hooked to his tractor? When he'd hit a speed bump, I was afraid y'all would fall out, but from the backyard I could see how much fun you were having! Oh— I'd better get on to *my* favorite memory, since that was part of his. Let's see—when you've lived as long as some of us have, it sure is hard to come up with only one, Robert! One of my favorites was when Steve, about age seven, won a bowling trophy at the awards banquet when we lived in Alaska. When they called his name, he began walking up there to receive his trophy, but about halfway up to the platform, he turned around and came back to his seat. We urged him to get up there, but he thought it was just a joke and didn't believe he'd won!"

"Yeah, I remember that, Steve," said Sellars. "You got 'most improved bowler' or somethin,' right?"

"I was surprised when they called my name," Steve

replied. "I didn't believe it was real because Mavis kept telling me every time they announced another trophy that they were gonna call my name—so when they actually did, I somehow thought she had put them up to it!"

Mavis laughed. "I know—I *was* picking on you. I was about fourteen, you were six or seven, but it was in my job description as a big sister to needle a younger brother a bit."

Renata was next. "I have no problem coming up with one of my favorite memories at all. Big surprise—mine was in Alaska. Remember that time we all went camping one summer? Robert, you and Ramelle had just bought a camping trailer that you proudly proclaimed would sleep six people—so we all drove to the Tanana River a few miles away for the weekend. We cooked our meals over an army field range, and the food was just so good in the outdoors. The water in that river was so clean back then that we could drink it—we made flavored drinks with it, didn't we? At night, we'd sit around and talk, and by day we would explore the woods around us while you men tried to catch some fish. That was so much fun."

"Yeah, that was purty nice," added Sellars. There were other folks there, too, several we knew, so it was a relaxing time fer me, too. Since I'm sittin' next to my honey lamb, I s'pose that means I'm next. I think one of my favorite times was when me and Duke worked together in Alaska. I was his mess sergeant, and he was the head cook there in the Black Rapids mess hall—that was where men came in from all over the country for cold weather training. And Duke and his crew put out some fine food. All of the men said so. In fact, his biscuits was so good, that ever day I declared, "Duke, them's the best biscuits you have ever made! Heh heh."

"Sellars, what's a mess sergeant?" asked Annika. "It sounds like you watched them make messes!"

"Naw, Honey, that ain't what a mess sergeant does.

In the military, the place where the soldiers ate was called the mess hall—that's kinda like your school cafeteria where y'all eat lunch. The mess sergeant was in charge, makin' sure everthang was cooked right and on time fer the soldiers."

"Oh. We know what it means now, 'cause we always eat lunch in our cafeteria at school," Annika replied.

"Papa, did you make cat head biscuits back then, too?" asked Alexa.

"Yep, they was purty big, not little like those people who invited us over to eat," answered Papa, smiling.

"Okay, Annika honey, you're next. Do you have a favorite memory you want to share with us tonight?" asked Nana.

"Um—I do have one. When I was little," and that brought forth laughter from the others, "I was so happy when Alexa was born so I would have a baby sister. I didn't like not having anybody to play with. She cried a lot for a while, but when she started crawling, Mama let me help take care of her. My sister is my best friend!" Everyone clapped.

Mama said, "Alexa, tell us what your favorite memory is now."

The little girl thought for a moment, then her face brightened. "Mama, my favorite memory of ALL was when we had that surprise birthday party for Papa. That was so much fun when we all hid, then jumped out and yelled 'surprise' when he came in the house. And he really was surprised, too!"

"I liked that surprise party, too, Honey," agreed Papa. "I had no idea that y'all were gonna do that, either."

Mama was next. "Okay, I'm not very old yet, but I have so many good memories! Bethany, remember when we were little and had bunk beds? Mom and Dad expected us to be quiet after we went to bed, but we had one of Mom's old purses in our room—I guess she had given it to

179

us to play with—so we tied a piece of jump rope onto the handle, and passed stuff up and down to each other? That sounds so dumb now, but we thought we were so cool passing things to each other. We were being quiet, but we weren't sleeping like Mom and Dad thought we were! Oh—that's not my favorite memory, but one of them."

"Hurry up, 'cause we'll be here 'til midnight at this rate," laughed Clark.

"Okay, okay. Just one more then: Mom, I don't know if you'll like this, but I still laugh about that time you were trying to open that packet of sour cream at the seafood restaurant and it somehow got all over your face! Oh, Dad, B, and I nearly burst trying not to laugh until you got up and went to the ladies' room. Whew! We laughed so hard at that, but we knew you weren't laughing at all."

Mavis continued the story: "The best part was that little girl who followed me into the ladies room and I could see her in the mirror as she stood staring at me while I was trying to get that sour cream off my face without disturbing my makeup—and it wasn't easy. And didn't you and B come in there after a minute?"

"Yes, we did," replied Bethany. "Dad wanted us to check on you and make sure you were all right. When we got in there, we saw that little girl staring at you like you were from outer space. You were obviously very annoyed, and looking at her through the sour cream, said, 'May I help you?' She shook her head no and just kept staring. Holly and I got out of there fast, and as soon as we got back to our table, busted out laughing again. Oh, that was so funny."

"We knew we'd better not laugh in front of you," added Mama. "And I thought Dad was having a coughing fit, but he was really trying to cover up his hysteria. Oh, what a time that was."

Daddy came next. "I've been told that I'm a man of few words, and with the time it's taking us to tell our favorite memories, I'd better be just that or we won't get

180

out of this dining room tonight! My favorite memory is when I asked Holly to marry me, and she said yes." Everyone just sat there in anticipation. "That's it, folks. I'm done," Daddy asserted.

"That was short and sweet," said Steve, "but I'm with Philip—we'd better move this right along. My favorite memory—among thousands—was when Mavis and I were young, and I had annoyed her one time too many. She hauled off to give me a swift kick, missed, and kicked the end table instead. I was about four, she was about ten, and she had quite a bump on her shin from that. Very satisfying to an abused little brother!"

"I'm next, and I don't think I can top some of these stories, but I'll try," said Dorothy. "I guess the time I burned my cake I was supposed to take to a church dinner. I was so upset, because I didn't have time to make another one. So, I just trimmed off the outer one inch of each layer, frosted it, and made marshmallow flowers to place around the edge of the cake. That took up enough room so nobody seemed to notice that the cake was smaller than it was supposed to be."

"How do you make marshmallow flowers?" asked Renata.

"You just use kitchen shears and cut each marshmallow in thin slices," replied Dorothy. The shears cause the slices to change shape, similar to a flower petal. Then arrange them in the shape of a flower. I sprinkled them with yellow-colored sugar, and they looked like daisies."

"That's really neat," said Mama. "I'll have to try those sometime."

"Okay, looks like we're on the home stretch," said Kurt. "I'm next, and I'll play a 'Philip' by being brief: my favorite memory was when Bethany took my picture wearing her burgundy wig from a high school play she was in. I looked so pretty in it." A brief silence followed his comment, then a few chuckles erupted.

"Ha ha, Kurt. I could think of some others for you, but since we're crunched for time, I'll just give mine," teased Bethany. "It's hard to top Holly's memory about the sour cream fiasco, but I'll try. Oh yeah: my favorite memory was when Mom and Dad let us 'camp out' in the living room every Friday night on those twin-size foam mattresses we used when we had friends over to spend the night. We must have had three or four, 'cause I remember having friends spend the night in the living room with us, so we had at least four mattresses. Anyway, we'd order pizza, rent movies, and Dad would pop some popcorn later in the evening. We'd sleep on those mattresses all night— they were really comfy—and Mom would make us pancakes and bacon for our Saturday morning breakfast. We'd lie around and watch cartoons for several hours, I recall. Both Mom and Dad worked all week, we had school and all our activities, so Friday nights and Saturday mornings were our family times, unless we had something else going on. I remember how much I loved lazing about on those Saturday mornings. Thanks, Mom and Dad! I never realized at the time the extra work that put on you guys!"

"Oh, we didn't mind," answered Clark. "Those mattresses sure came in handy for our Friday nights, didn't they? We enjoyed our family times, too, you know. I'm not one for much talking, either, so I'll get right to it: one of my favorite memories was the time Robert and Ramelle came to visit us in Cincinnati when Holly was two. They flew out there and landed in Covington, Kentucky, which wasn't far from Cincinnati. They stayed a few days with us, and we drove all over town showing them everything, and we even went to one of the local restaurants so they could experience the world-famous Cincinnati chili. While they were with us, they bought Holly a big toy box, which I put together. It had shelves on top, and Holly was thrilled with it—so were we. Next!"

"How do I always end up being last?" laughed Mavis. "Oh—I get it—that Bible verse that says 'the last shall be first' explains why, I'm sure. Ahem. Okay. My favorite memory, and one of many, I might add, was that time Clark and I took a trip on the spur of the moment. We lived in Lynchburg, and one summer, during the time Clark was attending college at Liberty, we were sitting on the patio one Friday evening—Holly wasn't even a year old yet. I made some comment about wishing we could go somewhere for the weekend. Clark said, 'Okay, throw a few things in a suitcase, and we'll go.' Well, you can't just throw a few things into a suitcase when you have a baby, but we managed to pack a few things, got in the car and headed north—and ended up in Gettysburg, Pennsylvania, later that night. We got a room for the weekend, then spent all day Saturday exploring the historical sights there. It was so much fun! We had Holly in her stroller, and she seemed to enjoy it, too. We headed back on Sunday, and it was one of many spontaneous trips we've taken over the years. But that was the first, so it was really special."

"Now I enjoyed hearing all of them memories," said Papa. But I'm gittin' tard of settin' in this chair. I'm goin' into the living room and grab one of them recliners." At that, everyone began getting up, and Mama said it was Asher's bedtime. The little boy had fallen asleep on her lap, so she took him downstairs to the family room where his crib was. Mavis and a couple of the women finished in the kitchen as the men made their way to the living room, too. Clark said he would take the dogs out, and I was glad to hear that. Duke and I jumped right up, and so did Zoe and Charlie. We went outside, but didn't stay long because a cold wind had started blowing.

As we came back in, I heard Mama telling the sisters that they could open one small Christmas present tonight, but we'd be opening all the rest the next morning. They clapped in happiness as they tried to decide which one they wanted to open. Finally, Annika picked a red package and Alexa picked one with festive snowmen on the paper.

Annika read the tag, which said it was from Steve and Dorothy. She ripped into it, and gasped in joy when she took out a pair of leather suede boots. "Oh, Mama! I've been wanting some pretty black boots to wear! Thank you Uncle Steve and Aunt Dorothy!" She immediately took off her shoes and began putting on her new boots. "Look! They fit just right, too," she smiled happily, going over to hug Steve and Dorothy.

Alexa tore the paper on the corner of her gift when Mama reminded her to first find out who it was from. "Oops!" said Alexa, causing laughter from everyone. She looked at the tag, and slowly read aloud: "To Alexa from Sellars and Renata." Then she started tearing the paper off again. She opened the box and started smiling, showing it to Mama. "Look! Isn't it pretty??" she exclaimed.

"What is it?" asked Annika, who was walking around the living room trying out her new boots. "Let us see."

"It's a cross necklace with a diamond in the middle," said Alexa.

"Isn't that a wonderful present?" said Mama.

"But you need to check out that there diamond—but it ain't really a diamond," commented Sellars.

"Yes," added Renata. "Close one eye, hold your other eye close to the jewel—and also hold your head up, facing the light. What do you see?"

Alexa did as Renata asked. In a moment, she exclaimed, "Look, Annika! There's something written in it!" Annika took the necklace and held the cross jewel close to her own eye.

Annika squinted, attempting to see inside the cross. After a moment, she stated: "I see it! 'Our Father, who art in heaven—"

"Oh, it must be one of those cross necklaces that has *The Lord's Prayer* written inside it!" exclaimed Mama. "I saw them advertised on TV. Wow! Let me see!" Alexa brought it over to Mama, who looked inside the cross, too. "Oh, how nice! You'd better let Sellars and Renata know how much you appreciate such a special gift." *How did they manage to get all those words inside that cross? It certainly isn't big enough—it's only about two inches high.*

Thank you, Sellars and Renata! I'm gonna keep it always, and I can't wait for all of you to see it, too." She motioned for Mama to pass it around to everyone. *Hey, I wanna look in it, too. It's kinda hard to believe, though. Are y'all trying to fool me?*

Alexa made sure each family member looked inside that cross. Papa looked, then did a double take.

"My goodness! How'd they git all them words inside a cross no bigger than a french fry?" The sisters giggled. "Now that's a fine present, ain't it?" Alexa nodded, trying to fasten it around her neck.

"Honey, don't wear it to bed. You might break the chain, which is delicate, when you turn over in your sleep. Just wait and wear it tomorrow. Okay, young ladies, it's bedtime for you. I imagine you'll be getting up early so you can open the rest of your presents!" said Mama. "Hug everybody, and I'm sure Renata will help us get you settled in the motor home."

"Of course," said Renata. "In fact, we are about ready to hit the bed ourselves, aren't we? It's been a busy day, and tomorrow will be busy, too." *Don't hit it too hard, Renata. You might break it.*

Sellars squinted at his watch. "Yep, I'm shore ready to turn in. Why, it's after ten, and although we usually stay up later than that, I'm bushed." And he yawned.

"I always get more tired when I'm traveling or being someplace else," said Mavis. "Y'all just do what you want to do. We'll all probably go to bed before long, I'm sure, judging from all the yawns I've been seeing."

"We'd better head on home now," said Steve. "It

won't take us long, but we'll be back in the morning to celebrate Christmas." Steve and Dorothy bid their good-byes, then each picked up a dog and headed out to their car.

Mama and the girls followed Sellars and Renata out to the motor home, with Nana and Papa deciding that they were ready to "lay down," too. So they hugged everyone else and headed on upstairs to their room. Kurt and Bethany went next, and that left Daddy, Clark, and Mavis with Duke and me. Daddy said he'd wait until Holly came back, and they'd head to bed, too. Clark commented that they'd probably stay up awhile.

Soon, Mama came back, saying that the girls were thrilled to sleep out there, but were so sleepy that they didn't say much at all once their heads hit their pillows. So, Daddy told me to come on downstairs with them—my doggie bed was right beside theirs. I was glad to "turn in," because I was tired.

Tomorrow was going to be another big day of family, fun, and best of all, FOOD.

20
Christmas Day and Such

I woke up to the smell of bacon, one of my favorite foods, but for a moment, I forgot where I was. *Oh, I'm at Clark and Mavis' house in Garner. Wonder if it's really early, 'cause it's still dark.* I looked closely at the windows, which were set higher on the wall than the other rooms, because the family room where I slept was in the basement. The blinds were closed. *Aha. That's why it still seems dark.* As my eyes adjusted, I looked around—Asher's crib was empty, and so was Mama and Daddy's bed. *Guess I'm a lazybones this morning,* I thought to myself as I stretched and yawned. I padded across the floor and headed to the stairs leading up to the kitchen. The smell of bacon was much stronger—my nose always has a mind of its own when it comes to bacon.

As I reached the top of the stairs, I saw Clark, Kurt, Papa, and Nana sitting at the small round kitchen table, drinking coffee. Mavis was taking a large plate out of the microwave, and I knew that was the bacon. I trotted over to her, smiling my best doggie smile and wagging my tail. Just then Duke clicked into the kitchen, too. I don't know where he had been, but he loves bacon as much as I do. He joined me in smiling and wagging.

"Okay, doggies, you need to get out of the way so I don't trip," Mavis admonished us, but her words had absolutely no effect on us at all. *I suppose Mama's right in calling me just a "nose with legs," because when something good to eat is around, my nose just leads me toward it.* Mavis put the dish with the bacon on the counter. Looking at Papa, she asked, "Dad, do you want your eggs fried or scrambled?"

"You know, I don't think I want any eggs this mornin,' Mavis," he replied. "There was plenty of Ray-melle's coconut cake left, and you know we always eat that for breakfast on Christmas morning. I'll just eat some bacon along with it. You get your coffee and set down here with us. We'll just enjoy that until the rest come in and join us." *But what about my bacon, Mavis? Even Mama gives me a bite or two when we have it at home, you know.* Duke boofed to get her attention. *That's right, Duke—tell her.*

"Oh, all right, doggies. I'll let y'all share a piece, then go into the living room or somewhere. We don't want y'all staring at us like you're starving—all right, fellas?" She took a piece of crispy bacon and broke it into two pieces, then dropped one of them for me and one for Duke. We, of course, snapped them up before they could hit the floor. *Oh, that is so good. I LOVE BACON,* I smiled at her. "Now that you've got your piece of bacon, shoo! Go on elsewhere!" She motioned us away. *I can take a hint, but I don't like it. C'mon, Duke. We're not wanted here.* We reluctantly headed toward the living room just as the front door opened. In came Annika and Alexa, followed by Sellars and Renata. The sisters hadn't yet combed their hair, but they were smiling.

"Sarge and Duke," said Annika excitedly, "we will get to open our Christmas presents in a little while!" She bent down to give us dawgs a hug.

Rubbing her eyes and yawning, Alexa added: "And Mama told us last night that we could hand out the presents to everybody since we're old enough this year. Yay!"

They headed into the kitchen, where I heard Papa say, "Well, lookie here at this sight for sore eyes. Mornin,' girls. How'd y'all sleep?"

I didn't hear what they said, because Sellars said to me, "Sarge, where's everbody at? I hear ol' Duke, an' I smell bacon, so I figger he must be in the kitchen. I'll head on in there myself. Coming, Renata?"

188

She started to answer when Mama, Asher, and Bethany came down the stairs from the bedrooms. "Good morning, ladies and gentleman," greeted Renata. "How are y'all this morning? Asher certainly looks bright eyed and bushy tailed!"

Asher laughed, saying "Asher happy. Open presents now!"

"Renata is happy about that, too, little man. Can you give Renata a big hug?" Asher nodded, and came over and placed his arms around her neck. "Oh, what a nice big hug. Thank you, Asher," said Renata, who planted a kiss on his forehead.

"Bethany and I had a couple of final gifts to wrap upstairs in her room," explained Mama. "I'm ready for a piece of Nana's coconut cake!"

"So am I!" added Bethany. "I don't want a really big piece, but I do want a glass of cold milk to go with it." They started to head toward the kitchen.

Renata said, "Ladies, that little table in the kitchen isn't large enough for the rest of us, so let's eat in the dining room. I'll come get my coffee and cake—but why don't I keep Asher company for a moment, Holly, while you get his breakfast and juice ready? Just call me when it's ready."

"Thank you so much, Renata. I won't be but a moment," as she and Bethany headed on into the kitchen. Duke and I followed them, hoping for another morsel of bacon. After all, Mama and Bethany didn't know that we'd already had some. Maybe we'd get lucky and get some more. *A dawg can always hope, you know.*

As we entered the kitchen, Papa and Sellars were making the sisters laugh, apparently saying all kinds of silly things. Papa had decided to tell them a story. He was telling Annika to think of something—anything—and he'd be able to make up a story about it for them. He asked Sellars to help him, and Sellars said he'd be glad to.

Annika thought for a moment, then she and Alexa

went over to a corner and whispered for a little while, giggling all the while. Finally, they came back, and Annika announced triumphantly, "Papa, I bet you won't be able to think up a story about what we thought of!"

"Let's have it," said Papa. "I ain't gonna be able to tell no story at all if I don't know what you came up with."

Both girls shouted in unison: "A plastic spoon!"

Papa looked horrified. "Sellars, looks like we got our work cut out for us. How in the world are we gonna come up with a story about a plastic spoon?"

"I dunno, Duke, but heh heh, it was yore idea after all. I reckon if you can start it, I'll try to join in to help you along. Good luck."

Papa thought a moment while Kurt, Daddy, Clark, Mavis, Nana, and Sellars looked on. Overhearing the situation, Mama, Renata, Bethany, and Asher stood in the doorway between the kitchen and dining room, waiting to hear what Papa would say.

"Papa, we're waiting anxiously to hear your story," said Mama.

"Yeah," added Bethany. "C'mon, Papa, you can do it."

Papa scratched his chin, then his face brightened. He took a deep breath, then plunged in: "Once upon a time there was a young boy who wanted to go campin' with his daddy. They planned on goin' to the mountains, and they had a tent, some sleeping bags, an' some food, too." *Now you're talking.*

Sellars joined in: "The daddy, whose name was Carl, told the boy, whose name was Jimmy, that they'd catch some fish in the stream beside their campsite. He'd show Jimmy how to clean all those fish they caught, and then they'd cook 'em over their campfire. Jimmy was gittin' excited about goin' campin' with his daddy."

Alexa said: "I haven't heard anything about our plastic spoon yet, Papa and Sellars!"

"Now you jest wait," answered Papa. "I'm gittin' to it." He continued: "Carl and Jimmy packed up, got in their car, and headed to the mountain campsite, which was about two hours away. Jimmy couldn't wait to help his daddy pitch the tent and then fish in that stream up yonder."

Nana and Renata, who were listening intently, were chuckling. Papa asked, "What are y'all laughin' at? I ain't said nuthin' funny yet, have I?"

"Well—no," laughed Nana. "I was just hoping those two are better at catching fish than you and Sellars are!" She and Renata laughed out loud then, and the others joined them.

"Now, ladies," drawled Sellars, "don't y'all go an' ruin this here story fer these youngins.' Jest you wait and see how it turns out." Then muttering to himself, he said under his breath, "I'd kinda like to know that myself!" *So would I, Sellars, so would I.*

Papa continued: "They drove on up to the campsite, and when they got there, it hadn't gotten dark yet, and Carl noticed that several other tents an' a couple of campin' trailers were set up around the site, so he picked a nice level spot for their tent. Telling Jimmy how to help, they got their tent set up in no time. They had brought some sandwiches to eat fer supper, with Carl telling Jimmy they'd have plenty of time the next day to fish all they wanted."

This time Annika asked, "Papa, where is our plastic spoon in the story??"

Sellars answered: "Now you jest be patient, young lady. We're gittin' to it—you want our story to be interestin,' don't ya?" The sisters nodded. "Well, then, we gotta put in some colorful details so we can git to that plastic spoon. It'll show up real soon." Sellars took up the story: "Carl and Jimmy finished eatin' their sandwiches, and Carl tole Jimmy they could walk around and meet their neighbors before turnin' in fer the night. Jimmy liked that idea, so they went over to the nearest tent where and old man and old woman was settin' in some lawn chairs. They had an' ol' huntin' dawg layin' on the ground between 'em. As Carl an' Jimmy came closer, the dawg raised his head an' started waggin' his tail, but didn't bark.

"The ol' man said, 'Welcome, gents. I'm Howard, and this here's my wife Ada. An' this,' he pointed to the dawg, 'is Killer. But he ain't gonna hurt y'all none, so rest easy.' Carl and Jimmy shook hands with the old couple, talked a few minutes, and went on their way to meet the rest of their neighbors."

Mavis interrupted the story: "Sorry, girls, but everybody wants to eat breakfast so we can open our Christmas presents. Papa and Sellars, will you finish the story later? I'm sure the girls won't mind, and—that will give you more time to come up with how to work in that plastic spoon!"

"Yay! Let's eat so we can open presents!" yelled Annika.

"Now Papa and Sellars, don't forget about our story later!" added Alexa. "Remember, Carl and Jimmy were meeting their camping neighbors. I sure hope that plastic spoon will be in the story soon!"

Papa looked at Mavis: "That's a good idea. I was kinda paintin' myself into a corner with that story, an' you rescued me!" *Wha-a-a-at? I didn't see you painting anything, Papa. Oh. I suppose that means something else. Humans and their "figures of speech"! Why don't they just say what they mean?*

Everyone began scurrying around: Mama told the sisters that yes, they could have a small piece of Nana's coconut cake IF they also ate some yogurt and drank some milk; Renata put Asher in his booster seat, and Mama placed his milk, fruit, and yogurt with a spoon in front of him; others were getting coffee, cake, bacon, and settling down at the kitchen table and dining table as they wished.

We dawgs stayed put where Papa and Sellars were sitting, hoping for a little more bacon coming our way.

I heard a knock at the door, so Duke and I went into overdrive by barking madly to protect our humans from harm. We ran to the front door just as it opened, and in came Steve and Dorothy, laden with festively-wrapped Christmas packages. "Down, boys! It's just us," laughed Steve. "We have another load, plus the dawgs to bring in, so you boys move on back and let us set these down." *Barking to warn everybody is part of our job. We must protect our humans. And, we're glad it was you guys instead of burglars. Besides, it's too early to have to chase anybody away.*

Daddy and several others offered to help them bring in the rest of their stuff, and Dorothy said thank you, that the rest of the packages were in the trunk, which was open. She and Steve would get the dogs out of their car seats themselves. *Car seats again? Poor dogs.* So, Kurt, Clark, and Daddy went out to get the rest of the presents. Duke and I retreated to a corner of the room so that we could see what was happening without fear of being stepped on.

Soon, the men had brought in everything, with Steve commenting that it had started snowing. I looked at the men closely, and I did notice a few flakes of snow on their hair and shoulders. Mama said she was hoping for a white Christmas, but she didn't recall anything on the weather about snow. Papa said that sometimes the weatherman got it wrong, and we just might have us a white Christmas after all. I wanted to jump up on the back of the couch so I could look outside and see for myself, but it was occupied by Sellars, Renata, and Clark. *No room there. Guess I'll have to wait until later to see for myself.* Steve and Dorothy brought in Zoe and Charlie, and everyone finished eating their breakfast.

The children were thoroughly excited now, not only because it was time to open presents, but because it was also snowing. I don't know why, but humans seem to get a big thrill out of seeing snow, playing in it, and throwing it at each other. I have played in the snow once or twice myself, but I'm so low to the ground that my tummy gets really cold! Mama bought me some booties one time for my feet when I was a little dawg, but I guess she never thought of finding me a tummy wrap!

"Attention, ladies and gentlemen!" Mavis was ready to make some kind of announcement. "Find yourself a seat, but before we open our gifts, as a family tradition, we always read the Christmas story from Luke 2 in the Bible, so I've asked Philip to do the honors this year. Nobody here enjoys giving and receiving gifts any more than I do, but 'Jesus is the reason for the season.'" There were several *amens* from around the room. "So, Philip, please read the true meaning of Christmas to us."

Daddy nodded and opened his Bible, then began reading: "In those days Caesar Augustus issued a decree that a census should be taken of the entire Roman world." He kept on reading for several minutes, talking about Joseph and Mary, who had a baby in a manger because there was no room for them in the inn. Then later, shepherds were out in the field watching their flock at night, when an angel appeared to them and told them some really good news. It was good news to them, anyway. Since the shepherds were scared to death, the angel told them everything was okay and not be scared. The angel said that this baby was born in a city that belonged to David, and that He would be the Savior of the entire world. *This David must have been a pretty important guy.*

All of a sudden, a whole bunch of angels came and started singing and praising God. They said something about "glory to God" and "peace to men." Then, when the angels left, the shepherds decided that they needed to go find this baby Jesus, and they figured out that David's city was really Bethlehem. So, they went there and found Mary

194

and Joseph, His parents, and Baby Jesus, lying in that manger just like the angel had told them. After the shepherds saw Him, they went out and told everybody they could find about Him. People were just amazed at what those shepherds said they saw, too. Daddy closed his Bible and said a few words about keeping the beautiful Christmas spirit of our Lord and Savior alive in our hearts today. Then he said a prayer, asking the Lord to bless the family and thanking Him for all His blessings, especially sending His Son Jesus to be the Savior to all who accepted Him.

"Thank you, Philip. We really appreciated your reading of God's Word and the prayer, too." Mavis turned to the sisters: "Girls, are you ready to pass out the presents for us? Now *hand* them to people—don't *throw* them just to get them done so you can open yours!" *You must know how impatient children are about opening their presents, Mavis. Wait—you were a mother before you became a grandma. That's how you know about kids and presents!*

The sisters jumped right up, and so did Mama and Bethany, who were going to help the girls with reading the tags, I suppose. While they were handing out the gifts, I took this time to look around the room at my family. Something Daddy had said touched a chord in my heart, and although I didn't really get everything he said, I did understand that I loved my humans. I glanced over at the couch: Sellars and Renata, who are as much a part of this family as any of the rest. How could any humans and dawgs not love them? I recalled my visit to their farm with Clark and Mavis, and how they had welcomed me there, even if Sellars' mama pig Tenderloin didn't much like me getting close to her babies.

Next to Renata was Clark. He is a quiet man (at least compared to most in this family), but when he says something, it is worth listening to. Clark knows how to fix just about anything, and he always seems to be thinking of others, not himself. I've loved him since I first met him as a little puppy. His quiet ways, gentle touch, and kindness won my heart right away.

Steve and Dorothy were sitting on the arm chairs next to the couch, and Steve was clowning with the sisters, trying to take all the presents they were handing out, causing much mirth around the room. Steve was the tallest person I had ever seen when we first met those years ago at Nana and Papa's house, and he is always ready for a joke to make people laugh. Dorothy is one of my favorite people because she is a wonderful cook, and we doxies love good food! And she's kind and sweet, also.

Uncle Kurt and Aunt Bethany were sitting on the floor beside the Christmas tree—at least, she was sitting there a moment ago. I'll never forget my visit to their house when I met their two conniving felines, Tate and Joey. Oh, Kurt and Bethany treated me well, as they always do, and I did come to a truce of sorts with those cats. We were pretty good buddies by the time Daddy came to get me and take me home, but I aged a lot in that week I was with them! It was much easier when I went back to visit them again with Clark and Mavis. I understood cats so much better and we got along fine.

On the other side of the Christmas tree, sitting on the loveseat, were Papa and Nana. I hardly know where to begin, because they are the bedrock of this wonderful human family of mine. Nana loves her family so much, and she shows it in so many ways. But Papa not only loves his family a lot, he knows, understands, and loves ME, too. He loves Duke, too, but since I was his first granddawg, I think I'm special to him. From the time I saw that wide grin of his, heard that hearty laugh, and felt those large, strong hands holding me, I was hooked. One of the first things he said was about food, so right away, he got my attention as a chow hound. I have since learned that he not only loves me, but he knows how I think and what I want. Yes, Nana and Papa are great. And, Papa needs my help sometimes, too.

Beside Nana was Mavis. She loves to laugh, enjoys being sarcastic, but has a big heart, too. She loves Duke like he was her own child, and I've heard others in the family say she has spoiled him. *I don't see a thing wrong with showing a dawg how much you love him!* Mavis loves the sisters and Asher a lot, too, and loves to play with them.

My eyes lighted on Mama and Daddy. Where can I begin to say how much they mean to me? They found me at the doxie farm when I was a scared little puppy. They took me home, and have loved me ever since, even treating me like one of their own children. Oh, Mama has done some crazy stuff now and then, like buying me booties (which I hated), and making me that hat and coat (which made me look ridiculous), but she has a big heart and a kindness toward all. She's a wonderful mother to my sisters and brother, has a beautiful singing voice (but sometimes my ears hurt when she hits those high notes), and is a lot like Mavis in her sense of humor.

Now Daddy is a lot like Clark in some ways. Both are quiet men, but when Daddy says something, it's usually important, too. I heard Mavis say one time that when she first got to know Daddy, she didn't think he could even talk—that is, until she heard him preach at church! She said he used more words in that one sermon than she had heard him speak in the months she'd known him! *Wow, that must have been some sermon.*

Sitting on Daddy's lap, Asher was bright-eyed and excited about all the Christmas presents. He wanted to go ahead and open his, but Daddy told him to wait until everyone had their presents, too. What can I say about Asher? He is my own special little boy. I take care to watch out for him, because I never want any harm to come to him, ever. I love the sisters, too, but Asher is just so cute and sweet, says funny things—oh, that reminds me. One day Mama got him all dressed up for church with his little suit, tie, shoes, and his blond hair slicked back. He came into the living room and told Daddy, "I handsome." Daddy thought that was really funny, but I thought it was rather truthful myself!

The sisters had finally finished handing out all the presents, and Mama told them to sit down beside her, where their presents were on the floor. Annika was the first baby in our home, and I was there to help Mama take care of her. Oh, I lived through some sleepless nights along with Mama and Daddy, and I learned to avoid getting whacked over the head with a toy when she was a toddler. When she could talk, it took us all awhile to figure out that "Fah-boo" was her version of my name! But those hugs from her little arms around my neck made up for all those dangerous toys I had to sidestep.

Alexa was the next baby I helped with, and she came along when Annika was eighteen months old. Oh, Alexa cried some, too, but I'm not sure if she cried less than Annika, or if I had simply gotten more used to having a baby around. Probably a little of both. In any case, I was still amazed at how few things a human baby could do for itself: she couldn't even sit up, feed herself, talk, get dressed, or much of anything for the longest time. Mama had her hands full with Annika toddling around, getting into everything, and Alexa being a little baby, needing everything. I don't know what Mama would have done if I hadn't been there to help her!

After the sisters got a little older and could at least walk, talk, feed themselves, and even go to preschool and kindergarten, along came the light of my family, Asher. He's now nearly three, but I just don't remember hearing him cry that much. He probably did, and I just learned to tune it out. One of my favorite memories was when he first smiled at me. He was definitely "a toothless wonder" then, because I didn't see a single tooth when he grinned at me. He was lying on the floor where Mama had placed him on a blanket, and I was fascinated by his constant flailing of his arms and legs. He wore me out just watching him! It was like he was directing a choir, but of course, no choir was present. I sat down beside him on the floor and boofed at him. He turned his head, stared for a moment, and then broke out into that toothless baby grin, right at me! Oh, I was thrilled, because that meant he liked me! I mean, he couldn't talk and tell me, now could he? The best he could do at that point in his life was smile, and it meant a lot to me.

Papa's voice brought me back to reality: "Hey, is it time to open presents, everybody? Mavis, how do you want us to do this—one at a time, or everybody at once?"

She thought a minute, and Mama said something to her that I couldn't hear. "That's a good idea, Holly. How about we go around the room, starting with the youngest, and we each open ONE present while everyone else watches? After that, it's every man for himself! If we make everybody wait until each person opens all the presents, by the time we get to Papa, the children will be worn out from waiting! How does that sound to everybody?" There were murmurs of assent around the room. I prepared myself by getting out of the way—I sat down beside Papa's feet. Mavis looked at Duke and said, "Buddy, did you know you have a present over here, too? Soon it will be your turn, you know."

Daddy said, "Sarge, you also have a couple of presents, so I'm sure you'll want to open yours when it is your turn." I jumped up and went over to Daddy, sniffing the gifts to see if I could determine which ones were mine. "Holly, when are the dawgs gonna open their presents?"

"Um, I don't know if we should go in the order of dog years or human years for them!" she laughed. "So, we'll just let them go after Annika opens hers."

"Sounds like a plan to me," commented Sellars. "When I was a kid, dawgs didn't git no presents, you know.

We was lucky to git anything ourselves, times was so bad back then."

"Same here, Sellars," added Papa. "I had a hard life growin' up, an' my mama did the best she could, but Christmas was just about like any other day around our house. We barely had enough to eat back then, so that's why something like a cookie was real special to me as a kid."

"Okay, Asher, it's time for you to open a present!" Mama said excitedly. "Which one do you want to open first—you get to pick the one you want!"

Asher looked at his stack of presents, seemingly bewildered by that. He said "Ummmmm," then immediately pointed to a rather large package, covered with shiny red paper with pictures of various toys: bikes, trains, building blocks, or trucks.

"All right, let's open that one," said Mama. "Look, Asher—the tag says this present is from Nana and Papa! Oh boy—I bet you'll love it." She helped the little boy tear away the paper, and then break the tape on the box. She carefully lifted out a Styrofoam mold, and I couldn't see what it encased, so I went over to get a closer look. "Sarge, are you the gift inspector?" laughed Mama. *Yes, Mama. It's my job to see what everyone gets!*

She turned to Asher: "Look! It's a toy train like your favorite TV show, Asher!" She lifted out little train cars, each colorfully painted a different color, but I noticed something a bit odd: each train had a face on the front! *The things they think of for toys.*

Asher squealed, and said, "Tootle Train! Asher like trains!" And he took one of the train cars and inspected it closely.

Nana said, "Holly, there's a track down inside the box—you can assemble it later, but the train runs on batteries, which I also put in the box. I know how annoying it is to have something requiring batteries, but not having

200

any!"

"Oh, thanks," Mama replied. "Asher, tell Nana and Papa thank you, Honey."

Asher walked over and hugged them both, saying "Thank you, Honey." Everyone laughed. *What's so funny? He did what Mama told him, didn't he?*

"Am I next?" inquired Alexa. She was poised and ready to go, having already chosen the package she wanted to open. *I bet she chose it because the paper had princesses all over it.*

"Yes, you are," said Daddy. "I see you want to open the princess present." *Daddy is almost as observant as I am!*

Not needing assistance, Alexa began to tear into the wrapping paper. "Ahem," said Mama. "What are you supposed to do before you open it?"

"Oh, sorry. I forgot," apologized Alexa. She looked at the tag and read it aloud: "To Alexa, from Kurt and Bethany." She smiled at them, then proceeded to finish demolishing the wrapping paper. Once she had done that, she knew immediately what their present to her was: a beautiful princess doll, because the box front had a window in it, revealing the princess doll inside. It had long wavy blond hair, wore a beautiful yellow satin gown with sparkles all over it, and a gold crown on her head. I knew immediately that this present would be a hit with "Princess Alexa." Her mouth flew open as she gazed upon that doll. "Oh, Aunt Bethany and Uncle Kurt, this is exactly the princess doll I wanted. THANK YOU SO MUCH! I LOVE IT!" She hugged them, then asked Mama to help her get the doll out so she could see the dress better.

"I know I'm next, Mama. Can I open mine now?" asked Annika. Mama nodded, engrossed on removing all the entrapments on Alexa's princess doll. *Why do doll companies make their dolls so difficult to get out of the box? Seems like it would be frustrating to young girls if nobody was there to help them.*

"I'll look at the tag first. It says: 'To Annika, with love, Sellars and Renata.' Boy, it is a pretty big box, and I don't have a clue what's in it, either," said Annika happily.

"I shore hope that toothbrush in there is the kind you like," laughed Sellars, who was obviously joking. "You *do* like green toothbrushes with big orange polky-dots, dontcha?"

Annika smiled knowingly. "Sellars, I'm pretty sure it's not a toothbrush, but I'm gonna find out right now!" And with that, she ripped off the paper with much determination. As she lifted the lid, her mouth flew open, too. "Mama, look! Sellars and Renata got me a winter coat like the one we saw at the store! I said I wanted that when we saw it. How did they know??" Sellars smiled, and so did Renata.

"Oh, a little bird told us," Renata informed her. "And he told us the right color and size, too." Annika had already taken out the coat and was trying it on. *I know that girl loves clothes, and I have to admit that it is a beautiful coat.* It was a dark brown chocolate color, and it looked like fur. It also had a hood.

"That is the coat you wanted," commented Mama. "It's faux fur, but it just about looks like fur, doesn't it? The thing is, I can throw this one in the washer and dryer! You will certainly stay warm, and it looks great on you, too! Thank you, Sellars and Renata."

Annika ran over to them and hugged them: "Thank you so much! This coat is just like the one I saw in the store with Mama. You tell that 'little bird' thank you for me, too!" Sellars chuckled and slapped his knee. *Why is that so funny? That bird got it right, didn't he??*

"Okay, now it's Duke's turn—the dawg, that is," said Mavis. "C'mere, buddy—let's open your present, and it's from Daddy and me." Duke began sniffing the gift, but he obviously didn't have any idea about how to open it, so I decided to go over and help him. I grabbed a corner of the paper and pulled. "Thank you, Sarge," said Mavis. "See, Duke? Sarge is helping you." With that, Duke also grabbed a corner of the package, and between the two of us, we managed to get the paper off.

Mavis intervened. "I don't think you can open this plastic bag, though—nor would I want you guys to choke. So I'll open that for you." She tore open the black plastic bag, and out fell something red. It looked like a blanket, but when Mavis held it up, I figured out that it was a garment of some kind. "Look, Duke—a doggie sweater! This will keep you nice and warm outside!" She and Mama proceeded to put it on Duke, but he was none too happy with the process. Once they got it on him, however, he seemed to like it—he sniffed it, walked around, kept trying to look at his back. I must admit that he was quite the handsome dawg in the red sweater.

"Now ain't he a good-lookin' dawg in that sweater," exclaimed Papa. "Is anybody gonna take any pictures today?"

"Coming right up," replied Bethany and Clark together. *Hey, they can say stuff at the same time like the sisters!* She had her camera phone, and immediately snapped a picture of Duke. Clark had his digital camera, and he also snapped a picture of Duke, who looked bewildered. Everyone laughed.

Now it was my turn. Nobody had to tell me, but I did have to go over to Daddy, who was holding a package for me. "Here you go, Sarge," he said. "This gift is from Mama and me, and I know you can probably open most of your present by yourself. You usually help us open ours, too." *You're right, Daddy. Humans just take too long, so if I can help keep things rolling, then I'm quite willing to lend a hand—er—paw.*

I quickly tore all the paper off my present, and from all my vast experience in gift opening, I used my sharp

teeth to bite through the tape on the plastic bag. All that
was left was for me to reach my long muzzle into the bag
and draw out whatever was in there.

"Believe I'd better do that," Daddy stated. "We don't
want your sharp teeth to ruin your present, ol' boy." Daddy
proceeded to pull out another garment of some kind. It was
also red, but had a few white stripes in it, too. Daddy held
it up: "Look, Sarge! It's your own sweater like Duke's!"
Mama took the sweater from Daddy and pulled me to her. I
knew that there was no use in trying to get away from
Mama when she had her mind set on putting clothes on me,
so I just resigned myself and stood there. She quickly put
the sweater on me, but I must admit that it felt pretty good.
The material was soft, it covered my back, and there were
openings for my two front paws. Duke was still wearing
his, too.

"Say cheese!" yelled Bethany, who had her camera
phone in front of her. *I love cheese, but I know I won't get
any. It just means that humans want to take my picture—*
so I stood straight, as tall as I could. Duke was looking
down at something on the floor, so I butted him with my
posterior to get his attention. The moment he looked up,
she snapped our picture. "Oh, that's a good one," she said.
"Both dawgs are looking straight at the camera." Mama
leaned over and looked at the phone. She agreed that it was
a good picture of us dawgs.

"Let's keep everything moving now," said Mavis.
Looking around the room, she eyed each person. "With my
great powers of deduction, here's the remaining order of
opening gifts: Bethany, Kurt, Holly, then Philip, Steve,
Dorothy, and Clark; then moi, Renata, Sellars, Nana, and
last but not least, Papa Duke. Hit it, Bethany!"

And so it went. Each person read tags, stated who it
was from, then politely opened the gift, showing it to
everyone. There were some nice gifts, but that's at least
twelve presents, and I didn't really bother to keep up with

who got what, or who gave it to them. Too boring for my taste. But they all seemed to enjoy opening their gifts.

As soon as Papa had opened his "first" gift last, then Mavis said, "Now we'll all open the rest of our presents—each man for himself. I've provided large trash bags over here for putting the paper, so let's try to get most of it in them! Enjoy, people!" The children screamed, Mama and Bethany whooped, and Sellars said heh heh. Paper was flying everywhere, and I had to move a couple of times so I could see what was going on—paper kept landing on me and I was afraid I'd miss something. Exclamations rang in the air:

"Oh, just what I wanted—I love this perfume! Thank you!"

"Ray-melle, look at these chocolate-covered cherries I got!"

"Wow! This new laptop carrier will come in handy! My old one is shot."

"Mama! Look at these fuzzy mittens! They match my new coat!"

"I got a coat just like Annika's, but mine's tan!"

"Tools! I got tools like Papa Clark. Asher fix things, too!"

And so on. Duke and I definitely had to keep our wits about us. We wanted to help with opening the gifts, but our humans were really quick, so we didn't help much. We mostly had to stay on the move to keep from getting buried under a mountain of wrapping paper—I guess Mavis's announcement about the trash bag fell on deaf ears. I noticed that Zoe and Charlie had moved to the doorway of the dining room, definitely out of harm's way. *Hey guys, aren't you the least bit curious about these presents? No, I guess not,* because they just sat watching.

With the gift-opening frenzy finally winding down, the last gift had been opened. The talk died down a bit, with everyone sitting around watching the children play with some of their new toys. Suddenly, Mama let out a whoop. "Woo hoo! Look outside, everybody! It's snowing really hard now!" Someone opened the front door so we could all look out through the glass storm door. It really was coming down hard, and the ground was white!

The children gathered at the door, with several adults standing behind them, and others were on their knees on the couch, holding the curtain sheers aside to peer out the picture window. I managed to squeeze between legs and make my way to the storm door, which was at my level. Large, fluffy flakes of snow were falling, and the grass and trees were partially covered in what looked like fluffy cotton. I loved this beautiful picture-postcard scene before us. Across the street, smoke was coming from the chimneys of several neighbors. Nobody was outside yet, because it was still rather early in the day. If it kept snowing, I was pretty sure there would be some kind of snowball fight outside later.

"Mama, can we go out and play in the snow?" asked Annika. "It has been a long time since it snowed. Can we?"

"We don't get snow in Georgia, at least not since we moved there," replied Mama. "Y'all can go outside later, maybe after lunch. But in a little while, we've all got to clean up Mom's living room. It looks like an explosion happened in here!" I know, Mama. *But nobody can blame us dawgs, 'cause we mostly just watched you HUMANS make this mess.*

They all stayed put for a while, watching the beautiful snow come down. *The world is always so quiet, too, when it snows,* I noted. *It's almost like the snow is some kind of sound barrier,* which I like, because it's so peaceful. I didn't see any squirrels running around the yard now, either. *Wonder where they go when it snows?*

Here I was, with all the humans in the world that I loved. I looked forward to Christmas lunch, which, according to Mavis, would be "an instant replay" of last night's Christmas Eve dinner. Each of my human family so enjoyed sharing another Christmas season together, I could tell. Not only did these humans love Duke, me, and those conniving cats (for some strange reason), but they also love each other a LOT. They are always doing things for each other, and when they are not together, they are either talking on the phone, sending text or e-mail messages, or just simply asking about the others.

I guess it's because I'm no longer a young dawg, but Christmas with my human family means so much more to me now that it did when I was a pup. Of course, I can't deny that the outstanding FOOD plays a big part of it, but now that I'm older, I realize that eventually things will change, and one of these years, some members of my family won't be around for one of our Christmas gatherings. Until that time, though, I'm going to enjoy every single minute! I have already learned that the great times I had this Christmas will one day turn into great memories I'll treasure for the rest of my life.

I already have tons of wonderful memories piled up—and I can think about them any time I want!

21
Planning Nana's New Year's Party

We were able to stay in North Carolina until after New Year's, and so did Sellars, Renata, Kurt, and Bethany. My family (meaning Daddy, Mama, and the children) spent a couple of days with Daddy's parents, Joe and Sheila, and his grandma Agnes, and I enjoyed seeing all of them, too. Some of his aunts, uncles, and cousins came over to a big meal—everyone brought something good to eat. Although Papa wasn't there to see that I got my share of good human food, the children managed to sneak me a few bites when the adults weren't looking.

My family is so large! Mama tells me that I haven't even met half of them, and at this stage of my life, I guess I probably won't meet the other half. I didn't run and play with all the children at Daddy's family like I used to, but I enjoyed watching them outside as I sat on the porch in a sunny spot. They had on coats and hats, and Mama had put my new sweater on me, but I didn't want to get it dirty—actually, Mama didn't want me to get dirty—so I just rested on the porch.

Instead of going back to Garner, we spent the rest of our Christmas holidays at Papa and Nana's in Sanford. Nana invited a few friends over while we were there for an "after-Christmas fellowship," and I enjoyed meeting some of their neighbors and friends I hadn't met before. Of course, Mr. and Mrs. Vance came, and so did Ashley next door, with her parents and little brother and sister. Several more humans from down the street came, and I enjoyed getting lots of attention and good food once again. *If I keep this up, I know Mama is going to put me on a diet—but right now, I don't care! I'm having too much fun.*

Papa was in his groove—he and Sellars joked with the children, told some of their funny stories, and live music from Papa with his "geetar" were all a hit. Later in the evening, Mama, Aunt Bethany, Papa, Renate, sang together, too. Annika and Alexa even sang a couple of songs all by themselves! Asher *could* have joined them, but he just wasn't in the mood this time. My boy is shy sometimes and outgoing sometimes—that evening just happened to be one of his shy times.

The major significance of the fellowship to me, however, was that Nana had good "finger" foods: I discovered that means human food that can be picked up and eaten easily. But I quickly found out that such foods, such as sausage balls, cheese straws, or pizza bites were just as easy to drop, so I got plenty of tasty treats that night! Nana told everyone just to eat when and where they wanted, so that made things so much easier for me to enjoy—some humans just sat on pillows on the floor, which was practically eye level for me. Oh, I didn't jump into anyone's plate, but I did sit nearby and look pitiful. *That still works every time.*

The humans even played a few games that Mama and Aunt Bethany came up with. These games weren't quite as silly as charades, but came close! One game seemed to be just conversation. The main stipulation was to avoid saying the word "yes." If a human did utter that word to another human, then the *yes* human had to give a popsicle stick to the other human. The one with the most popsicle sticks at the end of the game (there was a time limit) won. Papa loved that game. I was listening when a young boy came up to Papa and asked him if he liked playing his guitar. Of course Papa replied, "Yes, I shore do."

The boy laughed, and holding out his hand, said, "Mr. Duke, give me a popsicle stick!"

Not to be outdone, Papa replied, "Oh, are we still playing that game?"

The smiling boy replied, "Yes, we are!"

"Then give me back my popsicle stick!" Papa replied in triumph. The boy was shocked that Papa tricked him so easily. That exchange caused some chuckles around the room, too. *Way to go, Papa! It's hard to fool my papa.*

When Aunt Bethany called time and the popsicle sticks were duly counted, I was surprised by who won: Daddy! He doesn't talk as much as some humans, but when he does, he knows how to zero in on what's important. I guess he was able to get the humans to answer his questions before they knew what hit them! *Yay for you, Daddy!* The "prize" was a silly hat, which Aunt Bethany put on his head—it was red and had reindeer antlers on it.

I don't think he'll be wearing it anywhere else, though. But the children will enjoy wearing it, I know.

Mama and Bethany wanted to "hit the stores" in Raleigh for all the after-Christmas sales—they had received some gift cards for Christmas. Mavis and Dorothy said they'd like to do that, too, but Nana and Renata just wanted to stay home. So, early one morning after Christmas, the four ladies prepared to head for Raleigh. Annika and Alexa wanted to go, too, so after a bit of begging, Mama relented, cautioning them not to whine or say things like they were tired, hungry, or bored. The sisters dramatically promised, bowing down before Mama in gratitude like she was a queen or something. Asher was just content staying here and playing with his new toys.

After they left, Steve, Clark, Daddy, and Kurt watched games on TV, Nana and Renata sat at the kitchen table planning the New Year's get together, and Sellars and Papa just drank coffee and talked. I chose to sit on Papa's lap so I could hear what they were talking about, which turned out to be a good idea. Daddy put Asher down for a nap a little later.

"Sellars, you ever wonder what happened to all them people we met in the Army? Oh, I've run across a few of 'em over the years, but at our age, most of 'em are already gone now!"

"Yeah, I have. An' like you, I've met a few of my buddies and their families over the years, but only one or two we knew in Ft. Greely. You remember Sgt. Boggs—the one who worked in food service with us? One time many years ago, he was coming through Georgia on vacation—on his way to Florida—an' gave me a call. I never did figger out how he got in touch with me, but he had his wife and grandchildren with him. He wanted just to stop by for a few minutes and say hello. We tole him to come on, and we'd fix dinner fer 'em. So they did."

"What did y'all have to eat, Sellars?" asked Papa. *That's right, Papa. Find out the most important stuff.*

Sellars called to Renata in the kitchen. "Renata, remember when that Sgt. Boggs from Greely came to see us that time? What did we fix fer dinner that night?" There was a pause, then Renata answered.

"Seems like I remember making beef stew, several vegetables, and I had a couple of pies in the freezer," she replied. *Sounds yummy.*

"We ain't really had nobody much to visit us here from our 'old days,' Sellars. We've made a lot of friends here, that's for sure, but you know, it just ain't the same as it is in the military. Families just seem to grow closer, 'cause we know we won't be together forever like it is in civilian life. Of course, families move more now, 'cause of jobs and whatnot, but the military life was shore good to us."

"Oh, that's the truth," answered Sellars. "Do y'all ever git down to Ft. Bragg? We ain't that close to any military bases where we live, and I miss it."

"Yeah, we do, in fact. Ray-melle likes to shop in the PX, an' Mavis has gone with her a few times, 'cause Mavis says she likes to be around military stuff, too. I'll go, but just sit in the café beside the PX, drinking coffee. I always find me a couple of ol' war horses like myself who want to just set and shoot the breeze. I enjoy that a lot, 'cause some of 'em was in the same places I was, even if we didn't know each other at the time."

"Do y'all still have commissary privileges now? That's one thang that me an' Renata miss—gettin' groceries at the post commissary. They had some real good prices on stuff."

"Naw. Fer some reason, after I turned sixty-five, we didn't git to use the commissary no more. But that's okay; Ft. Bragg is a good thirty-minute drive, and we got us a nice grocery story just down the street—so the money I save on gas makes up for it. Besides, I'm always going to the grocery store for somethin,' and it just don't make no sense to drive to Bragg, anyhow, for a few thangs." *Y'all are talking about things I never heard you mention before, Papa. I don't even know what a PX or a commissary is— and Annika isn't here to ask you, so I'll probably never know.*

Nana and Renata entered the living room. "Gentlemen, we've just about got our New Year's party all planned out," Nana informed Papa and Sellars. *I notice that the other four men are engrossed in TV, so it's like they aren't even here.* "I know all the women will help, like they did several years ago. All we need you men to do is to rearrange the furniture to accommodate everybody, help carry stuff, and then put everything back afterwards. Will you do that for us?"

"Why, shore we will," said Sellars. "Me an' Robert— and them four zombies over there: Steve, Clark, Kurt, and Daddy—" he pointed to the men—"will be sure to help any way we can."

"Did I hear my name used in vain?" asked Steve.

"Welcome back to reality, Steve," said Renata.

"Ramelle and I have the New Year's thing all planned out, and we want you guys to help with furniture, carry things, and so on."

"Yeah, we'll do that. Right, guys?" He looked over at the other three, who nodded, but I'm not certain that they even knew what they were nodding about. *Goodness, that must be some game they're watching.*

In a little while, Nana asked Papa what he wanted for lunch—how about some of the men running over to Jackson Brothers and getting lunch for all of us? Daddy somehow managed to overhear that, and so did Kurt. They said they'd be glad to go for all of us. *I include myself, because I just love hamburgers and such—and I know Papa will give me a few bites of his.* So, they took everyone's order, and Kurt and Daddy left. The game on TV must have been over, because Clark asked Steve if he minded having the TV off. Steve nodded.

Daddy and Kurt returned shortly, and they all went to the dining table to eat (of course I followed): they had burgers, hot dogs, fries, onion rings, and apple or cherry turnovers for everyone. Daddy woke up Asher, who smiled when he heard that Daddy and gotten him a hot dog. And, Papa did give me a few bites, as he usually does.

Dorothy, Mavis, Mama, and Bethany, along with Annika and Alexa, returned from their shopping trip about the time it was getting dark. They entered the house carrying large shopping bags.

"My goodness! Did y'all leave anything at the stores fer anybody else?" laughed Papa.

"Yes, but there were so many people shopping today, it's a miracle that we got anything!" exclaimed Mavis. "Lines everywhere, people grabbing things—it was a madhouse."

"And that, my dear friends, is why I never go shopping if I can avoid it, especially after Christmas," stated Clark. Steve and the other men nodded, agreeing.

"But we found some great deals," added Bethany. "Kurt, remember that blue silk top I bought recently? I found a great scarf and belt to match it, and they were all on sale! I even got a cute pair of flats, too."

"Wow. That's fantastic," said Kurt, but his enthusiasm just did not match his words.

"Mama found me a pretty dress—and one for Alexa, too," Annika stated proudly. "Can we show it to you?"

"Sure," said Clark. "If it's okay with your mom, go try them on for us." That thrilled the sisters when Mama nodded yes, so they scampered back to a bedroom to try on their dresses.

"What treasure did you find today, Dorothy?" asked Steve. "Probably something for our kitchen—I mean, we only have three sets of everything!"

"Hey, watch it! And why do you think I got something for the kitchen this time?" Dorothy replied. "I don't *always* buy kitchen stuff. But, you're right this time. I did get a new wooden salad bowl set, complete with wooden tongs for serving." She took a large box out of her even larger shopping bag. She took out the set of bowls, and they were beautiful—polished, dark wood that looked heavy.

"Okay. We did need a new salad set, 'cause our old one has seen better days," conceded Steve. "I do like those." Dorothy gave the thumbs up sign.

"I know everybody wants to see everything we bought," said Mama in a joking tone, "but we're all tired, and you can see the rest of our stuff tomorrow if you think you can wait that long." The men all nodded vigorously, looking relieved.

The sisters came parading into the room just then, and as they got to the center, twirled around to show off

214

their full skirts. Their dresses were dark green with sparkles across the top, and the skirts were made of some kind of shiny, light fabric.

"Beautiful," commented Renata. "Holly, I love those dresses. The sparkly velvet bodices and full chiffon skirts are so dressy! They will be the prettiest girls at church, that's for sure." The sisters looked pleased. *Oh, so that's what those fabrics are.*

"Girls, go take them off now and lay them across the bed. I'll hang them up for you. It's getting late, so just put on your pajamas." With a couple more twirls, the girls headed off.

After a light supper of sandwiches and "whatever," they all ate and got ready for bed. Nana did mention the New Year's party again, and the ladies all decided to work on that tomorrow, since they still had two days to get it all together. After the meal, they all put on their comfy night clothes, then laughed and talked until bedtime.

I enjoyed today, listening to Papa and Sellars talk about military things, which was obviously a topic they both loved. I also look forward to Nana's New Year's party. I remember the last one when I was young, and I got a lot of good food, so I probably will this time, too. I never pass up a chance to consume good human food—we doxies are quite proficient in that area.

22
A Tribute to My Family

Mama and Daddy picked *me* when they chose a little puppy to take home from Mrs. Fitzgerald's dachshund farm all those years ago. My humans are sometimes zany, but we have so much fun, too. My brother and my sisters are growing up so fast, almost before my eyes! I'm not a young dawg anymore, but I'm healthy and enjoy my life. And, of utmost importance to me, Duke has turned out quite well under my tutelage, if I may say so. He's become a good buddy.

The cats? We just recently acquired a new cat whom my family named Thor, if you can believe that. THREE CATS IN THIS HOUSE! I can't do much to change Tate and Joey, Piper and Aslan, but then, they *are* adult cats, and they'll always be like they are. We've reached a truce, the cats and I—and I have yet to meet the newest member of Kurt and Bethany's family, Winston, except through pictures Bethany has sent in texts to Mama. Humans often say that dachshunds stubborn, but I tend to disagree. Oh, we know what we want and are pretty single-minded in going after it. And we usually know what our humans want us to do, but we often choose not to do it—at least not right away. But I like to think that we're just exercising our individuality as the noble breed we are. And why shouldn't I have a choice to do or not to do something? It's not like I want to harm anyone when I don't want to get down off the couch so a human can sit there. After all, I was there first!

Humans come and go, circumstances and situations change, I've learned—but above all, I have my loving family of humans to be with me. I also have my animal family, and I must admit that my humans pretty much treat us all very well—except that I don't get enough of their delicious

food. I'll always be on the lookout for some, though.
We chow hounds enjoy it so much, you know.

The World According to Asher

Since my favorite boy Asher is now three, one milestone he has accomplished in the past few months (in the human world, at least), is wearing "big boy underwear." Mama seems especially happy about that fact, and I suppose I am, too—with my sensitive nose, I certainly won't miss the diapers *at all.* I've also noticed lately how much he can talk—and boy, does he come out with some interesting observations! He just tickles me to death with some of his statements, and if dogs laughed, I would certainly be guffawing all over the place.

For instance, I recall one day when he had just turned two, when he and I were playing by ourselves—the sisters were at school, Daddy was working at church, and Mama was busy rounding up the laundry for washing. Asher and I were in the playroom, and I was watching him line up his little figurines on the table in there. He still loves those toys: a mouse, a dog, a cat, a dragon, a cow, and several others. He talks to them, he provides the different voices so they can talk to each other, and in general, weaves an entire story around them just about every day. I was getting a little impatient, because I wanted him to throw my ball for me, so I boofed to get his attention. Since I managed to do so, I picked up my tennis ball in my mouth and wagged my tail. I tried to give him my best doggie smile, too, but it was kind of hard with that ball in my mouth! So, I whined. He looked at me for a moment, blinking those big blue eyes, then said, "You a baby, Sarge. Where's you bottle?" That caused me to drop the ball and stare back at him. *Where did you get that from? And do I*

217

actually look like a human baby who drinks a bottle?

He nonchalantly resumed his play, leaving me to mull over what he'd said. *Aha. It came to me:* he had probably been told that same thing by his darling older sisters—I hadn't actually heard either Annika or Alexa say that to him, but that was the only way he could have picked up such a comment. Oh, I've heard them tell him he is a baby when they wanted to play a board game and he wanted to join in, meaning he was too little to understand the workings of the game. He didn't like it either, retorting with "I not baby!"

And Mama delighted in telling the family what he had said in the grocery store one time when she and Asher, by then two and a half, went grocery shopping by themselves. Mama said they saw a man wearing suspenders, and Asher commented: "Look! Him wearing a seatbelt!" Oh, Daddy and the sisters loved that one.

The other day after school, Annika promised she would play with him after she finished eating her snack. He waited a short while, then came back into the dining room and said to her: "C'mon, Granny—hurry up!" Annika replied that she wasn't a granny, but Mama heard what he said and chuckled from the kitchen.

One day he found a large, round black button on the floor in the bathroom. Mama and Daddy were in the kitchen, and the sisters were in the dining room beside it eating breakfast before school. I was sitting nearby in hopes that they would drop me a morsel, when Asher came out of the bathroom holding that big black button over one eye. "I a pirate!" he announced. Mama and Daddy burst out laughing, but it took the sisters a second to catch on. Then, they also laughed.

Alexa asked, "Asher, are you mean? Sometimes pirates are mean."

"Asher not mean. Asher nice pirate!" he replied.

I heard Mama ask Daddy, "Where did he learn about

pirates wearing a patch over one eye?" Daddy replied that Asher had probably seen something about pirates on TV.

Mama bought him some super hero pajamas a few months ago, and he dearly loves wearing them. They even have a little cape attached at the shoulders with that sticky stuff that holds them on there. In fact, when Mama puts them on him before his bedtime, she HAS to play the theme song on her cell phone while she holds him up, flying him around the house until the theme song finishes playing. He smiles, holding his arms out straight in front of him, as I imagine his super hero must have done. I've never seen any of those movies, but I've heard so much about him since Asher got those pajamas that I believe I could be an expert!

That boy also dearly loves looking at books with anyone. The whole world could be going crazy, but Asher and "whoever" blithely go right on looking at books like they are in their own little world. I know that is especially true when he and Mavis are together. Oh, he loves Mama, Daddy, and the sisters, of course, but since he doesn't get to see Clark and Mavis that often, he is thrilled when they come for a visit. Clark will ask what needs fixing around the house, and he happily putters around, working on swings, faucets, appliances, or one of the vehicles, while Mavis will look at books with Asher for hours, it seems. While they do so, the sisters enjoy watching Saturday morning children's programs on TV, and he likes them up to a point—but if Mavis says, "Asher, bring Grandma a book to look at," he'll immediately run to his "stash" which Mama has kept on a shelf in the corner of the living room. He'll bring several books to Mavis, and away they go—she'll ask him questions about some of the pictures, read parts of his books that he'll understand, and just be silly with him, much to his delight. They even pretend to eat food in Mama's magazines, make up stories about humans in advertisements, and just end up being silly, laughing together.

One thing I've noticed about my boy Asher, besides the fact that he is cute and sweet: he is very smart for his age. Months ago when Clark and Mavis visited, she was looking at his shapes book with him, asking him about the various shapes on the pages: circle, square, rectangle, diamond, even oval. He knew every single one of them. She apparently came to a shape that she was sure he wouldn't know, pointing it out and asking him, "Asher, now I bet you don't know this shape—what is it?"

He looked at it and quickly said, "Pent-a-gon."

Mavis was astonished. "Holly!" she called to Mama, who happened to be doing something in the kitchen. "This boy knows what a pentagon is! I bet I didn't even know a pentagon shape until I was ten years old!" she laughed.

"Oh, Grandma, you're silly," laughed Annika, who had managed to overhear the comment while watching her cartoon program. "You learned them before you were ten, or you wouldn't even have passed kindergarten!" she commented smugly, turning back to her cartoon program.

Mama answered from the kitchen: "Philip and I have taught him the shapes because he likes that book and seems to absorb things like a sponge," Mama replied. *Yikes. That sounds like a painful way to learn something,* I reasoned. "Honestly, he seems to pick up everything right away—it wasn't long before he knew all the shapes. He also knows his colors—that is, unless he is in the mood to say that everything is blue," she smiled.

Yes, my boy is very smart. When Mavis says silly things about his books with pictures of food, he loves it. "Look, Asher. There's a cupcake. Let's 'eat' it because it looks so yummy." And they'll pretend to get it off the page and stuff it into their mouths. Or, "do you see those hamburgers those people are eating at the park? What shall we do with them?"

Asher will yell out, "EAT HAMBURGERS!" And he'll proceed to "get" them and pop them into his mouth.

"Hey—" Mavis would say in mock anger, "I was gonna eat those, but you beat me to it!" Asher thinks that is so funny. *You know, Mavis, you remind me so much of Papa. That sounds like something he would do, too.*

As if reading my thoughts, Mama said, "Mom, you are so much like Papa. I think he used to do that with Bethany and me when we were little!"

"Oh, he's never been much for sitting around looking at books with children," Mavis replied. "But he probably had REAL hamburgers that he crammed into all our mouths!" That comment drew a laugh from Mama and the sisters, who smiled and nodded.

"I miss Papa," lamented Alexa. "I like to sit on his big lap and hold his great big hand," she said wistfully.

"Me, too," added Annika. "Papa likes to laugh, and he always makes me laugh, too. He says funny things, makes funny faces, and tells us funny stories." She paused. "Hey, Alexa! He and Sellars never did finish telling us that story about a plastic spoon they were making up for us at Christmas. Remember?"

"Yeah," replied Alexa. "Mama said we couldn't open presents until we'd eaten breakfast, so we were in such a hurry to open presents that we forgot all about that story. Wonder how Papa and Sellars would have put that plastic spoon into their story?" *I would love to know that myself. Why, I was really getting into their story about Carl and Jimmy going camping. I guess we'll never know now.*

Asher joined in: "Where Papa Duke at? Asher wanna hug him." *Kids, you might love Papa, but I love him more than all of you put together. After all, I've known him a lot longer than you guys. I knew him well before you came along, you know.*

Another thing I like about Asher, which I never tire of mentioning, is that he is cute and sweet. That platinum blonde hair and big blue eyes full of innocence—most of the time—are totally disarming to just about any other human, young and old alike, with whom he comes in contact.

Case in point: Miss Savannah, who has often come to our house. Oh, she thinks the sisters are divine, but she's always telling Mama that she's just gonna take Asher home with her one of these days. *Personally, I'd prefer that she took Piper or Aslan—or both of them—home with her!* The last time she came to see us, dropping off a delicious sour cream pound cake for her "beloved preacher and family," Asher looked up at her with those big blue eyes and said: "Savannah got on a BIGGGG brown dress." Mama looked like she was embarrassed, but Miss Savannah just burst out laughing.

"Why, Asher, my dear sweet boy, you are exactly right. Miss Savannah's dress is big. Why, if Miss Savannah put on an itty bitty dress, she just could not fit into it at all, now could she?" And she picked him up, hugging and kissing him on both cheeks. Mama murmured some sort of apology—but I didn't understand why she needed to. *Asher did speak the truth, didn't he? In fact, he always does. Miss Savannah's dress does look big to little Asher. I thought humans liked it when others were honest.*

"Oh, Savannah, I don't know where Asher gets some of this stuff. Sorry!"

"Now, Holly honey, you just leave him be. Nobody could call me skinny exactly, you know, and I am not offended one bit. And I imagine that to a little boy, my dress, which is kinda on the long side, is big to him. It's no secret around here that I love to cook—and eat—so no harm done."

After Miss Savannah left, Alexa asked Mama, "What did Asher say that was so bad, Mama?"

Mama went on to explain that Asher had said that Miss Savannah's dress was big, implying that she was fat. Mama said you are not supposed to call people fat, especially ladies, because that is not considered good manners. Both girls nodded in understanding. *Oh, okay. I get it—Mama is always telling me I can't have this or that to eat because I might get fat. I don't like to be called fat, but I sure do like to eat. Apparently, so does Miss Savannah.*

"It's not nice to say that somebody is ugly, either," piped up Annika. The sisters giggled.

Mama took time to explain with a *teachable moment*, as she calls such. "Girls, do you think God is pleased if we call someone a name that hurts their feelings? How would you feel if someone told you that you were ugly?" "Well," answered Alexa, "Sellars is always tells Sissie and me that we get uglier and uglier every time he sees us!"

"Yes," replied Mama, "but you know he is joking and means just the opposite. But just remember to put yourself in the other person's place when you say things, so you can be careful about how you speak, okay?"

"Yes, Mama," they replied in unison. *They always do that—they must practice when I'm not around.*

Back to Asher: I've seen pictures of Mama and Daddy when they were little, and they both had very blond hair, too, although now their hair is brown. The sisters' hair is still very blond, too. Strange. We dogs stay the same color throughout life—like, I'm not going to wake up tomorrow and be a red dachshund, for instance. I have noticed, however, that some ladies we know have a different color of hair at times. I heard Mama say something about a lady on TV being a "bottle blond," but I didn't know exactly what that meant until she had to explain it to Annika, too—that a "bottle blond" meant she had dyed her hair blond—and the dye was in a bottle—when her hair was actually brown or maybe gray. *Humans—why can't they just be satisfied with what they have? Personally, I'm proud to be black and tan. I wouldn't want to be a red, cream, gray, dappled, or piebald doxie. I wouldn't want to be longhaired or wirehaired, either. Some ladies even do something to their straight hair to make it curly. Or, if it is curly, they do something to make it straight. I will never understand that at all!*

In any case, Asher's hair is the lightest blond of anyone's in our family, at least right now. All of them, with the exception of Mama (and me, of course), have blue eyes—Mama's are green. When he smiles, showing those cute little white teeth, he has dimples, and sometimes I just have to give him a doggie kiss! Not only is he cute and sweet, but he loves me and treats me well. He's only a little boy, not really out of his babyhood that long (but don't tell him that—he thinks he is as old as the sisters!), but he never pinches me or pull my ears or tail, like some children are prone to do. And he is generous in sharing his snacks with me, too. I suppose the word I want to use regarding him is *gentle*. He's a gentle, sweet child, and I hope he always will be.

What a fine man he will be one day. I hope I'll be around to see him all grown up.

Alexa: the Princess

My youngest sister has a lot in common with Asher: they both act the same sometimes. When he smiles, he looks like Alexa did at his age, but his hair is cut short and is a lighter blond. She can make him laugh just about every day, making silly faces at him or just doing something which she knows will make him laugh. Mama is always saying that Alexa is the social butterfly in the family, which at first I didn't understand. Butterflies seem kinda useless to me, but when Annika asked Mama what she meant, Mama told her that being a social butterfly meant that Alexa is very friendly, outgoing, and is never shy at all. *Yep, that just about sums up the Princess, a.k.a. drama queen.*

Alexa is always saying to anybody who will listen—

even me—that Asher is just so cute! She loves him greatly, and although they do annoy each other at times (they are siblings, after all), they get along famously. Duke, my buddy, sure annoys me at times, too, so I totally understand that concept.

Alexa, although just as cute and sweet as Asher is, has a devilish streak as well. I've heard Mavis say that Alexa is "Holly, Jr." in looks and in personality. Apparently, Mama was "something" when she was young, too—always wanting to stay busy all the time.

Regarding Alexa's devilish nature, one Saturday afternoon Daddy was watching a football game on TV, but fell asleep on the couch. Mama had been baking chocolate muffins with chocolate chips in them (which, of course, I did not get to taste because chocolate is supposedly bad for dogs). Daddy was deep in dreamland, and I noticed that he had his mouth slightly open as he was lying on the couch. The children were sitting on the floor in the living room eating their muffins, and Alexa kept taking the chocolate chips off hers and popping them into her mouth. She glanced over at Daddy, suddenly smiling about something. She punched Annika, whispered "Watch this!" to her, and took another chocolate chip off her muffin, crawling over to Daddy. She popped that chocolate chip into his open mouth! The significance of this action was not lost on me: *Daddy hates chocolate!* Both girls began giggling as Daddy woke up to having something strange in his mouth. He suddenly sat up, grabbed a tissue out of the box on the end table, and spat out the offending chip. "What in the world??" he sputtered. Just then, Mama came into the living room as the sisters dissolved into giggles. Daddy sat up, glaring, then smiling as it dawned on him what had happened.

"Girls, which of you did this so I can beat you to death!" he said in mock anger.

"Did what?" asked Mama.

Alexa burst out laughing. "Oh, Daddy, I couldn't help it—I put that chocolate chip in your mouth!" The sisters rolled around on the floor as they continued laughing.

Even Mama and Asher began laughing. "You did what?" asked Mama. "You know Daddy hates chocolate, Alexa! It's amazing that he didn't strangle you. Now, anytime you want, you can put all those chocolate chips in my mouth, but not Daddy's!"

"Daddy eat chocolate chip," chuckled Asher, knowing full well his daddy didn't like chocolate, being equally disbelieving with the rest of the family about that fact. They all adored chocolate and did everything in their power to eat it whenever possible!

I mentioned that Alexa is a princess and a drama queen. Oh, I don't mean those titles in a negative way at all. I'll explain: she dearly loves to dress up in what she calls princess dresses, which are actually long fancy costumes from past Halloweens, plays at church, and the like. The sisters have a large "princess dress box" in the playroom with all types of fancy dresses in beautiful colors. Some have jewels on them, lace, flowers, and so on. She's been known to wear one all day on Saturday, until Mama makes her change into regular clothes if they are going somewhere.

Alexa also has several tiaras, or princess crowns, and even a scepter she carries around to order her subjects (the rest of the family) to obey her *(we never do, though),* or "grant" special favors *(like providing me with special powers),* which never work.

Nothing is dull or boring around the princess! She loves life and enjoys laughing, which she must have gotten from Papa Duke. Or Mama, who likes to act silly with the children at times, too. If Alexa is tired, she just falls on the floor pretending to faint. Mama still makes her get up and finish whatever chore she was supposed to do in the first place. *I've noticed that the sisters can play all day without stopping, but if Mama wants them to clean up their room or the playroom, they suddenly get too tired to move. Odd.*

My favorite thing about Alexa, though, is how she always hugs me and rubs my back. When we are on the couch together, she never misses a chance to rub my back or my ears very gently, and I find it quite soothing. Dogs know when humans love them, and I know for certain that Alexa loves me. She always has, even when she was just learning to crawl. I remember those big, toothless grins she used to give me when she was a baby.

I can't believe how quickly she's gotten so big!

Annika: A Doll

My oldest human sister, Annika, truly is a doll in every sense of the word, which humans use as the highest compliment paid to others. To them, a *doll* means that another human is either nice, pretty, kind, or sweet. In Annika's case, she is all of those things! Oh, she has her moments when she likes to annoy Alexa just for the sheer fun of it, but from what I understand about humans, siblings often do that. Sometimes she'll play the "copycat game," which drives Alexa to distraction. With everything Alexa says, Annika repeats it. If Alexa says "Sissie, stop it!" Annika repeats that, too, laughing. I've noticed lately, however, that she doesn't do that as often as she used to, so I am sure that Alexa is relieved. *So am I.*

The sisters have gone through phases, according to Mama, and I've noticed that as well. For a while, it seemed that everything that anyone said to them was extremely funny. Even if they were being scolded, they thought that was funny, too. Mama didn't think that was funny at all,

227

soon putting a stop to their laughter when she was being serious. I thought at the time that they were skating on thin ice, as Mama puts it, but Mama has a way of persuading them to behave properly: she has lots of ammunition in her arsenal of parental authority. Since they dislike cleaning up after themselves or doing other chores, Mama told the sisters that they could laugh all they wanted—while they straightened up the playroom they had left in shambles the day before. Wow, that got rid of their chuckles right away!

I remember when Mama and Daddy brought Annika home from the hospital. I was new at being a brother, and her crying really got on my nerves at first. I lost a lot of sleep in those first few months after her arrival, because she never consulted me about the best times for crying: she cried at night, thus waking me up, in the morning, interrupting my naptime, or in the afternoon when I was trying to rest. Very annoying.

As she grew and began to smile at me, though, I came to understand that I needed to help Mama more, since the addition of a baby to our family created so much more work for Mama. And our house was a lot more crowded with a baby around, too! I just didn't understand how a small baby, who started off smaller than me, needed all that equipment. Mama and Daddy had to get a crib for Annika to sleep in, a dresser for her clothes and blankets, a diaper stacker, a big receptacle for disposing of used diapers (oh, my sensitive nose got a workout on that), a stroller, a car seat, a rocking chair for Mama to sit in while she held Annika, a changing table, baby toys, a small bathtub of her own, and even a baby swing! Not to mention all the food she needed as she began eating real food and not just milk. All those things took up a lot of space—she even got her own room, for heaven's sake. I was relegated to a corner of the living room where they placed my dog bed at the time.

I eventually learned to sleep by burrowing way down underneath my blanket so I couldn't hear her crying as much, but as she grew, her crying during the night grew less often and finally stopped altogether. She even began smiling at me, and Mama called her "the toothless wonder," until those two little bottom front teeth came in. Then she wanted to chew on everything. I understood that, because I *still* like to chew things, even now.

When she started crawling, I learned to keep a watchful eye on her, but kept my distance. She would just as soon bonk me over the head with one of her plastic toys as hug and kiss me. A dawg learns these things, and as a full-blooded dachshund, I'm pretty quick to catch on. Mama would be in the kitchen while Annika was on the rug in the living room, which was right beside the kitchen. Mama would keep poking her head into the living room to make sure Annika wasn't getting into anything. If I thought Annika might pull a lamp or something off on her head, I'd bark to alert Mama.

I lived through that time, but Alexa was born when Annika was a year and a half. By then, I had learned a thing or two about babies, so it was much easier for me this time around. I made sure I kept my own dog toys out of their reach, because they had no qualms about chewing on my toys just like they chewed on their own. I never liked baby slobber on my belongings, you know.

Annika is the big sister now, and she is tall and slim with long blond hair, so much fun to be around. She likes to chase me in the house, and I humor her by galloping down the hall, hiding behind doors, and crawling under beds until she finds me. She loves to ride her bike, play basketball with her goal that Papa Clark set up for her beside the garage, and just constantly stay in motion. She just enjoys being active, very much like Mama did, according to Mavis. Both she and Alexa like to go swimming in the summer, too, and so does Asher now.

Annika is friendly, too, but unlike Alexa, seems to enjoy being by herself at times, while Alexa would prefer being with fifty of her closest friends at all times!

One thing I find very important is that Annika loves to eat delicious food just like Papa and I do. I don't know how she stays so slim— probably because she burns up all she eats. I've heard Mama say that Annika can eat as much as two other people, especially at a Mexican restaurant, where she can practically make an entire basket of chips, along with the salsa, disappear quickly. I think that's an admirable trait in a human. I heard her tell Mama the other day that she's already been thinking about her birthday party in the spring: she doesn't want a princess party, a party with bowling, or a party at a place with inflatables to jump on. She wants one that is more grown up—like a steak-and-baked-potato party! Now *that* is a party I can get my teeth into.

This definitely shows that Annika understands the important things in life!

Mama and Daddy, My Beloved "Parents"

When Mama and Daddy brought me home to live with them when I was such a little fellow, I was scared at first, but it didn't take me long to realize how much they loved me and wanted to take care of me. Right from the first, Mama spoke to me in a kind and reassuring voice, and her hands were always gentle when she held me. She smiled at me a lot, too, and although I didn't quite understand much about humans, I soon grew to understand that her smile meant that everything was going to be all right.

Daddy treated me well right from the start, too. He didn't talk very much, but humans don't have to say

230

anything for us dogs to understand what they mean. Daddy was a quiet man, but that didn't mean he didn't *think* a lot! Mama always said what she was feeling, like "That computer is being so slow today! I'm gonna pitch it out the window!" or "Yay! We had some rain today!" and so on.

I learned quickly when Daddy had something on his mind. He didn't have to say a word—I could just tell by the way he held his head a little to the side, thinking. Or, he often had a different expression on his face. We doxies, being masters at observing our humans, notice little details like that. I knew not to bother him to play with me when he needed his space.

At first, I was startled a few times when Mama would just burst into song around the house. I wasn't used to human singing, anyway, and seemingly for no reason, she'd just start singing while she folded clothes, unloaded the dishwasher, or dusted the furniture. I learned that other humans thought Mama had a beautiful singing voice, and she often sang at church and other places. She has taught the girls to sing their favorite songs, too, and even Asher now joins in on the last word or two of each stanza. She directs the children's choir at church, and also sings in the adult choir. I like to hear her sing now. Sometimes her singing relaxes me.

Daddy doesn't sing, but he loves to work on the computer, laptop, or his tablet, where I often lie at his feet so I can be close to him. Of course, he spends most days in his office at church or about town visiting church members or attending meetings, but when he's home in the evenings and on Fridays and Saturdays, he still has to do his work. He does play ball with me, throw my other toys for me to fetch, and take me to the vet when I need to go, but I DON'T LIKE GOING TO THE VET AT ALL. They know too well how to torture poor, defenseless dawgs with things like giving us shots, poking in our ears and elsewhere, and cramming awful-tasting pills down our throats. Disgusting.

Daddy sometimes gives me baths, and I don't like those much, either. I've learned to just endure them, but being dried off with a big soft towel does make me feel great afterwards. While I'm on the topic of baths, I don't understand why humans have to take daily baths. That's way too many as far as I am concerned. Why, they never roll around in the dirt like I do, jump in mud puddles (well, sometimes the children do), or get into the trashcan. I suppose that's just another one of those funny quirks about humans that I cannot figure out.

Daddy does one special thing that I love, however: he is a great grill master. Whenever he's grilling meats, I like to be close by in case he drops something, because the meats always smell so delicious, whether he's grilling hamburgers and hot dogs, or chicken, or steak. He seems to take pride in grilling, and I take pride in eating it if I ever get a morsel to taste.

Mama is a wonderful mother to her children *and* her four-legged children. She cares for her family all the time, making sure everyone is well fed, super clean, well dressed, and content. Both Mama and Daddy take their parenting jobs seriously, always trying to do right by their children and us animals. I've learned to obey her, because whether human or dawg, one is supposed to obey Mama, or suffer the consequences. One time I didn't want to go out when it was raining, so Mama picked me up and set me down in the grass, anyway. It was raining hard and I got very wet, something I hate. But I might as well do what she wants because she'll make sure I do it, anyway!

Daddy isn't quite as exacting about such things as Mama, but from my experience, that's the way it is in many human families. He makes sure I am safe, but doesn't watch me very closely. I've gotten by with a few things when Mama wasn't around but Daddy was!

All in all, Mama and Daddy have always taken good care of me, shown me love and concern, and always watched out for my well-being. I felt unloved at first when Annika was born, but I see now that Mama and Daddy's first priority was to take care of that helpless baby. Human babies just cannot do anything for themselves, so as parents, their time was absorbed by doing everything for Annika. They did everything for Alexa and Asher, too, until they've gotten big enough to do more and more for themselves.

Mama and Daddy represent love in this house, and I will never leave them. They are too important to me.

Piper and Aslan: My Feline "Brothers"

When Piper joined our family, he was just a tiny, black-and-white ball of fur who was scared of his own shadow. Really. I didn't have much to do with him because he is, after all, a cat. I've learned, however, that dogs and cats can have companionable relationships if dogs make it clear that they are in charge.

Piper came along about the time Alexa was two. He mostly squeaked rather than meowed back then, and I had to stay on guard so that the sisters wouldn't hurt him, thus causing him to bite and/or scratch them. I took (and still do) my responsibilities seriously regarding my family. If a cat was placed under our roof, however I happened to feel about cats, then he became my responsibility as well. I had to teach him to leave my toys alone, leave the sisters' toys alone, and to avoid scratching Mama's furniture. It kept me quite busy, as one can understand, with two small children and a cat to supervise. Mama couldn't do it all, so she relied on me to take up the slack.

Piper and I never got into any big scrapes, because he was smart and learned quickly. I congratulated myself on my leadership abilities UNTIL Aslan came along. Now that cat was the total opposite of Piper in every way. He was rescued by Mama and Daddy at only a few days of age, and Mama nursed him back to health. After he got well, that was the end of my relaxation—that cat wanted to play nonstop even if nobody else in the house did! If humans and animals wouldn't play, then he'd tackle one of Mama's real or silk plants to play with—much to her annoyance, I might add. He was, and still is, hyper. Although he's settled down a bit now, and is actually a pretty good companion to me, he's definitely given me a run for my money, so to speak (not that dogs have money, of course— but I like to use human sayings when they fit what I mean).

Piper had quickly learned the dividing line between cats and dogs, keeping his distance from me and giving me my own space. Not so with Aslan! He just barrels right in, ready to play, pouncing on top of me at the slightest whim. That does not allow me to have much time for relaxing, to be sure. I'm not alone in being pounced upon, either. Daddy is often attacked by Aslan when he is sitting at the computer. Aslan will jump up on his back, scaring Daddy half to death. And Aslan would probably stay on Mama's shoulder 24/7 if she allowed him to stay. He wants to be as close to her as he can just about all the time. I truly think it's because Aslan thinks of Mama as his real mama, since he was rescued so young. I've heard Mama say that it's kinda hard to cook with a cat on her shoulder, so she makes him get down. He fusses at her when she does, too.

All in all, my family is wonderful, and I think it is fitting that Mama affectionately calls our home "the circus." We're very entertaining—all of us.

Thor: I don't Know About Him Yet

Thor is pretty much in a class by himself, because he

is so young, but mainly because I see certain traits in him that make me wary. He is afraid of NOTHING. That is dangerous, not only to him, but to the rest of us as well. He's very young and energetic, manages to get on top of the refrigerator, on top of the computer desk—there's a silk plant up there, and he likes to hide in its leaves like he's in the jungle. He's got markings kinda like a tiger, but he isn't ferocious. It remains to be seen how he's going to turn out. He's certainly shown Aslan how it feels to be annoyed to death by a kitten—ha ha! *It is so funny that the fur is on the other paw now, Aslan.*

As he matures, I'll be watching to see how he turns out, but with a cat, it could go either way. He could turn out to be a leader among cats, or a pure pest. I hope he won't be the latter.

Kurt and Bethany, Tate and Joey: Aunt, Uncle, and Fuzz Brothers

I couldn't pay tribute to my "aunt" and "uncle" without also mentioning their two pesky felines, Tate and Joey. I say *pesky* not in a derogatory way—it's just that in my way of thinking, all cats are somewhat pesky. A dawg never really knows what to expect out of them: they lie there looking at you and blinking their eyes, appearing for all the world like they are innocent bystanders, but their tails are twitching madly: I've learned that if a cat's tail is twitching, then that means he or she is up to no good, most of the time. Now with dogs, our wagging tails represent joy, or at least that we are pleased about something. Not so with cats. Oh, if they're pleased, they'll rub a human's legs off, and doing that purring thing that sounds like a motor running. I never did quite get that myself. But perhaps that's because I don't understand cats in general, anyway.

235

Tate and Joey tried their best to cause me trouble when I visited Kurt and Bethany the first time. We've since become good friends, but I don't get to see them these days since they moved to Arizona. That was one extremely long trip out there when I went with Clark, Mavis, and Duke. I bet I'll never get to go out there again, so I don't know if I'll ever see the Fuzz Brothers again, or meet their newest feline, Winston. For some strange reason, that makes me sad.

Kurt and Bethany have always treated me very well. Although it's obvious to me that Bethany is definitely a "cat person," she still always plays with me and just lets me know she likes me. Dogs pick up on those kinds of things. It's innate. We know when humans like us or not. Kurt will get down on the floor and play with me as hard as I want—he tries to catch me, but of course, he's just not up to moving as fast as I do. I am slowing down a bit now, but then, so is everyone else in my family, except for the children and Aslan. They just make me tired since they seem to go nonstop unless Mama or Daddy make them sit down. Aslan, of course, pretty much does whatever he wants, just like Tate and Joey seem to do—nobody can keep him down. He can be so sweet, but he'll turn on you "at the drop of a hat." According to Mama, that means it wouldn't take much, even just dropping a hat on the floor, to get him riled up.

Bethany loves to cook, and I suspect she got that love from Papa, who also loves to cook—and eat, of course. She went to culinary school (that means a bunch of classes on how to cook different foods) and has been trying out new recipes ever since. Of course, I never get to try any of her dishes unless she comes here to Georgia for a visit, and that's not very often. She also taught herself to play her guitar, just like Papa did. Both she and Kurt have guitars and can read music, even though Papa can't—but I have always enjoyed hearing him play and sing. He puts his whole heart into his playing and singing, and we dogs understand heartfelt singing. We might not always understand the meaning of a song, but we clearly understand the emotions behind the singing of it.

With Kurt being a whiz about computers, there's just not much I can say, since I do not personally know much about them. Oh, I know that computers sit on desks or tables, have a TV face, and humans enjoy typing on them—well, most of the time. I've seen both Mama and Daddy get very upset at their computer, saying it froze up—and I don't understand how a computer could freeze up in the summer, but like I said, I don't understand computers. Or want to, either. I have better things to do than sit in front of a computer screen and look at it. Sounds extremely boring to me, especially when I could be doing something really great like chewing on a nice, juicy bone. (Humans often like things that we dogs think are just plain dumb.) I understand that Kurt's job at work is doing something with computers—I heard Mama tell somebody that Kurt writes software programs. That makes no sense to me at all. I don't have a clue what software is—it can't be something to wear, because Kurt writes on it. Bethany seems to know a lot about computers, but she once told Mama that she attended a company convention with Kurt and she didn't understand much about what they talked about in the meetings. It must be strange to have a job that very few other people understand!

Both Kurt and Bethany are fine humans. They love animals, especially cats, but I can't hold that against them. It's the love that counts, after all.

Winston's still very young and energetic, kinda like Thor, but I hear that Joey has taken him under his wing as a tutor of sorts. That's what Piper has done with Aslan, but I hope Winston isn't as hard to train as Aslan.

I'll just have to wait and see how Winston turns out, too.

<u>Steve and Dorothy, Zoe, Charlie, and Gizmo: Tall Funny Man, Cook Extraordinaire, Slabs of Granite, and the Gabmeister</u>

Uncle Steve and Aunt Dorothy are definitely animal lovers: they have Zoe and Charlie the dawgs, and Gizmo, that blabbermouth bird. They've had cats over the years, too. They also have children and grandchildren, but I've never met any of them. I've only been to their house a couple of times, and with our circus of a family, plus Kurt and Bethany, Clark and Mavis, and Papa and Nana, that pretty much filled up their house. I've heard the other humans talk about their children and grandchildren, and Dorothy has proudly brought photo albums to family gatherings, but I've never actually met them in person.

Steve is extremely tall and slim—he's the tallest one in my family. It's kind of hard to believe that he is Mavis's brother, because I can't see that they look alike at all. Steve does look like Papa, and Mavis does look somewhat like Nana, so there you go.

Dorothy is a fabulous cook, which automatically makes her one of my favorite people by default. Daddy loves her food, too, and although he isn't as open about it as Papa and I are, he loves her food nonetheless. Her Czechoslovakian Christmas cookies are his favorite, and she always makes sure to bring him some when we are all together for holidays and such. I think that is very thoughtful of her—bringing food to someone is a wonderful trait to have! I just wish I could eat those cookies, since Daddy enjoys them so much.

Steve took after Papa in the grilling department. He enjoys grilling meats, and I enjoy smelling them and eating them. Once in a great while, if I'm around when he's grilling, he'll give me a small morsel. He and Dorothy NEVER give Zoe and Charlie any people food—that might be why those dawgs act so bland all the time. If I had to eat cardboard-tasting dog food all the time myself, I wouldn't get very excited about life, either.

One thing I've noticed about Steve in the past year or so: he's starting to look a lot like Papa Duke, too. Oh, he's much taller and much thinner, and their skin and hair are different colors, but their eyes, nose, and mouth look the same. They sound a little more alike now than they used to, also. *Wonder if Steve has some more funny stories he can tell all of us?* I don't know yet if he's like Papa in that regard. I'll be watching and waiting, because I love those funny stories as much as my human family does.

I haven't seen Steve and Dorothy as much as the rest of the family, but they have been very kind to both Duke and me, always making sure to say hello and pay attention to us when we are around them. That sort of thing is important to us dogs.

We take notice when we are being ignored, because we dawgs understand a lot more about humans—when it comes to dogs—than humans realize. Bet they'd be really surprised if they knew how much we actually know about them. We know if they are sad, even if they are smiling. We know if they don't feel well, even if they don't say anything. We know when they are upset, too. Of course, some humans make it easy to know how they feel, because they display their feelings very clearly, like Mama, Mavis, Kurt, and Papa. But then others—like Daddy, Steve, Bethany, Dorothy, and Clark—can hide how they are feeling.

We dogs don't need them to tell us, anyway. When we know our humans well, we know them inside, too.

Sellars and Renata: Another Chow Hound and a Sweet Lady

As I've often mentioned, Sellars is so much like Papa

that he is what I call my "alternate papa." He and Papa love to eat (and so do I), so we're just naturally a trio of chow hounds. Sellars likes to laugh at Papa's funny stories, Papa loves to *tell* funny stories, and I just enjoy being in the midst of it all.

They both enjoy good music, too, although Papa can play the "geetar" and Sellars can't, but I know for a fact that Sellars sure can tap his foot in time to music. You ought to try sitting on his lap, like I have, while he's tapping that foot, too. I've had to hang on for dear life to keep from falling off! I can still hear Sellars' boisterous laugh, especially when he starts tapping his feet to music when I'm trying hang on. "Hey, look at this here dawg tryin' to stay up here on my lap—his ears is flappin,' an' he ain't too happy, neither. Heh heh." I just humor him by hamming it up. Whenever I have an audience, I want to give them something to enjoy, just like Papa does.

Renata is one of the kindest people I've ever met. And that means something, because I think all my human family members are kind. She is always doing something for others, and she never misses a chance to pat Duke or me on the head as she passes by. She even likes our feline trio, so to me, that's positive proof that she's so nice!

She can cook as well as Nana and Papa (but so can Sellars). I've heard everyone going on so much about her crunch cake that I wish I could taste it myself, but I know Mama would have my hide if I ever tried to sneak a bite. It would just be too much trouble, I'm afraid—it would involve getting up into a chair and even getting onto the table or countertop, so I'll just leave well enough alone. I'm not a spring chicken anymore, so I don't wish to fall and hurt myself. Besides, the children—Annika, Alexa, and Asher—always make sure I have plenty of other good things to eat, and there's always Papa, who's looking out for this granddawg.

Renata has a beautiful singing voice, too. When she

and Mama sing together, why, I never have the urge to howl at all. Mama sings the high notes, which makes her a soprano, whereas Renata sings the lower notes, an alto, according to what Mama told the sisters. Those terms don't mean a thing to me: I just know what I like, and that's their singing. Papa said he used to sing a lot when he was young, but I love to hear him sing now. I don't know if his singing is good or bad in human terms, but he's my Papa, and that makes his singing good as far as I'm concerned.

Sellars and Renata have traveled all over the country in that motor home of theirs. It comes in handy when they visit our family, too, making more room in the house for sleeping. Of course, I can sleep just about anywhere, anytime, and for any reason. Speaking of motor homes, that road trip that Duke and I took with Clark and Mavis when we went out to Arizona to visit Kurt and Bethany was pretty interesting, but all those miles of riding in the desert just got very boring. I mean, if you've seen one cactus, you've seen them all.

I just want to sum up what I think of Sellars and Renata: if something were to happen to Papa and Nana Duke, I'd be privileged to become *their* granddawg. After all, a dawg is a pretty good judge of character when it comes to humans. We just instinctively know if humans like us or not; and Sellars and Renata are definitely characters!

Nana and Papa Duke: Pack Leaders Who Love ME

It's kind of difficult for me to even think of the words to talk about Nana and Papa Duke. I've said so much about both of them since they *are* the pack leaders of this entire family. Everybody who has ever met Papa Duke loves him like I do, and Nana just is in a class by herself. Both of them make me feel like I am special, and for that, I will love them forever.

That first time I saw Papa when I was just a little pup will be etched into my memory always. I didn't know what to expect, because I had never met any of Mama's family yet, and was a bit nervous as we rode to their house. I wondered if everyone would like me, and I'd heard so much about Papa that I kinda expected him to be ten feet tall or something!

I was still in the car when he came outside, taking those long strides I've come to know so well (and *still* try to keep up with when he and I are outside together). As he got to the car, he reached inside the window and patted me on the head. That big grin of his just radiated warmth and love to me. I didn't mind a bit that he called me a *dash-hound* instead of my real breed name.

From that moment on, I loved my papa with all my heart, and he has returned that love over and over. He talks to me like I am—well—a human like him. He feeds me good human food every chance he gets. He loves having me on his lap, where he'll rub my head, ears, and back so gently. And you know what? Just the other day, he told me, "Sarge, you know that you an' me is gettin' old? Yore ol' papa cain't do as much as he used to, but I've noticed that you cain't, neither. Guess we'll just be two ol' geezers together. Right, Sarge?" I looked him right in the eye and barked to tell him I agreed. *I can't think of anyone I'd rather be an ol' geezer with than you, Papa.*

Nana (sometimes I still think of her as Grandma, but since the great grandchildren came, we all try to call her Nana). We now have Papa Clark and Grandma Mavis. Apparently, Papa Duke and I aren't the only ones who are getting old!

Nana loves to try new things, like new recipes, new games to play with her great grandchildren, new outfits to sew, new books to read. In other words, she's either cooking, sewing, buying something for someone, or reading her Bible or another book. I've also seen her putting puzzles together, a process that often takes weeks, because to me all the pieces look just alike, and there are millions of them! I haven't yet figured out that fascination with puzzles, either. If you lose even one piece, then you can't finish the crazy thing.

Both Papa and Nana love all of us so much. They are always so excited when they see me and the rest of the family, and Papa has said on many occasions that he thanks the Lord that he lived long enough to see his grandchildren and great grandchildren. I'm not certain what he means by that, but the humans seem to understand what he means. I've even seen Mama, Aunt Bethany, Mavis, and Dorothy shed tears when he said that. He didn't sound sad at all when he said it, so why were they crying?

Nobody will explain it to me, but that's okay. I love my human family so much and I am so thankful that all those years ago, Mama chose me out of all those dachshunds. Life with this family has been quite a ride.

No dog has ever had it so good, I'm certain.

Food: Er . . . What I Live For!

There are a lot of things I love, especially my family—they just make my life so much fun. There are other humans I've met along the way that I liked, too, and knowing them has enriched my life. As I was relaxing the other day, I thought about some of the things I like: playing with my dog toys, especially if Daddy or some other human plays with me by throwing my ball for me to retrieve; chewing on old socks, or even new socks, but Mama gets annoyed with me if I chew those; sitting in Papa's lap and listening to his funny stories; hearing Sellars laugh at something Papa says; being hugged by my sisters and

Asher; and getting to eat some yummy people food!

Food is, to me, the ultimate enjoyment. I am called a chow hound by my humans, and for good reason. Since I'm also known as "a nose with legs," how do humans think food smells to *me*?? I have a hard time controlling myself and will attempt to get some of it if somebody doesn't keep it away from me. Oh, I'm not trying to cause trouble or get into trouble, but when something smells so delicious, sometimes my nose has a mind of its own!

When we are at Papa's and Nana's, they have so much delicious food that you'd think they were trying to feed an Army. I've heard Mavis comment that the family always tries to eat like an Army, too. *What's wrong with that? If I ever got the chance, I'd do just that!*

I have a very long list of my favorites in human food, and a few of them are: any kind of meat dish—roast beef, pork roast, chicken, beef stew, turkey (like at Thanksgiving and Christmas), meatloaf, anything grilled—and I like veggies, too. That green bean casserole is just so yummy, but I also like mashed potatoes with Papa's delicious gravy on them, mac and cheese (oh yeah—I love cheese, too), peas, carrots—you get the idea.

Oh, I don't want to leave the impression that I think food is just as important as my family, because it isn't. Humans often just don't realize how important food is to us chow hounds, though. That is, except for Papa and Sellars, my honorary dawgs!

I have so much to look forward to: Nana's New Year's party, maybe even a trip or two—I'm not too old yet, if Mama and Daddy will take me somewhere. I wonder how the children will look and act when they grow up?

Life has its ups and downs, but with my family, it's all a crazy circus—but who doesn't like a circus?

23
Epilogue

Mavis Duke Hinton's Blog –
http://mavisdukehinton.blogspot.com

AN INTERVIEW WITH SARGE

Welcome, readers! Today we have a very special interview with the talented dachshund, Shadow, who wrote THE DACHSHUND ESCAPADES series of books. I am privileged to get him here for a short while, as he is an extremely busy and sought-after canine personality. Perhaps in another post, we can have him answer readers' questions. I am happy to interview him here today.

MDH: My dear Shadow, known as Sarge in your books, we are so glad you are able to join us today for this informal chat. We know you stay busy with your family, friends, and promotional activities. What have you been up to lately?
SARGE: Thank you for the honor. But just call me Sarge, because that's the name readers associate with my books. I decided to take on a pen name a few years ago, like lots of famous personalities. For instance, did you know that the movie star John Wayne's real name was Marion Morrison?? But I digress. Besides personal appearances, I do whatever I can to promote "my" books. Seems that a lot of dog lovers out there haven't yet heard of THE DACHSHUND ESCAPADES, but I'm doing my part to get the word out. Maybe your readers will tell other dog lovers about my books—and I thank you for doing your part as well.
MDH: Then here's your golden opportunity. What would you like to say, SARGE, to your audience of humans--those who already know you, as well as prospective new readers?

SARGE: If you are a dog lover in general, and a dachshund lover in particular, then THESE are "the" books for you! I know, I know--I've said that over and over, but it is true. Humans often don't realize just how much we canines understand in the scheme of things. Read my books and you'll be quite surprised at what WE know about YOU.

MDH: I understand that your second book, I AM DACHSHUND, the sequel to I AM SARGE, introduces your doxie buddy, Duke. Share a little about that with your readers.

SARGE: I am thrilled to do so. In this second book, my family members are prominent characters once again. I sort of take Duke under my paw and mentor him to become the proud dachshund he ought to be. I also meet new people, have new experiences, and share more of Papa Duke's entertaining stories. In I AM SARGE, folks seemed to enjoy the fence story, the Purple Heart story, and the fishing story; in I AM DACHSHUND, Papa relates even more outlandish escapades, notably his encounter with alligators, and another war story involving haystacks. I accompanied him and Nana on a trip to visit Sellars and Renata in Georgia. Now THAT was quite an experience! In DACHSHUNDS FOREVER, I go on a trip out West to visit Kurt and Bethany with Clark and Mavis. Oh, the things I saw and the humans I met! Duke and I call that "the trip of a lifetime."

MDH: You mention Papa Duke quite often. Tell us a little about him personally, since you seem to know him so well.

SARGE: I regret to say that I never had the honor of meeting Papa Duke, although I've heard about him all my life. The entire family misses him since he passed away in 2000, so I thought my books would be a wonderful way to keep his memory alive. Besides, the three great grandchildren never got to meet this wonderful man, either, and they love hearing stories about him like I do. So—why not write them down as a tribute to what he meant to all my family? In fact, that is the name of my fourth book: A DACHSHUND'S TRIBUTE. It's to Papa and all my family, in fact. I've heard about him my entire life, so I really do feel like I know him. I know we would have been good friends, just like I've written.

MDH: That sounds like a wonderful way to remember someone so special to you. Who would you say is your favorite character in your books?

SARGE: That is a tough one, because I love all my family of humans AND animals, but it would HAVE to be Papa Duke. I love my "parents," Philip and Holly, who adopted me when I was a young pup. I love my two "sisters," Annika and Alexa, although they've pulled my ears more times than I have toes to count, and my "brother," Asher . . . hmmm . . . and I love my "Aunt" Bethany and "Uncle" Kurt, Clark and Mavis, Nana Duke, of course . . . but Papa adored my breed and dogs in general--and they loved him, I'm told—he so enjoyed sneaking "human food" to them. As a chow hound myself, I know he and I would have hit it off right away. What dog wouldn't love a human like Papa Duke?? All the characters in my books are real people and real animals, you know. In some cases, I've had to change the time frame in order to make things work, so to speak, and I've changed a few names as well, but my tales are mostly true. The writer in me did gild the lily a time or two (winks).

MDH: For my part, your books are fascinating reading, and I look forward to reading any others you plan to write as well. You do plan to write more books, don't you?

SARGE: When I first wrote I AM SARGE, I planned on three books—a trilogy. Then, when I was writing DACHSHUNDS FOREVER, it kept getting longer and longer, so I divided it into two books. That's how A DACHSHUND'S TRIBUTE came about. And I planned to stop after this one, but I have so much more to say that I'll probably write more books. I owe that to my loyal readers, you know.

MDH: That is good news, Sarge! There are millions of doxie lovers out there, and I know readers have enjoyed hearing from a real dawg. We humans think we understand you, but as you have so aptly stated in your books, we really don't understand you as well as we think we do.

SARGE: Thank you for acknowledging that tidbit. I still have a few surprises up my sleeve—er, paw.

MDH: I regret that we must bring this interview to a close since you have another engagement, but thank you for joining us today. We'll do this again soon, especially when you have a release date for your new book you hopefully do write. Perhaps readers out there have questions for you. If so, the next time you join us, perhaps you would be so kind to answer some of them. Meanwhile, keep on promoting your stories—dog lovers out there will buy them! By the way, where can readers purchase THE DACHSHUND ESCAPADES books?

SARGE: Readers can Google my titles, or simply "THE DACHSHUND ESCAPADES" online and see what pops up—there are tons of websites selling them, like Amazon, Barnes and Noble, Books-a-million, Christianbook, etc. My books are available in two versions: e-book and paperback, too. Even local bookstores will order them for readers if the books are not available on the shelves. Thank you so much for having me today. I'm starring in a dog food commercial the first of the year in the U.K. Be on the lookout for it! PLEASE BUY MY BOOKS, DOXIE LOVERS!

MDH: Er . . . thanks. With that quite flamboyant marketing ploy, we will sign off for now. Farewell, readers.

& A Word to Readers &

Thank you for choosing *The Dachshund Escapades* books. It has been my pleasure to write about my family and share them with readers, and these books are my way of keeping beloved memories alive. I'm entertaining the idea of a fifth book in this series—there is just so much more to share.

Robert "Papa" Duke passed away in 2000 at age 86 before I began my writing career, but I could not bear to write about his passing. Since his great grandchildren never got a chance to meet him, I first wrote these books to introduce my father to them. We often tell them his now-famous stories as well. When Alexa was six, she told me, "Grandma, I really miss Papa Duke." I replied that she had never gotten to meet him, but she said, "I know, but I can still miss him, can't I?" Mission accomplished!

"Pappy" Sellars went home to be with the Lord right after Book 2, I AM DACHSHUND, was published. I could not bear to write his passing into my stories, either. I still keep in touch with Renate (how her name is actually spelled), and I send her copies of each book as it is released. We often reminisce about all our good times together with our families.

My mom, Ramelle "Nana" Duke, left us in January 2013 at age 85, after a lengthy illness. She had the opportunity to know Annika, Alexa, and Asher, and had also read Books 1 and 2, but Book 3 was not published before she died. She did read the manuscript, however, so she got to enjoy the continuing saga of Sarge's antics. I like to think that she has been smiling over my shoulder as I completed this fourth book in the series. As a Christian, the Bible promises that I will see all three of them again when I meet my Lord someday!

Blessings to you all, Mavis Duke Hinton

ᘒ **About the Author** ᘒ

In her 23-year career as an English teacher, **Mavis Duke Hinton** taught all levels of English and related subjects, with the final five and one-half years online to students across the USA and several foreign countries, retiring in 2013. She grew up in a military family and lived in several U.S. states as well as Europe during her childhood.

Ms. Hinton has also been an editor for Christian and secular organizations, including Liberty University and the North Carolina State Budget, as well as a police officer. She has taught Bible studies to all ages, from preschool children to adult women, and has spoken in educational conferences as well as women's groups from time to time.

Married for forty-four years to her husband Clark, a retired science teacher, they have two married daughters and three grandchildren. She has published three other Christian fiction novels in THE DACHSHUND ESCAPADES series: *I Am Sarge*, *I Am Dachshund*, and *Dachshunds Forever*. She has also published several magazine articles.

She spends her time in church activities and hobbies: writing, reading, traveling, cooking, and marketing her books. Ms. Hinton especially enjoys time with her friends and family. Recovering from two knee replacement surgeries earlier this year, she plans to keep on writing and going strong until the Lord takes her home.

Website: www.MavisDukeHinton.com
Amazon author page:
www.amazon.com/author/mavisdukehinton
Email: dawgwriter@hotmail.com
Facebook: www.facebook.com/MavisDukeHintonsBooks
Twitter: @writer4dawg

℘ *If you enjoyed A Dachshund's Tribute* ℘

Please take a moment to leave a brief review on this book's Amazon page. I appreciate it, and future readers will, also.

Thank you!

Printed in the USA
CPSIA information can be obtained
at www.ICGtesting.com
LVHW090958141223
766500LV00006B/102